Mathew Paust

To Patsy —
I hope you
enjoy this
satire.
Matt Paust

Also by Mathew Paust

Executive Pink (a satire of presidential politics)

If the Woodsman is Late (stories)

Copyright © 2013 Mathew Paust

ISBN-10: 0615756751

All rights reserved. No part of this publication may be reproduced, stored in a retrieval system, or transmitted in any form or by any means, electronic, mechanical, recording or otherwise, without the prior written permission of the author.

Published in the United States by Bartleby Scriveners Assoc., Gloucester, Virginia

All names, characters, places and incidents in the fiction stories are products of the author's imagination or are used fictitiously. Any resemblance to actual people is unintentional and coincidental.

Howard Schechtman. Schechtman designed the book's front and back covers. More of Mr. Schechtman's art can be found on his Web site www.howi3.deviatart.com

Dedication

To Linda Seccaspina, Jonathan Wolfman, James M. Emmerling and Rena Oblong for their inspiration and encouragement during serial posting of a draft of this novel in the Open Salon writers community.

Human progress is neither automatic nor inevitable... Every step toward the goal of justice requires sacrifice, suffering, and struggle; the tireless exertions and passionate concern of dedicated individuals. – Martin Luther King Jr.

A man who was completely innocent, offered himself as a sacrifice for the good of others, including his enemies, and became the ransom of the world. It was a perfect act. – Mahatma Gandhi

Listen, son. You and I are professionals. If the manager says sacrifice, we lay down a bunt and let somebody else hit the home runs. – Frank W. Wead

SACRIFICE

PROLOGUE

Please don't call me Spock. That was the plan, to call me Spock. It's what the bloggers reported when they first began posting rumors I was a guinea pig in a "top secret government project" testing prototypes of an experimental drug intended to shift priorities within the human brain. This would empower reason to triumph with little effort over the baser instincts. In theory the effect would give anybody under the drug's influence a leg up in situations where emotions ordinarily cloud rational thinking, when the brain's limbic system -- the so-called "lizard brain" -- takes control. This frequently leads to personal excesses up to, in the extreme, war.

The bloggers, before they were silenced, got some of it right. My name is Alfred Pierce Geddes III and I am the former White House Chief of Staff-cum-Special Congressional Prosecutor-cum-Federal Penitentiary Inmate #76490263478-cum-paroled participant in arguably the most controversial pharmaceutical research ever conducted. I am not, however, the living embodiment of the popular collaboration of Gene Roddenberry and Leonard Nimoy, whose character, the half-human half-Vulcan Mr. Spock, addressed with his emotion-free, purely rational approach the weekly critical problems his fellow Starship Enterprise crew members encountered in their five-year mission to...*boldly go where no man [had] gone before.*

Interwoven in the drama of my involvement in this extraordinary experiment is the private dynamic between me and Warren Hendrian, with whom I have a long and uneven history.Hendrian has been my colleague and my nemesis, depending on circumstances and contexts. Our mutual esteem sprouted and grew collegially on the campaign trail with the presidential candidate we both served. It soured into adversity after we followed her into the White House and then peaked into deadly enmity when, as Special Prosecutor, I ordered a grand jury probe into his financial undertakings. That investigation's leading to my own crash from authority and into a judicial finding of criminality was the most abrupt turnabout of fortune I had experienced to date. This was not the end of what I liked to describe at one time as a shit storm of ironies. It was Hendrian who engineered my prison escape in the guise of Project Vulcana ostensibly "for the good of humanity."

Not that the above isn't what those in charge of this research had not hypothesized. At first. In fact, "Vulcana" became the project label after the name tacked onto the drug's early prototypes. Ordinarily one might expect a project of this magnitude to take years during which peers and government regulators bring intense scrutiny to bear on the health and behavior of test subjects before a drug is approved as effective and safe. Not so in this instance. A sense of urgency existed, which grew with accumulating evidence of opposition from powerful forces. This was the mindset existing when I joined the project, and it continues to this day.

Highly skeptical initially, I am now convinced Vulcana can be the last-ditch solution to what seems an inevitable countdown to self-annihilation of our species. How can Vulcana save our butts? I've seen it work with my own eyes. Hell, it's worked on me. As a weapon of mass intervention? I believe so. I believe in its potential to sway our collective mind to a heightened level of empathy, weaning us from our instinct for self-preservation at the potential cost of community preservation. Working in tandem with this hyped-up empathy would be an increase in Spockian rationality to reassure our squirming lizard brains that this is OK, that saving the community is the overall most efficient way of saving ourselves. Psychologist B. F. Skinner called it "beyond freedom and dignity," which grates on the ear. A century earlier Alexandre Dumas said it with more panache: "One for all, and all for one."

It was the "good of humanity" promise and the bonus of

SACRIFICE

unprecedented sexual prowess that kept me positive at those times my personal demons seemed in charge. Vulcana's most risable feature is its erection-at-will characteristic. It was the goal that lit the fire of interest in engineering the drug, coming on the heels of Wilde Laboratory's phenomenal success with Primrose Lane. Touted initially as the woman's answer to sildenafil citrate, the small rose-tinted tablet soon proved superior to the male versions as it not only induced orgasms during sexual arousal but in fact helped induce the arousal.

Hoping for a grand sequel, Wilde's researchers moved back to the male side of the stimulus spectrum, seeking to augment the erectile enhancer with an aphrodisiac effect. They succeeded, to a degree.

The project's supreme irony emerged with discovery of the empathy component as a side effect during adjustments to improve the drug's X-rated properties. Dangling these dual inducements, Hendrian, my nemesis, tapped me to become Wilde Laboratories' first human guinea pig.

MATHEW PAUST

DR. KNOE

A squirt of adrenalin into my bloodstream alerted me to the slim figure wending through the maze of reading desks. Capt. de Maupassant. Damn. Headed my way. My quickening pulse and a surge of gut chemicals told me the sadistic bastard had me in his sights. Sure as hell he did, skinny, smirky little punk. The perpetual twist at the corners of his mouth seemed to say he knew something I didn't want him to know and that this knowledge, whatever it might be, gave him a greater power than his badge alone conferred. His voice contributed to the irritating impression, soft, too soft and insinuating for a prison guard outside of a Mel Brooks farce.

Trying to refocus my eyes from the fine print of the Oxford edition of Moby Dick, I started at the severely pressed dark gray uniform trousers and worked up past the tightly clasped nylon garrison belt past the starched white shirt with its official gold bling and the knobby neck protruding from the open collar to a pale, twitchy ferret face, which, studied this close, seemed to mock the pair of quite ordinary weakish gray eyes that almost disappeared under the brim of his dark gray uniform cap.

"Mr. Geddes?" The voice aided the eyes' betrayal.

"Yes, Captain?"

"Can you come with me? You have a visitor." Oh, shit. Day gone to hell. I never had visitors. Never approved any. Mostly just reporters anyway. The only potential visitors on my list were my two kids, who had yet to set foot in the place, and, of course, Ruth, who had written me several warm letters but said Secret Service escorts advised against a personal visit.

"Who is it, Ghee...I mean, Captain?" I enjoyed confusing him with the name of his namesake French author, with whom he was

SACRIFICE

unfamiliar. He pronounced his last name *de mo-pass-ent*, accent on the "pass." Mumbling the name, as he did, it sounded as if he were calling himself a peasant, appropriately.

"Can't tell you that, Mr. Geddes." His voice carried the smirk.

"Aw, come on, Ghee...I mean, Captain. Is it someone on my list? My wife, perhaps?"

"Can't tell you that, Mr. Geddes." Stubborn edge now. He adjusted his stance, planting his heavy black tactical shoes further apart.

"Can't or won't? I have a right to approve any visitors, even a family member." Getting testy, against my better judgment. I have never liked suspense.

de Maupassant resented my tone. He sighed heavily and leaned forward, bracing himself with a hand and bringing his face so close to mine I could see a patch of eczema on the cheek under one of his eyes. Flies would have died instantly and dropped to the floor had they cruised past his mouth and caught a whiff of the rancid, sickly breath it emitted. He hissed: "I can't tell you, Mr. Geddes, because I do not know."

Shit. I did not like this. I could have refused, but somehow I suspected de Maupassant knew more than he was revealing, which pricked my curiosity. So I followed the little shit into a cramped, though private visiting room where my pique grew to dismay to find Warren Hendrian and a woman seated behind a metal table, its legs bolted to the floor. The guard said nothing, merely backed out of the room, pushed the door shut with a jarring slam of steel locks, and took up a position outside the transparent wall that made up one side of the room.

Had Hendrian been alone I might have risked punishment by leaping over the table and head-butting him. The fat old balding toad. He sat there with the smug grin on his face he always wore when he thought he'd one-upped me. Of course, he had one-upped me, big time this time. The wily little bastard had turned the tables on me, squirmed out from under the investigation I'd started and brought it back twofold in my face. I presumed he was here to celebrate my two-to-five sentence for prosecutorial misconduct and had brought his new girlfriend along to watch him gloat. "Hello, Al," he said with the smarmy lilt in his voice he used for such occasions. "How they treating you?"

I tried to keep my voice calm, evenly paced, just north of nonchalant. "Not bad, Warren. Come here to gloat?" I glanced then at the woman seated beside him. In a flash Warren was no longer in the room. His body remained at the table, but he no longer had any presence. The woman's aggressive sexuality had obliterated everything else within range. The air left my lungs in a rush and excited blood pumped into areas it hadn't visited much in recent months.

All she revealed to me was what I could see across the gunmetal table from where I stood. This vantage gave me a partial view of a trim powder-blue jacket and polka-dot blouse that didn't really register with me until later. What commanded all of my attention was her face. Correction, what commanded all of my attention were her eyes. A striking shade that couldn't decide between green and blue but dominated with an inordinate size and so clear and steady it was obvious they didn't care.

At first the eyes dared, boldly, with a seemingly ruthless interest, as if watching a bug crawling into the range of a flyswatter. The effect was so riveting I couldn't tear my gaze from them to look at the rest of her face. Yet, I could sense from the aura around them her features were symmetrical and pleasingly landscaped. A quick glance downward revealed full lips slightly pursed. Working against the eyes, which continued to stare hypnotically into mine, her mouth conveyed a relaxed poise that softened the overall expression to one suggesting a playful nature.

As my subconscious mind processed these sensations my inner monitor whispered a cautionary note that as I'd been in prison awhile now I might be responding a tad unrealistically to an ordinary female's ordinary charms. Before I could begin an inner debate on the matter Hendrian's voice, sounding far away, intruded on my reverie. "Al, this is Dr. Elizabeth Knoe."

"Dr. No?" Illusion-bursting, this, but I tried to grin in a friendly

SACRIFICE

way. I must have sounded incredulous, as the woman allowed a modest smile, then turned quickly to Hendrian, revealing dirty-blonde hair she'd arranged in a casual off-centered way that covered the tops of her ears and gave her a jaunty look. A pair of small gold hoops dangling from her earlobes glittered in the incandescent light from bulbs recessed in the ceiling. Her turning to Hendrian stirred the air around her bringing me a whiff of her subtle perfume, an unfamiliar scent that enhanced her mystique.

"I like him," she said, then turned back to me, smiling more easily. "A sense of humor can be a saving grace in a place like this." Her alto voice throaty with the muted confidence of an idling Jaguar.

I nodded and smiled back, feeling I should say something but not certain what tack to take. I swept my smile to Hendrian. His bland features still twinkled smugly. I swung back to Dr. Knoe, suddenly feeling foolish for gaping at her. "Uh..." I started to say.

"I have a proposition for you, Al," said Hendrian, winning my newly focused attention.

MATHEW PAUST

PROPOSITION

I should explain at this point the method in which I am approaching my current narrative. It's essentially the same as I used in my White House journal, prepared from notes made on the fly. The advantage of a not-so-distant retrospective interpretation enabled me then to employ the best elements of hindsight, i.e. a clarity of focus that can result in pulling back a tad from the immediate as well as a knowledge of which details among many rise in significance to advance the tale. For ultimately a tale it becomes and is so meant to be.

This is not to say my approach is necessarily foolproof in providing the best and safest personal history of pertinent events. I am acutely aware of unseen traps and pitfalls lined with sharply pointed sticks very likely lying in my path. Clearly it was premature exposure of the White House journal with its reckless mention of my official designs on Warren Hendrian that played a key role in producing the sorry predicament in which I find myself now embroiled. Alas, too often the most important lessons are learned too late.

"How would you like to have a permanent erection?" Hendrian lobbed this across the table after a little awkward chitchat in which I participated dazedly under the curious spell of Dr. Elizabeth Knoe.

"Say what?" The impulse to risk solitary confinement or worse by head-butting him returned. What mitigated my desire were his face and tone, more serious than I knew he employed with sarcasm. I glanced quickly at Dr. Knoe, who was staring levelly into my eyes. Still, I had no inkling of comprehension as to what was coming down. Flabbergasted, best describes my state of mind.

Hendrian continued, "A permanent erection. You know I'm with

SACRIFICE

Wilde Labs now?" I shook my head, confusion rioting through my brain. "Congressional Liaison. Dr. Knoe is Wilde's Director of Psychiatry. She's conducting a research project."

I imagined several clever things to say to the disturbingly attractive shrink about her impact on my physical state, but I held my tongue. Hendrian had just deferred to her, so I waited for her explanation. When she started speaking it took me a moment – too long actually – for her words to make much sense.

The irony of Hendrian working for Wilde Laboratories was more than enough to assimilate in one bite. It was controversy over the pharmaceutical Primrose Lane, the female answer to Viagra, that threatened to bring down Ruth's presidency before she'd completed her first term. Wilde Laboratories had developed and was marketing Primrose Lane. Hendrian was her national security adviser. What sort of unholy temptation had lured or persuaded him to surrender what I knew to be a vital part of his character for this? It couldn't be money. He had inherited a fortune before even becoming involved in Ruth's campaign. Sex? Some kind of blackmail? He was gay, but this was no secret and, so far as I knew, his domestic situation was stable. More stable than mine by a long shot.

"...took his own life." Her purring voice at last cut through the disjointed clanking in my head.

"I'm sorry, doctor, could you back up a tad? You want me to take some kind of drug that's already driven someone to suicide? Did I hear this right?"

She did. I listened this time, When she finished and asked if I would participate, be the next guinea pig, I laughed.

"Lady, you want me to take a drug that will give me a permanent hard-on while I'm here in prison? You are joking! You think I want some drooling troglodyte cutting my dick off and feeding it to me in a hotdog bun?" I turned to Hendrian, who was scribbling something on a yellow legal pad. "Haven't you already gotten your revenge? Get the fuck out of here! Both of you!"

Hendrian waited until I stopped huffing. His face never registered a reaction to my little rant. When I was breathing evenly, he said, "Not here."

"Huh? Not what?"

"Not here, Al. So far as I'm concerned you and I are even now. OK? I'm offering you an early release from this place, to be paroled into our custody, if you agree to participate in the research."

A different kind of respiratory rush was building now, but I tried to hide it. Took a deep breath and fought to keep a grin from seizing my face. "You can get me out of here? You? I thought you were a drug pusher now. Please enlighten me."

"Satin Edie." It came out barely a murmur, as if he wanted no one but me to hear, excluding Dr. Knoe and anyone who might be listening on a wire. This told me all I really needed to know. Edith Glick was still Speaker of the House of Representatives and a close friend of Edna Usher, CEO of American Enterprises, the umbrella for a number of corporations including Wilde Laboratories. No need to talk about the machinations now, or, actually, ever.

I nodded with enthusiasm. "Gotcha, Warren. Cool. Get me the hell out of here. I'll take your drug. Doc?" I turned to the shrink, my face stretched into an impossible grin, "will you be working with me on this?"

She unpursed her lips for a quick Mona Lisa signal of intriguing inscrutability. "We'll see," she said.

SACRIFICE

REVEAL

That first morning at The Cottage was a rebirth, several rebirths. The prospect of my first undisturbed dawn in years. I got up when I saw out my window the beckoning rosy leer of a new day. The room was still dark when I awoke about an hour before. I'd noticed the blue digital 5:07 on the nightstand clock so I swallowed the Ritalin tablet I'd placed beside it and dozed another half hour or so in the comfortable bed until the amphetamine cleared my head.

Fascinated by the prospect of witnessing the sunny spectrum bully its way into view along the horizon I found a terrycloth robe hanging from a peg next to the bathroom and made my way to the deck into the morning's chill. I used my hand to squeegee dew off one of the wicker-backed chairs and sat at a table made of oak planks. Squeals from a flock of excited seagulls greeted me as a half dozen of the little dinosaur descendants swooped into view silhouetted against the fresh brightening blue of a cloudless sky and flapped their way to a destination somewhere behind a stand of cedars.

The only noticeable motion besides the gulls' momentary appearance was a sparkling on the blue-black water's surface that wriggled in from the growing glare at its outer edge. An intermittent timid breeze off the water brought odors of cedar and loblolly pines mingled with the distinctive cocktail of fecund and decomposing marine life found around serious bodies of water. The richly nuanced tang of brewing coffee...

Coffee?

My chair creaked inquisitively as I torqued around in time to see the cloaked figure stepping silently through the kitchen door. Slowly the figure moved toward me. Its movement seemed oddly familiar, feminine. As it drew closer I saw the head, the way it tilted to one side, the hair, fluffed out over the ears...Ruth! My former boss and erstwhile sporadic lover, when she was president.

"Ruth?" Trying to keep my voice just above a whisper, it broke, one fragment coming out falsetto. The figure laughed softly, confirming my suspicion.

"How are you, Al?" Her small hands held two ceramic mugs of steaming coffee, which she lowered with almost simultaneous double clunks on the table. I was standing when she turned, her hands now outstretched from an identical terrycloth bathrobe. We hugged, for me with disbelief, which quickly warmed into an electric affection revived from years of denial. Her odors inundated me, the hint-of-mint shampoo she favored at play with a musky perfume and her more intimate aromas together awakening sweet and poignant memories in me as I hoped my closeness did in her. She slipped out of my arms before what was happening could become more. Sat in the chair next to mine, ignoring its dewy surface, and slapped my knee. "Al!" Her voice still muted but potent with joy.

We sipped our coffee and watched each other as the maturing daylight brought us incrementally into clarity. Ruth's face still held its beauty, its impish energy and the steel gray eyes that penetrated with a discerning, brutal honesty. The poise of her jaw, now allowing dimples of playful humor, appeared no less capable of hardening for the duration of a prolonged fight.

"My god, Al, you're gray. Oh, no! You're going bald!" She laughed again, louder this time, and reached to grab what was left of my hair. I pulled back and grabbed her wrist, immediately releasing her.

"Still have the reflexes, Ruth. And men don't dye their hair."

Up to her hair flew the hand I'd just released, then the other. She fluffed the loose curls, smiling girlishly. "I don't, either. Never have, never will."

"That's what Reagan said, too. You're more honest than the Gipper. Ruth. Damn but it's good to see you."

SACRIFICE

Our banter continued awhile until the sun had popped completely into view, an enormous glowing orange yolk with a yellow bonnet reaching into the blue. Ruth turned quickly to glance at the house. She turned back and leaned toward me. Took my hand. "Al, I need to make this quick for now, but so much has happened. There's so much you don't know. We haven't nearly enough time for me to bring you up to speed before the others are up, but let me say this: you're involved – we are involved in something much much bigger than anything we've done in our lives."

"Ruth, what the fuck? I'm about to get an erection...well, obviously I have one already, but, you know what I mean. A permanent one. That's a pretty big deal, I know. Pretty big for me, anyway and no doubt pretty big for Wilde Labs. But I have to beg to differ that a permanent hard-on, big though it may be, is bigger than anything I've done in my life. We, did you say? In our lives? Please excuse my vernacular, but I say again, what the fuck?"

"Al." She stared at me. The damned jaw was set. Dimples gone. "Al." She'd say my name twice when it was time for war. What the fuck? This time I kept it to myself.

"Yeah, boss."

"That's better. Sorry, Al, but this has to be short and not so sweet. You're not getting a permanent hard-on. That's a cover story."

"Say what?" I took a long swallow of coffee and clunked my mug down more heavily than I'd expected. Coffee flew out unto the table. I said it before she could repeat it: "Cover story?"

She explained, briefly roughing out the battle plan that looked to take me to the end of my life. Later, I hoped – and still do – than sooner. "There are forces, serious, dangerous forces that have an idea of what we are really working on. They would want to stop us at all costs if they could, because if the pharmaceutical we're testing does what we hope and expect it to do, its widespread application could undermine the psychology that drives our consumer-obsessed economy.

"Our pharmaceutical, which for now we're calling Vulcana, could introduce a measure of sanity in the global marketplace, and sanity, as we know, is precisely what would put out of business the people who sell addictive products, junk and unhealthy and needless products and who persuade us to vote into office people to whom our collective best interests as a species mean absolutely nothing.

"Vulcana would suppress the greed instinct and would enable us to argue into submission the fear instinct, which is the root of all our self-destructive tendencies. Vulcana is named after the fictional character known as Mr. Spock in the old Star Trek series. Mr. Spock was motivated and guided by reason rather than his primitive brain.

"Our species has not evolved fast enough to stay ahead of the destructive power of our technology to manipulate both our environment and ourselves. Vulcana will enable us to make that evolutionary leap in time, we hope, to keep humanity from destroying itself."

This rush of information overwhelmed me. I felt myself slump in my chair as Ruth talked. When she finished, I picked up my mug and choked down my coffee. She evidently had either already emptied her mug or had forgotten it. We stared at each other. Something alien had descended between us, making us virtual strangers. I started to say something, but stopped because I had no idea what I wanted to say. Finally a thought did present itself. It didn't seem as significant as I'd hoped it might be, but it would be enough to break the awful silence.

"Why me, Ruth? Of all the people you could get to test this new drug, why on Earth have you chosen me?"

The former president took a deep breath and exhaled slowly, as if she'd taken her first drag on a newly lit cigarette. Her face registered deep concern. The lines reaching out from the corners of her eyes and mouth, which I had noticed in the early dawn light, stood out now and made her look as worn as anyone might be expected who has endured eight years in the world's most stressful job. When she spoke, her voice as well betrayed her weariness.

SACRIFICE

"My dear Al. We've chosen you because you have already taken Vulcana."

She might have said this several times, as her words no doubt sent me into an immediate shock of denial. At some point I recovered adequately to inquire as to when and how. She explained that in one of the deliveries of Primrose Lane and my Ritalin refills she'd received monthly at the White House, a bottle had accidentally been filled with laboratory samples of Vulcana. The mistake was discovered the next day and a frantic-but-successful recall mission immediately conducted. The errant bottle was retrieved and replaced with my Ritalin but the recall was too late. I'd taken one of the Vulcana tablets that morning.

"It's a psychotropic drug, Al. It works on the neocortex, strengthening it so it can more easily override the brain's limbic system, the so-called "lizard brain." We watched you carefully after that. In fact, you've been secretly monitored ever since."

"You mean my...the assassination..." Ruth was nodding sadly.

"But..." I went into a full-speed-ahead fugue state, only vaguely aware of the kitchen door opening until the ghost stepped out, walked to the table and sat on the other side of Ruth, facing me.

MATHEW PAUST

QUESTIONS

Anybody watching us who didn't know what was up might have thought Joan Stonebraker and I were having a stinkeye contest. They wouldn't have been too far off the mark.

"You look pretty good for a zombie, Joan." I tried to keep from smiling, and failed. She did look good. Chestnut hair, dyed, of course, and some age lines in her face, but the kinetic energy I remembered her exuding, punctuated by a sparkle in eyes that missed nothing and always seemed a step or two ahead, had not waned. She might no longer have been Special-Agent-In-Charge of the Secret Service's White House Protection Detail, but she was on the job. No question there.

She cracked a half smile of her own. "You didn't come to my funeral, Al." Her voice was low and familiar, a tad warmer than I remembered. Before I could speak she added, "I know, I know, you went to Tonga's. I understand."

"I suppose he's here, too. I feel like the butt of the biggest goddam joke in the universe. You all have some heavy explaining to do, my friends. Wrong drug or no wrong drug. You know?"

"No, Al." It was Ruth. "Tonga's dead. No connection with this. Pure coincidence."

Joan said, "Washington PD believe it was drug related – street drugs – just as we thought. Wrong place, wrong time, mistaken identity, the usual screw up with stoned-out punks."

"I'll bet that played right into your game. I'm assuming I'd already taken this...Vulcan stuff?"

The former president said, "No game, Al. And yes you'd already taken the Vulcana tablet. We saw it as a perfect opportunity to test the paranoia theory."

SACRIFICE

"O-kaaay." It came out as sarcastic as I could muster.

"Godammit, Al..." said Warren Hendrian, who had joined us. Ruth held up a hand to cut him off. She continued, "The concern was very real, Al. Two lab rats had gone into catatonic shock. We didn't know why, but Dr. Knoe hypothesized it might have been a result of extreme paranoia. We...I decided that if anything was going to set you off it would be what happened to Tonga Cooke. And that's when you confirmed our suspicions by what you told Joan."

I felt like a bug under a microscope. "You left me twisting slowly, slowly in the wind."

"Dr. Knoe thought you'd be the perfect subject. She was ready to intervene if it looked like you were in any danger."

"Danger? Of what? Going nuts? Wasn't the presidency in danger? From me? Either my going nuts, which I thought I was, or by not serving you competently?"

"Warren had your back, Al. Anyway, that was not a problem. You did your job just fine. And best of all, you were Wilde's first success with Vulcana."

"What about the real assassination attempt, with Lauri Walquist? Was that phony? I mean, was that a test, too?"

Hendrian tried again. "No, Al. That was real. I advised calling it off when it became apparent how delusional you were getting..."

"Wait!" Several things were building to push me off center here. We were still on the deck and the sun was overhead with its annoying glare. There was my predicament, the sense of being boxed in and out of the loop with more questions sprouting with every revelation. I was getting hungry. And now Hendrian's smarmy tone telling me I was delusional. The little shit seemed to relish my discomfort. And yet I knew the last thing any of us needed was for me to fly off the handle. I hoped my neocortex was still in charge here, at least enough to choke down once again the recurring impulse I was having to grab him and slap some respect onto his pudgy face.

That's when I laughed, when I heard in my head how stupid I would look if I actually said what I was thinking. I figured it was time to toss the ball back into play. "You know, I knew you were reading my journal, Warren. You surely don't believe I would have written that stuff had I not known you were reading over my shoulder?" I scored with that one. Hendrian's jaw dropped as it always did when I slipped one past him. He started to speak, but I wasn't quite finished.

"I knew somebody was messing with me. How could I not? I had plenty of legitimate reasons to suspect there was a rat in the White House, and you were the obvious prime suspect. And I was right."

SACRIFICE

STAKES

Time for my debriefing with Dr. Knoe, who suggested I call her Liz. She wanted to do it outdoors as it was a gorgeous early April day, cool enough that we wore light jackets. Hers was a forest green with a light gray North Face logo over her left breast. Her attractiveness had not diminished but it took a different tack. The bluish greenish eyes were still attention traps but she'd stopped the staring. And she smiled more. Seemed more at ease with me. Her figure was trim and she moved with an athletic grace. Young enough to be my daughter, I guessed, which injected a mitigating dash of superego into my rising id.

She led me down a path through a wooded stretch along a bluff above the water's edge until we reached a clearing that put us at the mercy of blinding sunlight ricocheting off the water into our eyes. Someone had put a wooden park bench there and we settled in for the interrogation.

"Better this way, I think. You seemed uncomfortable with the others," she said. Even her voice was friendlier.

I told her there was too much baggage to sort through with the others and too much I didn't know, that I was Rip Van Winkle.

"Back then I felt alone with what I knew. Completely alone. Didn't know who I could trust or if I was losing my mind. Now I find I was alone with what I didn't know. In the dark. Still am. And I don't see the point anymore."

"Maybe if I explain it allegorically, Al. I grant you it's hard to comprehend. This is cutting edge. A philosopher might say it's existential." She crossed her legs. Thighs a tad heavy I could see through the faded jeans sheathing them. I'm glad we were both looking out over the water where a fishing trawler was anchored.

A couple of men were leaning over the side pulling on something. Nets, I guessed. I was glad for the distraction. If she'd had those eyes fixed on me I doubt I could have paid attention to what she was saying.

"I'd just as soon you gave it to me straight, Liz." I turned my head toward her enough to see if she was still watching the boat. I saw with mixed feelings she was.

"OK. You're the CEO of a multinational corporation that buys politicians, hires foreign labor at slave wages and, worst of all, sells addictive poison to children in the form of fat and and sugar and toxic chemicals. You could make a healthier product but it would cost you an extra two cents per retail sale to do so. This two cents comes out to seven million dollars for you per year. You don't need the seven million, but it would never occur to you not to want it.

"You'll never be prosecuted because you're breaking no laws that anyone could prove – not even for giving school lunch programs kickbacks to push your shit in the cafeteria.

"OK. You're a greedy pig. You know it and you're quite content with this knowledge. In fact, you laugh about it with your friends. You and the many other corporate monsters like you are squeezing the life out the human species and depleting the Earth of its capability to survive. Until now the only hope to survive this suicidal descent is that somehow we can evolve to a higher plane before we reach the end of the road.

"The higher plane CEO would see far enough into the future to understand that concessions are necessary to sustain the planet and its people. He or she would not only see, but would have the mental capability to override those primitive impulses vying for control.

"We're running out of time, Al. The next stage of evolution is out of reach."

"So we do it with this drug? We give everybody the drug like we do with flu shots? And that will make everybody see the light?" I didn't want to sound patronizing, but it seemed to me that's how

SACRIFICE

it came out. This didn't phase Dr. Knoe, noticeably.

She turned to me with enough of a grin that revealed awareness she was out on the ledge. "Not everybody," she said, barely above a whisper. "Just the pigs." The intensity had returned to her eyes. A sharp, chilling gust off the water stirred up dust around us and whipped under my jacket. A squadron of squawking gulls – probably the same ones I'd seen that morning – struggled for control in the buffeting wind.   I nodded yes at Dr. Knoe and tried to smile.

MATHEW PAUST

BUT...

Time to slow down here, break out of the linear narrative and do a little catch-up reflection. For the sake of the story, you can assume I'm still alive and at least sane enough to put this together from the notes I kept in those early days after my parole. Granted my White House journal was published prematurely and without my permission, which played a role in the setup that led to my landing in prison. Now they tell me this was all part of the plan, the research project. Get me out of office, disgraced and behind bars.

It's the old establish-our-man's-credibility trick that supposedly helps undercover ops penetrate their targets. It works in the movies. Problem now is, as I see it, I'm discredited but haven't been given any target to penetrate. I didn't even get the permanent erection Hendrian promised me. Not that I was looking forward to such a bizarre phenomenon but it's another example of the accumulation of bad faith around me since I took that damned pill.

Then, while I was in the White House, I had something to center around, a mission, protect the President in an environment where I could trust no one. With my own sanity in question I had to include myself on the list of untrustworthies. At the same time I knew I could sacrifice my own safety, my life if need be to keep Ruth from harm. Now, two weeks after arriving here I wasn't sure I could trust even her.

"You're distant, Al," she said one afternoon in my room where I'd gone for some privacy to muse and work on this, my journal. She'd knocked softly on the door and announced herself. I sighed and invited her in. Ordinarily I'd have been delighted.

"No shit," I said, trying to smile. She was perched on the edge of my bed, dressed casually in jeans and a sweater. I'd turned the

SACRIFICE

chair at my desk around to face her. The pained expression on her face didn't waver. "You don't trust me anymore, do you." She said it as a statement.

"How can I, Ruth? You hold all the cards." Then, to erase the sense I was whining, I added, "You know I've never put much faith in faith."

This won a gentling of her face. She shifted her weight, bouncing a tad on the bed. "You trusted me before."

"I was trying to protect you. It was my job and I adored you."

"That past tense hurts, Al."

"It's a new game, Ruth. The roles are different. It hurts me, too."

"What if I promised you I'm trying to protect you now?" Her eyes were fixed on mine. I looked away.

"I'm skeptical, Ruth. You said something about how important this project is, that it could save the human species from self-destruction. If it's that important, and you know what's going on and I have barely a clue..."

"It is, and you will have more than a clue. It's just too much to try to explain all at once, so soon. You gave up on Liz...Dr. Knoe. I don't want you to give up on me."

"Ruth, if you start talking like that, about offing the pigs and all that crap from the sixties, I'll bust out of here. That's a promise. I don't care what kind of surveillance you have on me. That kind of off-the-pigs shit didn't do a damned bit of good in the sixties and it won't work now. Never will. It's kids' stuff."

"We're not talking about offing anybody, Al. Nobody needs to get hurt. You know I'm nonviolent. I haven't changed. If I ever do, please shoot me."

Of course I laughed with her but she was still on my list.

DUH

The water was just hot enough that it gave me a mental flash of first-degree burning as I lowered myself into the steaming half-full tub. Short of scalding it was nonetheless hot enough to excite to a near madness of ecstasy the itching up my calves and down my back, a mystery of discomfort I preferred to ignore rather rather than delve into the arcane and tedious trial-and-error clinical procedure of trying to determine allergens or some other cause of the subdermal phenomenon. After rubbing my ankles and calves with my hands in an acknowledging ritual I lay back and luxuriated in whatever the heat was doing to bring the itching forward and call its bluff as my muscles relaxed and my thoughts drifted up with the steam.

When practical I much prefer soaking in a bath than dashing in and out of a shower, which had been my only option in prison the previous six months. I found it curious this was my second week at The Cottage and my first bath there. Something to do with the psychological adjustment, maybe. I had to reach a certain level of surface relaxation before I could take the plunge and really shut everything down and float.

My epiphany came with the lollipop-green bar of Irish Spring soap moments after I dipped it into the seriously hot water. I worked the bar over shoulders and under armpits, basking in the reassuring authority of its ruddy Ulster fragrance. I was being sanitized and deodorized, re-baptized in the font of social accession. It occurred somewhere from the soap's foaming anointment of my left armpit on its journey to the right that I recognized my liberation from all that had been burdening me since my ingestion of the psychotropic Vulcana years before.

It came down to responsibility and the marvelous spiritual awakening there in the bathtub that I no longer had any. None.

SACRIFICE

No responsibility for anybody or anything, not for the President, not for the human species, not for my estranged family nor anyone I might have loved. I no longer had a lick of responsibility for even myself.

I felt a leaden cloak of which I'd not been consciously aware rise from me in the steam and drift toward the ceiling vent and out into the atmosphere to a destination I cared not one whit where. I felt like leaping out of the tub, drying off and dancing nude out onto the deck and off the deck and into the woods and awaaaaay to a place I cared not one whit where.

Quickly coming to my senses, with nonetheless my new sense of freedom unmitigated, I soaked a tad longer, opened the drain, arose and rinsed off with a tepid spray from the overhead shower spigot. My mind picked up speed as I dried off and continued through my morning toilet drill. By the time I'd dressed and was ready to head into the kitchen for breakfast I had worked out a plan.

I shall interject at this point in the narrative a little explaining:

It may seem contradictory that despite my mention earlier of my White House journal being published prematurely, without my consent, I'm disseminating this one as I write it. My aim is to obviate any intervention, redaction or tinkering with my words by anyone. I forward each segment as soon as I have written it to a trusted associate who arranges to have it posted it on an Internet blog. My whereabouts are confidential at this time and are not known by even my associate. I shall reveal the necessity of these precautions as my narrative progresses.

You may be growing impatient that many obvious questions have not yet been addressed. This, too, I shall attempt to remedy as soon and as smoothly as I am able. The posted segments are shorter than I would like, but I'm keeping them to a length that more easily accommodates the medium in which they are being published. Several questions I intend to answer soon include:

● How could one dose of a psychotropic drug have such a lasting effect?

- Why am I so important to this project?

- Even if Vulcana does what I am told it is supposed to do, and, in my case, has already done, how is this going to change anything in our species' self-destructive surge toward extinction? In simpler words, is somebody pulling somebody's leg here and, if so, what the fuck for?

- What's with this permanent erection business? What in hell does it have to do with the price of eggs or the salvation of humanity or any other damned thing?

At this point I shall break off and wish you well until we publish the next segment. I am grateful to those of you who have followed this narrative thus far despite the understandable frustrations with what must seem at this point a preposterous scenario. Preposterous, of course, it is, but you have my promise things will begin to make more sense very soon.

SACRIFICE

DAMMIT!

She caught me trying to hide. I'd taken to getting up before anybody else, making coffee and some breakfast and taking it back to my room and then going out only when nobody else seemed to be around. The strategy was working, partly I imagine because nobody seemed to want to bother me. I assumed this was consideration on their part to give me time to adjust to my new circumstances. They would have been correct in this to a point, but I was also trying to put together a plan for escape.

"Not so fast, buster." The voice came from behind me as I carried a cup of freshly brewed coffee and a cherry fritter on a small plate back to my room. The voice was unmistakable. I kept walking, but turned my head and said over my shoulder, "Coffee's hot. Grab something from the kitchen and join me."

When I got to my room I turned to wait for her but she was right behind me. In we went. She marched to the captain's chair I'd found and put next to my desk, and I set my coffee and fritter on the desk and sat in the old-fashioned wheeled wooden banker's chair in front. I held out the fritter to my guest, but she waved it off. Her eyes were blazing. This was not a social call.

I shrugged, bit off a chunk of the fritter and chewed, keeping my eyes expectantly on hers but determined to wait for her to speak first. She held out until I'd swallowed and taken a slug of coffee. When she spoke her voice was softer than I was expecting. "I shouldn't be surprised you don't trust me, Al. I guess I wouldn't trust me, either."

"What makes you think I don't trust you?" I tried to match her tone but suspect the irony in mine was detectable. She confirmed my suspicion by lifting an eyebrow, smiling with a corner of her mouth. "Well, shit," I said, "Nothing's sacred anymore. Why am I not surprised. That wasn't a question."

She remained still, let me take the lure and run. I did: "Why bother? Aren't we on the same side? How do you do it? Hidden cameras?"

She shifted in the chair, still staring at me with amusement. She was wearing a plaid, pleated skirt and played with her legs a tad as if to tease me with a possible peek. I saw this peripherally, keeping my eyes steady on hers. "Where do you send your journal entries, Al?"

"You seem to know, Ruth. Why the game?"

She ignored my question. "Who do you suppose owns the cloud?"

"Aw shit."

"Not to worry, my friend. Your story is safe. Any other cloud and your stuff would make fascinating reading in all the wrong places."

"So you know I'm determined to escape. Doesn't that worry you?"

"No, Al. You're not getting out."

"Who's gonna stop me?"

She sprang out of the chair and reached for my hand. I pulled it back, bringing a smirky pout to her lips. "Have it your way. Come." She strode out of my room. Looked back to make sure I was following, as if I had a choice.

Out on the deck she motioned me into one of the wicker-backed chairs. She remained standing. Suddenly the squadron of gulls I'd seen my first morning on the deck swooped out of the same copse as before and flapped across the expanse of water view into the cedars. Ruth was holding what looked like a smart phone or a TV remote. She pointed it at the cedars and the gulls came swooping back across. She pointed it at the copse and the birds did a repeat.

"What the fuck, Ruth?" First time in my memory I'd used that word in her presence. She didn't appear to notice.

"Do you want them to land on the deck so you can pet them?" She turned to face me, smiling widely. I'm certain my face registered the idiotic dumbfoundedness I felt. I shrugged. "What's

SACRIFICE

the point, Ruth? So you have some fake seagulls flying back and forth. I suppose you're gonna tell me they shoot rockets or death beams, too?"

Ruth walked over and placed a hand on my shoulder. With her other hand gripping the remote, she pushed a button bringing whatever the hell it controlled flapping back into view. But instead of heading into the cedars again this time they hovered. She studied the remote. I could see it had a screen filled with symbols just like a smart phone. She did something with her thumb. POW! The sound, so near my elbow I felt the concussion, was that of a large firecracker exploding. It left my ears ringing. I turned to see what had happened and saw the coffee cup I'd brought with me to the deck had shattered into pieces, splashing lukewarm coffee everywhere, including on me.

Then I noticed the bright green beam of light linking the tabletop, where the cup had been, to one of the birds still hovering overhead. A plume of black smoke rose from a quarter-size hole at the end of the beam, which now was burning into the deck itself.

Ruth must have touched the screen again, as the beam vanished and the birds flapped away out of sight.

DAMMIT! (cont.)

Ruth's fingers clawed into the tender area between my shoulder and neck when I tried to pull away. "Don't be silly," she said into my ear. She released her "Vulcan death grip" when I ceased struggling. My face glowered when I turned it toward her to see she was smiling, albeit with a cast of grim determination. "What the fuck," I said again. "Just turn the goddam thing off and let me go. I'm no use to you. I'm not going to attack any pigs for you or save the species or whatever the hell else you have in mind. If I refuse to cooperate you can't make me do a damned thing.

"I've served you and I've served my country. In return, you fucked over me with some goddam drug and then you fucked over me with some goddam kangaroo court and now you're trying to fuck over me with whatever the hell it is you want me to do next. Well, I'm sick of your goddam fucking bullshit. Just let me go. I'm going whether you want me to or not. Kill me if you have to. I don't give a shit anymore what you do." I turned away from her. She removed her hand from my shoulder, pulled a chair over next to me and sat down. Then she reached across and jammed something into my shirt pocket.

"Keep it," she said as I pulled out the piece of plastic and saw it was the remote she'd used to activate the gulls. "It's yours. Those birds are not for you, Al, to hold you here. They're part of the defense apparatus we've set up to protect us from those who seriously want to keep us from doing what we're doing. They'll kill us if they have to." She paused while I tried to persuade myself I was awake. I had not yet succeeded when she added, "They would rather find out what it is we're doing, what we have. They'll do whatever it takes to get that information."

Finally I could see some humor and knew I was indeed awake. I managed only to choke out a chuckle or two but it was enough. I

SACRIFICE

said, "They haff vays to mek us talk?" I laughed full out then. Ruth joined in briefly, patting my hand. It was a strange laughter for both of us. It didn't last long. Her voice when she spoke next was low and resigned, almost morose. "I should think so."

Ruth explained that one of Wilde Laboratory's initial test subjects for Vulcana had threatened to sue after he developed an erection that remained longer than the advertised warning of four hours for commercial products using phosphodiesterase inhibitors.

"He became extremely agitated after the second day. He said he would sue. Wilde reminded him of the release documents he'd signed when he entered the research program. Liz...Dr. Knoe tried every available medical procedure, including tranquilizer injections. They even tried to bore him down with extended readings of...I'm sorry, Al, certain passages of your journal...not by her, of course, but Warren read some and then there was a lab assistant, very homely and, ah, unappealing in looks and manner, who read with a droning nasally voice that actually put the poor guy to sleep, but the erection remained."

I raised a hand for her to stop. "Was this after you published the journal?" I grasped as I was saying it how self-centered and vain I sounded, but could not hold it in. I tried to grin.

"No, Al, they used some chapters we left out of the book." She smiled. Hers seemed more genuine than mine had felt. I wanted to run away now more than ever.

"Anyway, long story short," she said, "he escaped...er, left the facility on his own and evidently turned up at Magdalene Medical Center in Richmond. We learned later he took his own life. Shortly afterward an FDA administrator contacted Edna and we knew the cat was out of the bag.

"Fortunately, after the subject escaped, we took the precaution of moving our research facility to The Cottage. Nobody knows of this property, yet. Edna acquired it as a gift from a venture capital executive she'd met on a cruise to the Bahamas. I understand the gentleman is deceased."

"Ruth, that doesn't seem like much of a reason for somebody to want to kill us, unless it's somebody who wants to avenge the guy with the hard-on. He was a freak, right? I mean, I took the same drug and...well, you know. Everything worked the way it's supposed to."

"Dear Al." She moved her hand to my thigh and rested it there. "No, actually, the drug you took was a later variation, with the libido enhancer suppressed. Yours simply amplified certain parts of your neocortex to give it an edge over your limbic system, what they call the lizard brain. As Liz explained it to me, only one dose was needed to kick-start the neocortex into an advanced state of predominance. The effect should be permanent, and so far as we know in your case, it hasn't diminished in effect the slightest bit."

"But I gather you're not finished with me?"

"That's right, Al. Wilde's latest variation hasn't been tested on anyone yet. They frankly do not know precisely its effect. "

"What if I refuse?"

"That will be up to you, of course, but there've been some developments outside our little domain here we're hoping will persuade you to see the need to help us."

While Ruth was speaking I noticed some movement near the door to the kitchen. I saw a man I didn't recognize standing just outside the door staring at us. I had a feeling he'd been there awhile.

"Ruth," I said, nodding toward the man.

SACRIFICE

FEEDBACK

Backing away again from rote sequence here. Trying to avoid narrative slavery without losing the thread of my story. Objective is to draw you into my milieu more with suggestion than with graphic or metaphoric pyrotechnics. I am fully aware this approach runs counter to modern, post-modern and coyly cinematic literary expectations. Please trust me, this is no *dîner avec André*.

At the moment I am bound by a sense that a predictable expository design might distract from the underlying message I'm trying to convey. This, despite knowing that as a rule most messages, excluding the most sublime, benefit from direct delivery. I'm hesitant because this one is anything but sublime and is possibly too shrill in its implications to play without laying some foundation. Thus I proceed cautiously as I ponder which details to release and how and when.

Many of the events I'm describing are happening as close in time to my filing these dispatches that any statutes of limitation which might apply to any of the described actions are no doubt still ticking. I feel relatively secure from physical discovery, yet am taking the precaution of transmitting these installments via a network of satellite-connected relays to the operator who is making them available to you. I'm comforted by how many readers are commenting regularly. The more who know of these events the safer I feel.

Be aware, however, there are possible risks for bloggers who can be linked to these dispatches even though most of the events they describe should be safely out of play by now. I cannot help but recall the WWII Japanese soldiers who, never getting word of the surrender, lived out their lives in uniform on obscure Pacific islands honing their bayonets and staying true to their emperor.

I find comfort knowing there are others following this story, readers who can ensure that a record of these events is less likely to be expunged by those who would wipe away every trace of it from human memory. By merely reading my words you become repositories of a knowledge vital to the safety of our species. You may feel inclined to preserve this account and see that its message is dispersed to others and to future generations beyond the reach of the inevitable would-be expungers.

At the same time your comments are helping to guide the narrative in a direction that keeps alive my promise, which, if not implicit thus far I do hereby pledge, that all will be explained in due time. I see from some of you I might have overplayed the "permanent erection" element initially. I apologize if this has misled anyone to anticipate something a tad more titillating than I have intended and still intend to expose. At the same time I am fully aware that, as with many other aspects of perception, titillation most often arises in the head of the beholder.

Philosopher Jim, a close reader, loyal and helpful in his comments regarding the unfolding of this saga, has suggested the appearance of a contradiction in my temperament. Despite my taking the pill, Vulcana, that supposedly gives my superego supremacy over my id, I lose my temper with Ruth.

A tantrum such as mine in this circumstance indeed derives from the more primitive part of the brain. The implications that drive my emotions here are dire. They would be for anyone in any context. Yet I manage to get a grip on this reaction to my sense of powerlessness and of being manipulated. I have my emotions under control in a relatively short time. I suggest the ordinary person would have come unglued, go bonkers, at the very least become paranoid - and quite justifiably so.

Some of you may be chafing a bit that I left you hanging last time with a mysterious man standing on the deck where Ruth and I have been talking. I would apologize for the melodrama except I saw it as a reasonable device to keep you from losing interest.

There was a man standing just outside the kitchen door. When Ruth invited him to join us I recognized him immediately but could not recall his name. It came to me at the same instant Ruth reminded me he was Anthony Cromwell, formerly animal control warden-in-charge of a detail that assisted in the White House sting operation to nab some suspected assassins and who, when I confronted him in exasperation for being in the Rose Garden during such a critical time, startled me with the calmly delivered comment, "People are animals, too, sir."

Cromwell had ended up besting the Secret Service and FBI contingents in that operation and saving the day. Afterward, Ruth lured him away from his position with the D.C. Division of Animal Control and hired him to head up security at The Cottage. I had assumed this job was held by Joan Stonebraker, who had headed the White House Secret Service Detail. Stonebraker, however, was assigned now as special agent-in-charge of security for Ruth as a former president.

"I'm leaving now for the weekend," Ruth told me after she'd introduced Cromwell and instructed him to show me around The Cottage. "Herman wants to take me to New York. He and his trio have a gig at Birdland. He's quite excited." She winked, then leaned over and whispered in my ear: "Call me if anything comes up, Alfie."

MATHEW PAUST

WHO?

"Who is the most dangerous person in the world right now?"

It's a question I'd pondered once or twice as White House chief of staff but hadn't had occasion to consider even remotely in the years since. In those executive days it was asked usually in a strategical sense and only by the president. I found it annoyingly incongruous to hear it now coming from the mouth of Anthony Cromwell.

We were in his office, a fairly large room at the other end of the house from mine. He sat behind a metal institutional desk at facing 90-degrees from the door. A bank of several video monitors stared at him from a shelf against one wall. The monitors appeared to be connected to cameras scanning the property around us. I was in the only other chair, an old-fashioned unpadded wooden creation on wheels and with wooden arm rests. I'd rolled it to face Cromwell at an oblique angle so I could glance occasionally at the monitors without being rude to my host. The room was neatly kept despite several overloaded bookcases and boxes of books and documents arranged on the floor. Even Cromwell's desktop was neat, with only an LED lamp, a laptop computer, a stack of two or three yellow legal pads, a coffee mug holding ballpoint pens and a box of Puffs tissues.

"Dangerous? In what way? You mean somebody like Ayatollah Arsham? Bernard Kunkle? Me?" I'd been brought up to speed that Cromwell had gotten a doctorate in linguistics since I'd last encountered him but I wondered if he was still as flat and humorless.

"Arsham and Kunkle are rooks in comparison, sir. Potential Hitlers but incipient thus far. The world's gotten too small for those types to spread their wings without brushing counterforces they're better off not upsetting."

SACRIFICE

"So I'm off the hook, too? Oh, and Cromwell, I thought we'd settled this 'sir' bullshit way back. Please. You outrank me now. It's Al."

"Sorry, Al. Old habits die hard. To answer your question, which I'm trusting was a joke, actually we're thinking you might be a key to gaining access to the target." He rocked back in his chair, which looked identical to the one I was using, setting up a clacking and pinging of springs.

"Target, eh? I wish we could stop using these militaristic terms, you know? I haven't agreed to anything yet, and the idea of 'targets' worries me, especially as I've been led to believe I am the target at this point." I clacked back in my chair, too, bumping into a stack of boxes directly behind me. "Have you considered oiling the springs in these chairs?"

"Oil, yeah. Good idea. I've gotten used to it, and I don't have many visitors, but I see where it could be irritating." Not nearly so irritating as your stiff manner, I thought.

We fenced a tad more about what makes someone dangerous and what type of danger concerned us until finally my irritation got the best of me.

"OK, Cromwell, dammit. I give up. I don't know who the hell you're referring to and obviously you have someone in mind. So, please, I'm still unsettled by all this. Hell, I may never become settled. But please quit beating around the bush. Who? Who's the most dangerous man - you did say 'man'? - in the world?"

"The President."

"Ruth?" Are you nuts? Are you all on drugs...excuse me, pharmaceuticals here?   Or am I still hallucinating? I was hallucinating before, right? Some of the time?" I'd taken to rocking in the chair now, kicking up a minor cacophony of squeaks, clacks, bumps, pings and scraping noises.

Cromwell leaned forward abruptly, almost matching my noises with his own. "Easy, Al. No, of course, not. Besides, she's no longer president. I mean the one we have now. President

Morowitz."

I believe my jaw was hanging down at this point. I was agape in the non-Christian sense. Slackened by dumbfoundedness. I had a sudden sense of being Alice pushed through the looking glass. I wanted to look around for the familiar forms of Misters Tweedledee and Tweedledum or, more appropriately, the Mad Hatter. I needed, desperately, something soothing to drink.

SACRIFICE

TINK

"Do you have another one of those?" I asked, nodding toward the clear plastic bottle of Aquafina water on his desk. He turned his head and stared at the bottle for a couple of seconds as if surprised to find it there. Then he ducked down and I heard, in addition to the protests from his chair, a crinkling that came from under the desk. He reappeared with a similar bottle and looked at me with an undecipherable expression. We both rose at once, filling the room again with the tangled intrusive sounds of aggravated steel springs and old wood. I retrieved my water from him and returned to my chair, my brain scrambling to measure implications and possible questions and arguments I could render if what I feared he had meant was what he meant.

"Dangerous? Morowitz is so weak and insignificant newspapers are giving away free magnifying glasses just so we can see him in the cartoons. He's damned near microscopic!"

"I don't read the papers, sir...I mean Al, but you don't need to exaggerate. I'm..."

"Not exaggerating, Cromwell. The Washington Times is giving out little plastic magnifying glasses as a promotion."

"Look, I'm not arguing with you. Morowitz's stature is admittedly diminished. That's what makes him so dangerous. He's too malleable, too easily manipulated. A weak president in the most powerful office in the world makes him more dangerous than a tyrant."

I got it. The logic snapped my myopic cognition into focus. "Of course! Rather than go after the manipulators, the Kunkles and the corporate barons who use money and veiled intimidation to have their way, we get there first and manipulate the man whose main weapon is his knowledge of them and his ability to rip their veils away and expose them to the angry masses. That's it. Am I right? With pharmaceuticals, right?"

I watched Cromwell's face go through a curious transformation as I said this. It started with his eyes, which widened at first, their brown irises darkening as the pupils expanded bringing his countenance to a piercing intensity. Almost as soon as this focus seemed about to reach an alarming vortex the skin of his face stretched laterally and suddenly I recognized he was smiling, an expression I'd never seen on him before. He chuckled.

"That's the old Al, sir...I mean..." The smile vanished, replaced by the old Cromwell-trying-to-bluff-with-a-pair-of-treys look, his usual look and which he actually was pretty good at but which he now betrayed with a slight sag of embarrassment. Were he able to read my face he'd have known I was thinking, What do you know of the "old" Al, you Boy Scout upstart?

He recovered quickly and stood. "Come on. There's somebody you need to meet." He led me down a couple of halls past doors with no indication as to what was behind them. The more I saw as we walked the more I came to realize that although The Cottage at one time might have been residential it was since converted into something else. We took an elevator down at least two floors. The door opened to another hallway, a lengthy stretch with an odd odor and a subterranean feel.

"The man you're about to meet is a little different," Cromwell said as we started along the dimly lighted corridor. "He's our resident genius. Our chief of research. He designed Primrose Lane, which, as you know, put Wilde Labs on the map. He designed Vulcana, the drug you took accidentally when you were in the White House. He's now developing pharmaceuticals that will change the world."

"He works here?"

"Sir...Al, the contract that's out on you is garden variety compared with the one on this man. The most secret, deadly agents of the governments of much of the so-called civilized world are out to find this man. They will kill anyone to get to him. Right now this place, The Cottage, is the most secure and best protected location we could find. You will know before you've finished that bottle of water why it's so important to protect this man. Here we are." He had stopped in front of what appeared to be a steel door in a steel frame. As with those we'd passed earlier, there was no window, sign or indication of any kind as to what we would find behind it.

I became aware that the annoying crinkling noise I'd been hearing after leaving Cromwell's office was me nervously squeezing the plastic Aquafina bottle. I took a deep swallow of the unchilled water and looked for a place to set the bottle.

"That's OK. The noise doesn't bother me and it won't bother Tink."

"Who? What did you say?"

"Oh, sorry. We call him "Tink." I have his name in a file in my office but I don't think anybody else knows it. It's a odd name. Tell you the truth I can't even recall it. He's Tink. That's what he goes by." Cromwell produced a plastic key card and inserted it into a receptacle in the door.

"Does he know we're here?"

"Oh, yes. Nobody ever comes down here without clearing it first. In fact, we're five minutes late. I should mention that Tink always wears a kilt. I've never seen him in anything else. He...ah, well, you'll see for yourself, but he, ah, has an erection. He tests most of the drugs on himself. He liked the effect one of the earlier forms of Vulcana had on him and, ah, decided not to, um, tinker with it. He never leaves the lab here...well, I don't need to say any more. You'll see."

Cromwell waited until a green light flashed in the key receptacle and pulled the door open.

MATHEW PAUST

GLADYS

Her smile greeted us at the door with the radiance of a November sun blooming through morning haze. She glanced first at Cromwell then brought her hazel eyes to me, flicking them quickly over my face before resting them on my eyes where they slipped inside to explore the mysteries lying beyond my quivering optic nerves. "Hi. I'm Gladys," she said in a voice that sounded so shy it was barely audible.

She led us through a space crowded with electronic apparatus, some of which winked at us with digital displays on small screens. One piece appeared to be a sophisticated microscope and beside it an off-white plastic box about twice the size of a microwave oven. A digital display panel in front gave no clue of the object's purpose, but a hinged lid on the top was up. I leaned over as we walked past and saw an oddly configured cylinder inside giving the device the appearance of miniature top-loading clothes dryer.

"It's a centrifuge," she said, noticing my curiosity. I smiled appreciatively and nodded as I tried, futilely, to think of something to say. Gladys was slim and petite. Her brown pony tail bounced playfully as she led us through the laboratory maze, hips tilting this way and that as she navigated around tables and work benches laden with equipment.

We came to a more comfortable-looking room, with a couch and several padded chairs. Lighting was lower here, apparently limited to a row of recessed ceiling lights and a couple of reading lamps. I could see two people seated across the room facing each other. They seemed to have been engaged in conversation but both turned their faces toward us as we entered. One face belonged to Dr. Knoe. The other, which I didn't recognize, was a man's. The man stood up.

"Sir...er, Al, this is Tink. Tink, Mister...er, Al Geddes," said

SACRIFICE

Cromwell. The man who strode toward me appeared to be about my height and weight but at least 30 years younger. His face sported an oddly wide smile, a Cheshire Cat smile that stretched what looked to be an already wide face into a horizontal oval with a grill of gleaming teeth. Atop this flattened visage sprouted a massive tangle of six-inch-high hair tufts that clearly had not been combed since their host had emerged from the womb. And, yes, he was wearing a red-and-green plaid pleated kilt that draped tellingly over a mid-range protuberance the more curiously noticeable for his apparent effort to conceal it.

"Yup, it's real never goes away teeheehee want one?" he said in a tense, energetic voice by way of introduction. He'd evidently seen my quick glance down before focusing back on his face. Before I could respond he added, "All it takes is another pill the one you took was an early prototype I've invented many better versions since then I have some right here teeheehee."

I opened my mouth to speak, but he started in again, "I have pills that make it go down but I don't use them teeheehee why would I want it to go down with these glorious bimbos around teeheehee. I have..."

"STOP!" Gladys barked, placing a smooth dark-chocolate hand in front of his face. Then, more gently, "Tinkydo, I don't think they want to know all that right now. OK, sweetie?" She reached over and patted one of his cheeks, both still bunched up from the unceasing ear-to-ear smile. I studied her face for any sign she might be putting him on or had taken offense at the "glorious bimbos" remark, but found only merriment. Not so evident with Dr. Knoe, whose face remained impassive as she studied mine with her unwavering cryptic gaze.

Cromwell had filled me in on Gladys Alabi, a Nigerian national with doctorates in chemistry and neuroscience and a masters in digital spectroscopy who worked for Wilde Laboratories as Tink's assistant. Difficult as it was for me to comprehend at first that Gladys served under a man whose formal education ended with a bachelor's degree in mathematics, I imagined it must be ten times harder for her to accept. Not so, she assured me.

"Tink is a true genius," she told me before our scheduled meeting while Tink and Dr. Knoe finished up the discussion they'd been having. "He's an autodidact. Taught himself to break free of the bonds of conventional thinking and into a realm very few people can manage. I consider myself fortunate that I can keep up with him conceptually, but I'm usually a step or two behind him at reaching the important benchmarks. On my own, without him leading the way, it would take years to get to where he can reach in a week."

One of Gladys's jobs, she acknowledged with an affectionate note in her voice, was to help him relate to others. "I'm sort of like his translator, you know? He speaks in rapid bursts, whatever's on his mind just comes tumbling out and it's not always in the right sequence and he often expects you to understand considerably more than you probably do. I'll be with you in the meeting, mostly for that role."

She explained that Tink had hired her after first contacting her through a website for Nigerians living in the U.S. He'd been flirting with someone named Gladys who approached him in an email claiming to be an heiress who needed his help to escape political opponents of her father.

"It was one of those typical scams that have given my homeland a bad reputation. Tink was having fun spoofing with whomever was pretending to be this Gladys and ended up contacting me through this group. He was so impressed with my credentials. I think he was thinking of photos the other Gladys had sent him while he and I were getting acquainted online.

"I hope he wasn't disappointed in me when we first met. I don't think so, though. Oh, hell, I know so." She laughed. It came out of her throat a low, rolling series of chuckles that seemed to inspire an even brighter sparkle in her eyes.

Cromwell tapped me on the shoulder and nodded toward the other two when I turned from Gladys. Tink and Dr. Knoe were staring our way, Tink nodding his head and gesturing for us to join them.

SACRIFICE

ENOUGH OF THE ONE-WORD TITLES!

Were Tink's arrogance helium the walls and ceiling of our little room would have blown outward, the gas then ripping the entire building from the ground, and lurching it into the stratosphere.

"Big Pharma? Hah! I'm Big Pharma teeheehee I've left the rest of them in my dust all the big guys who buy all the politicians and scare all the presidents I can give you any kind of drug you like for anything teeheehee you wanna grow hair? where? anywhere, on the bottom of your feet or on your butt or anywhere you want I have drugs for it I have drugs to make you sleep and make you high and make you brave as a lion and smart as Stephen Hawking I've cracked the code teeheehee nobody else can do what I can do..."

He paced, he sat, he sprang up after a couple of seconds and paced some more, then sat, then sprang up, then down, then up, down, up. The words flew out of him like bats from a Mexican cave at midnight. I've given you a word-for-word transcription of some of what he said because I had a digital recorder rolling all the while. I had to slow it down playing it back to make out individual words. While he spoke I had no clue what he was saying but Gladys Alabi would gently stop him every now and again, patting his forearm - the one he wasn't waving dramatically at that particular moment - and he would stop, sometimes in mid-word it seemed, and turn to her, smiling his ubiquitous smile, and she would whisper in his ear and then turn to us and translate.

"He wants to show you his mice," she said at one point, and we moved into yet another room.

I prepared myself for an expected assault of raunchy animal odors and was surprised to find none. The laboratory smelled vaguely of pine, probably from a detergent. Its cages were glass cubicles arranged in three tiers along one wall. Metallic hoses led from each enclosure to what appeared to be a central ventilating system. I would guess about six dozen rodents - mostly mice with a few larger specimens, probably rats - inhabited this laboratory condominium.

The rats and some of the mice seemed to recognize Tink when he entered the room. They scurried to the glass wall nearest him and stretched upright against it, dipping their heads back and forth and scraping their paws on the surface.

"Hello, Randy and Minnie and Ralph and Woodrow and Max and Murgatroyd and Benjamin and..." This went on and on as he quickly worked his way along the enclosures, leaning down to put his face up to each one as he softly spoke the name of its occupant, which, in turn, bobbed its head up and down in excited communion. Some of them, showing tiny pointed teeth as their mouths opened and shut, seemed to be chattering to him, but Tink's voice was all I could make out.

As Tink greeted his friends, with Gladys next to him apparently exciting the rodents with her presence as well, I glanced at the others. Cromwell stood by the door, his face a noncommittal mask, while Dr. Knoe, nearer me, had her eyes fixed upon mine with an intensity that continued to baffle and excite. Knowing that Philosopher Jim, who is following this narrative, has indicated a persistent interest in seeing some kind of heterosexual relationship consummated soon, I will say that I did speak to her at this time, but only to break the distracting tension of her unwavering focus upon me.

"This is becoming surrealer and surrealer," I said, trying to convey lightheartedness and hoping to win a chuckle or at least a smile from this inscrutable woman. She blinked.

"You ain't seen nuthin' yet, Al." Her voice was so soft I wasn't sure I'd heard what I thought I'd heard. I gambled.

"You mean there are more looking glasses to slip through?"

She stepped closer, which I surmised in the dimly lit room only because I saw her eyes growing larger and larger. Her breath reached my neck carrying a minty sweetness that wafted up and

SACRIFICE

engaged my nostrils with a sharp recognition that caused me to envy Tink his kilt. She patted my face with a hand that brought a musky nuance into the mix, letting her fingers linger a tad longer than necessary before withdrawing them from sight. That's when she allowed the tiniest of smiles to enter our psychic proximity. The eyes, enormous and steady, seemed anticipatory. At this point I knew I had no choice. I was damned if I gave her an intentional sign of deference.

"Doctor," I said, my voice unnaturally hoarse from the surge of hormones, "I ain't no Alice."

MATHEW PAUST

TINK IS PINK

Tink beckoned us over to a glass cage containing a mouse whose black and white markings gave it the appearance of a miniature Holstein cow. The mouse sat on a cushion of shredded paper bedding, staring placidly at Tink, it's pink nose and whiskers twitching rhythmically.

"Morganstern," said Tink, who was kneeling, his face even with the mouse's several inches from the glass. A flood of words followed so rapidly I had no idea what he was saying. Gladys, kneeling beside him, explained that Tink initially had named the mouse Morganstern but they were now calling him Mighty Mouse.

"You'll see why. He's our star test mouse," she said, then, "Pink, I think we're ready now."

I turned to Dr. Knoe and tried to whisper out of earshot of the others, "Pink? Isn't it Tink?"

"I think so," she said, her charismatic breath jigging me away from my train of thought for a second or two. "Is that what she said? Pink?"

"Maybe I didn't hear her right. Maybe..." I caught Cromwell's eye and motioned him over. "We're supposed to call him 'Tink,' right?" Cromwell narrowed his eyes and stared at the two scientists a moment. "'Tink,' I think," he said. "What's the problem?"

"I heard her - Gladys - call him 'Pink.' It sounded pretty distinct. I was just wondering," I said.

Cromwell scratched his scalp through thinning hair, his face crinkled in thought. "Tink, Pink, what's the difference," he said, his voice low and with just enough timbre to reach our ears

SACRIFICE

without disturbing the others. "It's just a nickname, anyway."

Dr. Knoe took my sleeve and guided me several steps further from the other two. Cromwell backed up to stay with us. "It matters," she said. "Nicknames are often more important than given names. Nicknames tell us more about the individual and may mean more to the person with the name.

"If we've been mistakenly calling him 'Tink' when in fact his nickname, for whatever reason, is 'Pink,' it likely has distanced us from him in a way that could be detrimental to our mission here. He may not mind the least bit, of course, but if he does his regard for us as discerning associates is bound to be diminished by our mistake. He might in fact be laughing at us, which could degenerate into a greater misunderstanding or even a practical joke that could end in disaster.

"We simply cannot take the risk."

She was right. My discomfort at being in the middle of a situation that could go haywire at any moment due to miscommunication, with stakes as high as they seemed to be, was interfering with my ability to think clearly. "I agree, Doctor. Shall we clear this up now?"

"I would wait until after we're finished here. Maybe talk to Gladys alone and get her take on it. Maybe we're still not hearing it right. Gladys can straighten this out for us, but I wouldn't interrupt the flow of things right now. She's motioning us over. I think they're ready for us."

As it turned out we had been hearing it wrong. "Pink" was the correct nickname. Pink evidently hadn't noticed our mistake, Gladys told us, and she herself had not been sure she'd heard the others correctly with their mispronunciation.

"I thought perhaps it was some regional vernacular," she said. "I don't make a point of reading lips and it just sounded to me as if you were pronouncing the first letter a little harder than we were. If Pink noticed he said nothing to me. We've never discussed his nickname. I have no idea what it means or why he's chosen it."

This now clarified, I will proceed with the correct nickname henceforth, although I believe the confusion among people supposedly working closely on a strategically vital project should be part of the record.

Pink was ready to begin his demonstration. As we approached, he held out a hand, palm up, upon which the little mouse perched, nose and whiskers twitching and an expression of bonhomie on its face the likes of which I'd never imagined a rodent of any kind could manage.

SACRIFICE

CAN MIGHTY MOUSE SAVE THE WORLD?

Its contrail of implications continued to rattle my nerves for several heartbeats after the shriek blitzed through the laboratory. It started as a cry of disbelief that lasted for less than a second before ramping up in intensity and pitch to an unearthly keening that sent a shockwave of fright through my nerves and into the roots of the hair on my head and neck, bringing each follicle to quivering alert.

The piercing commotion occurred behind me at about the instant I'd turned my head for an impulsive gape into the eyes of Dr. Knoe. The look of heightened-yet-manageable expectation in them might have kept my hirsute response from becoming comically exaggerated.

We'd been watching a demonstration the likes of which I couldn't have imagined while sober. In fact the spectacle aroused in me a rare sense that maybe indeed I could use a drink, and a stiff one at that. (The pun slipped out unintentionally, but I'll leave it alone at least for now.) Our demonstration consisted of Morganstern, aka Mighty Mouse, mounted atop the rear of a rat at least six times his size. The rat, Freda, was cooperating fully, even presenting herself with a angle that made it easier for M to engage her, which he did, grabbing her on each haunch and delivering a seemingly endless series of vigorous thrusts that suggested a miniature jackhammer pounding a hole in a patch of stubborn street concrete.

The romantic tryst did not begin so connubially. Pink, explaining that the two had never seen each other before, placed M into a cage adjacent to Freda's. The rat eyed M for a moment and then rushed to the glass wall separating their cages, baring her teeth and emitting a sharp hissing sound. There she gathered herself into a combative stance, her haunch muscles bulging with the tension of coiled springs and pressing her face against the glass. The hissing grew into a guttural sound that reached us easily through the glass. The sound, which Gladys said was growling, might have been the roar of a tiny chainsaw. M's reaction was peaceable. He sat facing the rat, nose twitching, appearing not the least bit intimidated by Freda's warlike posturing on the other side of the glass.

Pink reach out and grabbed a metal loop atop the glass panel. He slid the panel up so there was nothing blocking access by the two rodents to either cage. M moved first. He walked slowly forward straight to Freda, who seemed frozen with surprise. When M reached her he sniffed her face and then rubbed his nose against her, working back toward the outsized flaps of her ears. He rubbed his nose inside the nearest flap.

At this point Freda's tension eased noticeably and she began rocking her head back and forth as I'd seen other rats do when Pink approached their cages. Freda wriggled into a presentation stance even before the mouse was himself in position to mount. She started producing a meek cooing sound in her throat. The cooing continued after M climbed aboard and initiated copulation with the much larger animal.

This activity had continued without interruption for at least five long minutes before I turned away to glance at Dr. Knoe. When I looked back at the cages I saw Pink on his knees in apparent extreme agony, rocking back and forth and holding his head in his hands. Freda was lying on her side and M was nuzzling her with what appeared to be affection, moving up to her head and back along her exposed belly. He emitted an intermittent series of squeaks as he appeared to be either grieving or trying to resuscitate his lover.

Vague words eventually emerged from Pink's wails. Gladys explained that Freda evidently had died from the excitement, that the copulation with M had gone on much longer than rats normally experienced.

"Her heart just couldn't take it anymore," she said. She led us from the lab back to the sitting room and then returned to Pink,

SACRIFICE

whose grief seemed inconsolable. Cromwell went to the electric coffee maker while Dr. Knoe and I sat facing each other. I had hoped she'd join me on the couch. As it was, our thoughts -- at least mine -- were completely distracted by what we had witnessed and by the terrible sounds still coming from the lab.

Cromwell returned with cups of coffee for each of us. When I realized he intended to sit on the couch I moved closer to one side to allow for some distance between us. I caught Dr. Knoe's lips form a quick smirk as she watched me slide from the center. I smiled back, but the smirk by then had vanished.

"Mighty Mouse never did that in the cartoons," Cromwell muttered, perhaps hoping to lighten the mood.

"Guess not," I said, to be polite. A flick of my eyes revealed no readable reaction from the good doctor.

MATHEW PAUST

MOURNING FREDA

By the time our coffee had cooled enough to be sipped without lip or tongue injuries Pink's wailing from the lab had ebbed and Gladys rejoined us.

"It must be hard to do his research if Pink gets so attached to the lab animals," I said, suspecting it was the wrong thing to say but feeling a need to say something that seemed substantive. When Gladys merely looked at me quizzically without response, I added, "I mean, surely there are other casualties. All of these little fellows can't survive the testing."

Cognition appeared in Gladys's sparkling brown eyes. "Oh, you think Pink is upset because of Freda! Because Freda died?"

"Well, isn't that..." I stopped, feeling nonplussed, not wanting to sound too obvious or merely stupid. She picked up the thread before I could think of a way to continue.

"Of course Pink and I love all of the lab animals, as if they are pets. We're sad Freda died. Of course. But what you probably don't understand at this point is that Morganstern - Mighty Mouse, that is - is heartbroken. It's Morgie's grief that Pink is empathizing with. Pink is grieving with Morgie and will probably sleep on the floor in front of his cage tonight to keep him company. Morgie is devastated by what happened."

"But..." I knew I should keep quiet, but I was feeling dizzy from the surreality of what was happening. I needed a rational paddle in order to stay afloat. I began to fear I might suddenly burst out laughing in near hysteria, something I am prone to do in bizarre situations. More than anything right then it was necessary for me to participate in a straight-faced non-ironic, no bullshit dialogue.

Gladys's voice helped. Low-registered and unrushed, she spoke in an understated manner that had a soothing effect even before her

SACRIFICE

words began registering. Her vital yet gentle gaze enhanced this calming sensibility, focusing on my eyes without challenge or expectation but as if enjoying privately what she saw. I cannot rule out that what was happening was a more collaborative phenomenon, that she saw the effect of her natural, unpretentious beauty reflected in my face and that this had a reassuring effect on her that transmitted back and forth in mutually building strokes that engender a pulse-quickening reach toward spiritual communion if not out and out jubilation.

"Morgie's upset because his empathy failed to warn him Freda was becoming too excited," she said. With a quick glance around the small room I saw that Cromwell and Dr. Knoe were staring at Gladys with rapt attention. At least it appeared that way, maybe because that's what I was doing.

"The mouse could sense the rat's excitement level?" I wanted to inject some realism here.

"The drugs we've administered to Morgie have enhanced his senses exponentially," Gladys explained. "Both his id and his superego have merged into a cooperative arrangement with the neocortex fully in charge. On a level of course much more primitive than ours Morgie is nonetheless vastly more the master of his perceptual interpretations, his impulses and his reactions than the ordinary human.

"Pink and I are grieving Freda, as well, of course, but she was a control animal, an ordinary Dumbo Rat. A sweetheart, but she had not been enhanced in any way."

Gladys's rational-sounding explanation loosened my tongue. "How do you know this is what happened? How can you possibly know what the mouse is thinking?"

"Of course we can only hypothesize," she said, shifting her weight in the chair she'd taken next to Dr. Knoe. A white lab coat largely obscured her body's femininity, yet the confident grace of her movements left little doubt a primal beauty thrived mere millimeters beneath. "We monitor him very closely, constantly, both in person and from a digital video system that records his every move 24-7. His behavior patterns are more familiar to us than our own." She laughed modestly. Smiling and waving off Cromwell's gestured offer to get her a cup of coffee, she produced a crinkly plastic bottle of Aquafina from her lab coat, unscrewed the cap, took a serious swig and set the bottle on the floor beside her chair. She continued her explanation, "We've been adjusting his cellular modifications by micro-increments.

"Our goal is to bring his intuition and consciousness so closely in harmony that each augments and supports the other no matter what outside stimulus might chance to confront him. I realize this is pretty technical stuff. It's especially tricky to explain because it's cutting edge research. We're out there where nobody to our knowledge has ever previously ventured.

"Let me put it this way, if Morgie had sensed Freda's crisis in time and withdrawn from the coupling and calmed her heart rate we might have been ready to proceed to the next step. It's possible the stimulus that prevented a successful outcome was your presence in the room, Mr. Geddes. You were the unknown factor, and this alone might have distracted both Morgie and Freda from an optimal communion."

"Me? Jesus! I'm sorry!"

Dr. Knoe jumped in. "No, Al. It's not your fault. You just happened to be the unknown factor in an ongoing experiment. We would have had to confront that circumstance eventually. This just moves our timetable back. Nothing critical."

"May I ask what the next step is?"

"Certainly," said Dr. Knoe. "You are the next step."

Somehow I sensed this was what she would say an instant before she spoke. I wondered if this meant my intuition and consciousness were already in the kind of harmony they were looking for. But I couldn't tell them this. I started feeling unusually protective of my thoughts. Instead, I simply bleated, "Me?"

Dr. Knoe chuckled softly. "Yes, dear Al, you. Morgie here, our

SACRIFICE

Mighty Mouse, is the Laika of Project Vulcana. You shall be our Yuri Gagarin."

MATHEW PAUST

HASHING IT OUT

The Yuri Gagarin analogy was dangerous. If Dr. Knoe meant to push me into actively engaging the concept behind Project Vulcana, something I'd done only superficially up to then, she was putting Vulcana at considerable risk, because she had to know I was unstable at this point. Comparing me to the cosmonaut had the immediate effect of jarring me out of a passive acquiescence to what I'd been seeing and told. Bits of thought dallying in the back of my mind -- questions, half-assed answers, tentative alibis and other, vaguely definable fragments -- seized the moment to coalesce and launch a volition I'd forgotten I had.

"Look," I nearly shouted. "I don't know who has clearances or not in this place and frankly I don't give a shit. But if you all believe the president is the most dangerous person in this fucking world, you're wrong!

"You wanna know why? I'll tell you why, godammit, because the most dangerous person in the world is right here in this room! It's me! You're nothing but a bunch of goddamned megalomaniacs and I'm the one you're trying to railroad into being your suicide bomber. Me! Well, fuck you! I refuse to play your goddam sick fucking game. I don't care what you do to me. Send me back to prison. Kill me. Feed me to the rats. I don't give a shit anymore. Do whatever the fuck you want, but I'm out of it. Out! You got it? Leave me the fuck out of this!"

During my brief rant I snuck a couple of peeks at Dr. Knoe and Gladys and was surprised to see no change in expression on their faces. Both were directing their gazes at me, but remained still. Dr. Knoe's face was its usual blank mask, but Gladys's seemed amused, merry, even. I shut it down when it became obvious to me that although my words bordered on hysteria, my voice, despite a greater decibel output than usual, sounded almost

SACRIFICE

relaxed. I was acting, I realized, and then knew they knew it, too.

"Feel better?" Dr. Knoe said after a distorted passage of time during which I wrestled with the one thought I'd verbalized that lifted my thinking to a higher level than I'd been on. Dr. Knoe's voice sounded patronizing.

"No," I said. "A little more in control, maybe. But not better. No way better."

"The dangerous man idea?" she asked.

"Absolutely. You'll want me to get next to the president and slip him a mickey, which either knocks him out so you guys can turn him into Mighty Man. Or it does the job right off the bat and I turn him into Mighty Man. But what if it kills him or drives him nuts? I mean it worked on the mouse and it might work on me but what if it has a different effect on the president, turns him into Nero? The world is precarious enough as it is. Who are we to take such a risk, diddle with its fragile balance?"

"Somebody's got to do something." It was Cromwell. He was pouring himself another cup of coffee. I'd forgotten he was in the room. He hadn't sat, just sort of hovered, unobtrusively, floated quietly here and there. His voice now startled me.

I said, "That sounds like something Tresckow would've said to Stauffenberg."

This animated Cromwell. Coffee slopped out of his cup as he practically jumped across the room to stand in front of me. "No!" he said in a voice louder than I'd ever heard from him. "We're not talking about killing anybody. We want to give the guy a pair of balls so he can stand up to Gallston and start acting presidential. That's all we're trying to do."

It made sense. Stewart Gallston, the aide everyone assumed was the quiet power behind the throne, the former advertising executive who had financed and engineered the president's rise from an obscure but oddly charismatic New York councilman to a seat in the legislature, then the governor's mansion and on to the White House, sticking to him all the way like snot on a brat's sleeve. As the future president rose in prominence a progressive blogger had compared the relationship to Truman's sponsorship by Tom Pendergast. The blogger said the main difference was that after Truman's election to the Senate, "he cut the umbilical cord and kicked Old Tom under the bus where he belonged."

The idea was intriguing but my skepticism remained insurmountable. "What do we know about their relationship? How do we know it's as sinister as it might seem? How do we know changing the president's personality will change the dynamic between the two? And more importantly how do know it will work out for the best? It could backfire."

Gladys jumped in. "We know quite a bit about both men, from their body language, their public statements, what's been said about them by people who know them. Pink has everything in a database and has run "what if" programs.

"The most important thing we know about the president is he stood up for a fellow cadet at the academy and it cost him a favored position among the ruling circle there. The cadet was unfairly accused of an honor violation. He'd been unpopular and it was an excuse to railroad him out, to use your expression, Al. The president stood on principle. It took integrity and courage to do so. We know he's strayed from those qualities in his political career, but we believe we can bring them back, put that spine back into play. We know we can."

Cromwell: "Al, the Western democracies are on the brink of revolution and you know it. The Club of Rome knows it. They want it. They want an excuse to begin the slaughter. Where do you suppose the initiative to federalize all local police originated? Government control of telecommunications and the Internet? The quiet construction of concentration camps in every state? You haven't been in prison that long. You know what I'm talking about. The president's practically neutered. You mentioned Stauffenberg. That's not so far off, Al. Even if Vulcana works and the president stands up to Gallston, and thereby the Club, there's no guarantee he can stop what's happening, turn this thing around and head us back to sanity, we have to try. Don't you see

SACRIFICE

it? We have to take a shot. It could be our only chance.

"We need your help."

MATHEW PAUST

BACK TO THE GARDEN

I stared at Cromwell, the man who had once told me with a straight face and no context other than to justify his presence during a Rose Garden sting operation, armed with only a tranquilizer gun, "People are animals, too, sir," and wondered once again if in fact I was losing my mind.

"You need me?" I asked. "Me? You think that because I accidentally took some experimental drug five years ago and didn't freak out that this somehow qualifies me to be your human guinea pig for more experimental drugs? You once told me people were animals, Cromwell, and I thought then that one of us was nuts. Guess what? I'm back to thinking the same thing. Only this time I'm hoping it's me that's nuts because that lets me off the hook. Surely you don't want to be messing around with a nut in this plot to save the world?"

Cromwell's face remained impassive although he seemed to be hiding behind his coffee cup, sipping noisily and peering at me over the rim.

"This requires a certain amount of faith," he said finally. "We're all relying to a certain degree on faith here. Faith in our methods and in our intention with this project and ultimately, for you especially, in our good will."

"You're scientists," I blurted, turning to Gladys. "Since when does the scientific method involve faith?"

Her face still expressed merriment. I couldn't remember if the expression was different when I met her, but it didn't seem forced. "I think Anthony means reasonable expectations, Al," she said. "It's allowable in science to have reasonable expectations based on experience and what the data reveals.

"We feel confident that this will work the way we're expecting it

SACRIFICE

to."

"And if it doesn't?"

"There's always an element of risk. We can never be one hundred percent certain. We're hoping you will see the critical importance of what we're trying to do, despite the very minute risk involved, and share our reasonable expectation that we'll be successful."

As a former trial lawyer I resented evasive answers. I couldn't let this one go. "I repeat my question, Gladys. What if it doesn't work the way you expect it to? What could go wrong?"

She sighed deeply, shaking her head and looking at the floor between us. At last the merriment appeared to have vanished, replaced by a look of puzzled concern. A warm smile was back when she looked up.

"You got me there, counselor," she said, surprising me with her apparent knowledge of my background. Somebody had briefed her before I arrived, which bothered me a tad. "There's really no way to know what could go wrong. Theoretically I suppose there are an infinite number of possibilities. Beyond our reasonable expectation that nothing will go wrong, I'd have to say your guess would be as good as ours.

"But I repeat that the likelihood of something catastrophic happening is so remote as to be incalculable."

As she explained her faith that disaster was virtually not in the cards my resistance, tempered by a cynicism that rarely disappointed me, had begun oddly to shift. It was as if she were reaching me between the lines in the same way pharmaceutical commercials seduce TV viewers despite the rapidfire recitation of hideous side effects the wonder drugs being hawked can cause. I found myself identifying with the legendary Gagarin and subsequent astronauts strapped in their potential coffins on a rocket awaiting bravely a launch they knew damned well could whisk them into the void of no return. Where did their courage come from? Many of them had families. How did they justify the risk?

"What if I refuse?"

The three of them looked at each other, revealing nothing.

"We could strap you in anyway, whether you cooperate or not." It was a new voice. Ruth had entered the room so quietly she completely surprised me. I believe she surprised the others, as well. All four heads swiveled as if linked electrically and faced the former president. My response was automatic.

"Not a good idea, Ruth. You know how stubborn I can be."

"Ve haf vays to mek you...more compliant," she said. I laughed and I believe Gladys did, too. But I was thinking rapidly, as I knew this was crunch time.

"Another case of ends justifying means? You know what Einstein thought about that: Perfection of means and confusion of aims seems to be our main problem. You expect the president to stand on principle but you would betray principle yourselves."

Ruth came back without hesitation.

"You vaccinate a child with a weakened virus to enable that child to fight off the strong ones."

"Corruption is corruption, Ruth. Once you yield, how can you trust yourself to stop?"

"You've worked in the White House, Al. We did it every day. You have to know when to fold 'em. I remember when you first told me that. I'm telling you now's the time to hold 'em. The stakes are too high to get all tight-assed. I remember when you told me that, too."

"That was politics, Ruth. We're talking about fucking with Mother Nature now."

"Didn't know you were superstitious, Al. But if that's how you want to play it, we fucked with Mother Nature when Adam took that first bite of the apple, you know. It's way too late to take back that bite, and the power of knowledge it cursed us with is all we have now to get us home. We're on our own. Tell me I'm wrong , Al."

SACRIFICE

Oops, it was apparent I'd bitten off a tad more than I could chew. Damned, but she was good. I stared at her. Same dumbfounded stare she'd won from me many a time before. Well, maybe not many a time, but at this moment it sure as hell felt like it. I fought to keep from grinning my concession, struggled for a gap in her argument. I was stubborn. There'd been times when I was able to find that gap quickly enough to jam a shoe or something in, keep the door from slamming shut, but this wasn't one of them. I sighed. Grinned.

She slammed the door and turned the key: "You know, Al, getting back to Einstein. Pretty smart man he was. He also said this, as I recall, something about it being appallingly obvious that our technology is ahead of our humanity. I think that's it. Close enough, anyway. That's our stake here, you know. If we can't get our humanity up to speed soon - damned soon - we're gonna lose it, bubba.

"Think on it tonight. She put her mouth next to my ear and whispered, "Want some company?"

The grin dropped away with my jaw. Her warm moist breath, which she'd sweetened with something minty, slithered straight to my groin. She added, "Herman's divorcing me."

PILLOW TALK

She stayed the night. Broke a precedent we'd followed over our several years of intermittent trysting after her neurotically patriotic husband found himself unable to perform marital intimacies with a United States president. He eventually overcame this quirk but evidently was taking a new assessment of the whole relationship thing with his wife.

Our discussions didn't enter this realm at all. In fact there was virtually no discussion of any nature when she came to my room with a bottle of cabernet, a wedge of brie and a single-stack box of rice crackers. Having eaten a sandwich I'd made for myself not long before her arrival I ignored the refreshments and immediately embraced her and began kissing her mouth and neck and ears and neck and... The bottle thumped on the rug. Ruth reached away for a moment to toss the cheese and crackers out of harm's way on my desk and then returned with full ardor to the task at hand. We were essentially undressed by the time we hit the bed.

We were still not completely undressed half an hour or so later when we'd finished our grunting, giggling, moaning carnal reunion opening act and agreed to use the shower in my room before sampling the wine and cheese in preparation for a lengthier more nuanced celebration of a fine auld acquaintance we both obviously had not forgot. This plan went awry when we commenced the second act in the shower, which lasted until we'd exhausted the hot water. Our repast was all the tastier for its delay, despite leaving cracker crumbs between the sheets.

"For an old fart you're friskier than I expected," she murmured, nibbling on one of my earlobes.

"It's young things like you that bring it out in me. Hey, you didn't call me Louie. I'm sure that helped." She chuckled.

SACRIFICE

"God," she said. "I musta been pretty desperate back then, huh. You know something, Al sweetie? After our first little tête-à-tête, you know, the one on my couch? I never let Louie in my britches again. Not one time!"

"That was a tad more than a tête-à-tête, Ruthie. And you were not wearing britches."

She punched me, fairly hard, on the nearest shoulder. "I'm just trying to be a lady, OK? But if it makes you happy your tongue drove me nearly crazy that night. I thought I was gonna hafta call in well in the morning. There, that better?"

It was. Amazing how effective a little ego stroking can be on a man with an open mind. Her reminder of our first intimate encounter was already wriggling its way into my libido where additional nuances remained to be explored. With perfect timing, she pushed the overdrive button by way of a little coy modesty, attributing my current prowess to the Vulcana prototype I'd taken accidentally half a decade prior.

"Oh, I know it's not just me." She leaned over and kissed me full on the mouth, then raised herself several inches above my face, her auburn hair hanging on either side in damp, musky curtains. She deliberately brushed my chest several times with her hardened nipples. "It's that damned pill you took, isn't it? I'll bet you're this good with every bimbo who catches your eye."

And so yet another celebration of our friendship proceeded, this time among the cracker crumbs and wet spots, our oral emissions less fevered, more articulate now as they approximated terms of endearment and deep, deep affection repeatedly up to the explosive concluding exclamations followed by joyful whimpering notes of utter contentment muffled in each others flesh and then probably a little snoring until, I'd say within about five minutes -- maybe a little longer -- we returned to full if languorous consciousness.

"Was this part of the plan? Get ol' Al in the sack and sweet talk him? That's how it was with Gagarin, I imagine." I decided to bring it up first because it was indeed the elephant in the room and I thought it the gentlemanly thing to do. Nonetheless I braced myself for another punch on the shoulder. It didn't come.

"I couldn't say how they got Gagarin on board," she said, her executive voice now in charge, "but if I had to guess I'd go with patriotism. His country needed him."

She was always good with comebacks. I wasn't half bad. Probably why we got into politics. "How do you know that wouldn't have been enough for me? You've set me up and blackmailed me, knowing all the while you'd eventually have to come clean with me. Isn't it a little late to be singing God bless America?"

The former president planted an elbow in the mattress to give her a slight height advantage, and leaned in to make her point: "I'm not singing, Al. You know better. But if I were suddenly to break into song here you would cover your ears and run for what's left of your sanity. You'd hear me trying to sound like Barry McGuire."

"...you tell me over and over and over again, my friend, ah, you don't believe..." I heard myself starting to sing, softly, those angry stirring words that had drawn me, Ruth, Warren Hendrian -- hell, the most promising incipient minds of our generation -- to shrug off the dry-rotted bindings of our Dobie Gillis Eisenhower rearing and look for the first time beyond what we were told to believe and ordered not to mess with.

Ruth patted my cheek -- one of the two on my pillow -- and rolled back to her side of the bed. Somehow I knew what was coming next. My prescience was not disappointed. She arched her back and let it fly: "Yeah, my blood's so mad feels like coagulatin'." Her alto voice was surprisingly good. I joined in, "I'm sitting here just contemplatin'. I can't twist the truth, it knows no regulation. Handful of senators don't pass legislation and marches alone can't bring integration when human respect is disintegratin' this whole crazy world is just too frustratin'."

We shouted the chorus: **"AND YOU TELL ME OVER AND OVER AND OVER AGAIN, MY FRIEND, AH, YOU DON'T BELIEVE WE'RE ON THE EVE OF DESTRUCTION!"**

SACRIFICE

GLADYS IS GONE!

If it had to happen I'm glad it happened when it did, Gladys's disappearance, because I had not made up my mind yet. I'm not suggesting Ruth's powers of persuasion had diminished over the years. Not at all. Actually, considering the relief she provided my frustration from the forced celibacy of imprisonment and the simple joy of our reunion all in all, I'd say she was more persuasive than ever. But as I've mentioned, I'm stubborn, especially when it comes to expectations of others for me. If I'm to do something I need to have bought into it all the way. I need to own it. It must fill me with passion. I wasn't there yet.

It was later in the day of my tryst with Ruth. She'd arisen before me, showered and headed to the kitchen to make breakfast for us. I joined her there soon afterward and we'd eaten on the deck, eggs and whole grain rolls with honey, enjoying another glorious sunrise, this one in relative silence. Afterward Ruth went off to her study in another part of the house. I returned to my room to read and bask in the remnants of our jolly time together. This included a pair of baby blue silk panties I found wedged between the sheets, which I draped over the back of my chair, and the combined scents of her toiletries, including a poignant trace of the sophisticated perfume she favored and a muskiness she exuded naturally and which always seemed to linger after she'd departed.

I was reading The Way of the World: A Story of Truth and Hope in an Age of Extremism, by Ron Suskind, when the trilling ringtone of Anthony Cromwell's call pierced my concentration.

"Al, have you seen Gladys today?"

"Gladys?"

"Alabi. Gladys Alabi. Pink's assistant. He says he hasn't seen her today."

"That's unusual? I guess it must be, or you wouldn't be calling me. Where does Pink think she might be?"

"He says she left yesterday to visit her mother. She was planning to spend the night with her but would be back in the morning, as usual. She does this nearly every weekend."

"I see. Where does she live? Her mother."

"Couple hours drive from here. Usually one of my security people drives her. She drove herself this time. We don't like to do that, but something else had come up and Abby wasn't able to go. Gladys said her mother had the flu or something. She wanted to be with her."

"Have you tried calling her?" I felt foolish asking this, but I was getting a sense from Cromwell that he was a tad discombobulated. I assumed he already would have taken the obvious measures to locate Gladys if it were important. The fact that he was asking me if I had seen her was curious.

"Oh, yes, sir. She's evidently left her cell phone off, something we advise against. It's possible she's in a dead zone, I suppose, but I've tried several times over the past hour. The last time I tried I got a message indicating the phone was out of range. The phone might be on the blink, but that's never happened before with our equipment, to my knowledge."

"I gather Pink is worried?"

"Oh, yes, sir. Quite upset. He asked me to call you. I wonder if you would mind talking with him?"

"Of course, Cromwell. Is he in the lab now?"

"Yes, sir. I can meet you here, in my office, and I'll take you down there."

Cromwell's offer to take me to the lab was more than welcome. I had a hard enough time remembering how to get to his office. He was waiting for me outside his door, sipping from another of the crinkly plastic water bottles. I declined his offer of one for me. Pink was waiting, too, just inside the lab door.

SACRIFICE

His appearance had changed so much I might not have recognized him under other circumstances. Mainly it was the absence of the kilt that struck me, along with the missing erection the kilt was intended to conceal. Pink was wearing baggy jeans and a green-and-yellow College of William and Mary sweatshirt. His crotch contain no hint of a bulge. Even his hair was different. The spikes had been combed flat. He looked quite ordinary.

"Pink," I said extending my hand. He took it in a firm grip and we did the ceremonial pump to acknowledge our mutual acceptance of civilized conduct. He responded with an articulate, "Mr. Geddes," at moderate volume. He voice was of a pitch somewhere between alto and baritone.

Cromwell spoke: "I'll leave you two. Call me if you need anything." He pivoted 180 degrees and strode off toward the elevator. Pink invited me into the lab and led me through to the small conference room. We sat facing each other in the comfortable chairs. "How can I help you," I said. "Oh, and, Pink, it's Al, please. 'Mr. Geddes' makes me look around for my dead father." Pink acknowledged with a nod and silent laugh.

"OK, Al. Thanks for agreeing to see me. I'm worried. She's never done this before."

"That's what Cromwell said. What do you think might have happened?"

"I think she's been abducted."

I suspect my jaw dropped. Either that or I'd been unconsciously mouth breathing. I snapped it shut and said, "Abducted? Why would you think that?"

"I don't know. It's just a feeling. I'm rather intuitive, you know."

"So I've heard, but, frankly, I'm wondering if you're the same fellow I met two days ago. You look quite different...er, and last time you spoke so rapidly we needed Gladys to translate for us. If I were a detective I'd have to say something isn't quite adding up here."

"Teeheehee," youmeanlikethis? I get like that when I'm hyped, when I'm working. I can't work now, Mr...Al. I can't concentrate. I'm so worried about Gladys. Something's happened to her, I just know it."

"I see. I suppose this would explain the...er, the jeans instead of the kilt?"

"Oh, I see what you mean. The erection thing. I can bring it up and put it down whenever I like. It's all mental...well, mostly. I like it up when I'm with Gladys because she likes it that way, too. We...we're in love, Al, if you haven't guessed by now. Most of the others haven't seen me like this. Mr. Cromwell sees me more than anybody besides Gladys. I've already taken the most recent version of Vulcana. I've taken all the versions. I try every new combination on myself. I..."

"Hey! Hey! Hey! Wait a minute, Pink! Wait just a minute! If you've already taken the stuff then why am I here? I'm supposed to be the Yuri Gagarin. That's what everybody tells me. So what's really going on here? What am I really supposed to be? Sounds to me like you're the Yuri Gagarin."

"Teeheehee. I'm the secret Yuri Gagarin. I'm the secret phantom of the la-bór-a-try (he pronounced it like Boris Karloff did). You're the star, Al, the one everybody will be watching. The one who's going to SAVE THE WORLD!!"

"You're skeptical."

"I'm always skeptical. I'm a scientist."

"Well, Pink, I'm no scientist, but I share your skepticism. I have my doubts that Vulcana will work and I'm also not so sure we should be meddling with evolution, and it seems to me that's exactly what we would be doing."

"We just work here, huh? Teeheehee."

"OK, look. Back to business. What if -- and I say this just as a hypothetical -- what if Gladys wasn't abducted? What if..."

"What if...she betrayed us? Cromwell asked that, too. My love would not betray me, Al. I know this in my heart."

SACRIFICE

"So what do we do?"

"Cromwell wants to send a team out. I told him I will quit if he does that. No more Vulcana. No Mighty Mouse to save the world. I told him I will find Gladys."

"You?"

"Me. And you. Will you help me, Al? Come with me?"

"Holy shit, Pink. I'm on parole. If they caught me outside they'd put me back in prison and throw the key away. I can't do it."

"They won't catch us. Anyway, Ruth will protect us. She still has connections."

"That's naïve, Pink, with all due respect. Ruth is already on thin ice with me here in this house. I'd like to help you, but I don't see how I can do it. Besides, wouldn't it be better to have one of Cromwell's people with you? Somebody who's trained for that kind of thing?"

"Al, the key to finding Gladys is going to be her mother. I know her mother. Her mother will not talk to Cromwell or any of his people. She doesn't like me, either. You, Al. She likes you."

"How can you say that, Pink? I've never met Gladys's mother. How can she possibly like me?"

"She loved your book, Al. You're her hero."

"Oh my God!"

MATHEW PAUST

PLANNING ACTION

The next time I laid eyes on Ruth she was in full executive mode. She'd converted her office into a situation room. The maintenance crew evidently had scrounged a small conference table and moved it into the space in front of her desk, which they'd pushed back against the wall. Seated around the table now in folding chairs were, besides me and Ruth, Cromwell, Pink, Joan Stonebraker, one of Cromwell's security people and Warren Hendrian, who had arrived by speedboat with a bodyguard from American Enterprises. The bodyguard remained outside the room. A yellow legal pad, Bic Gel pen and a crinkly plastic bottle of Aquafina water were at each place on the table. In addition, Cromwell, Ruth and Joan Stonebraker had iPads at their places.

"No iPad for me?" Hendrian asked in his usual whiny manner. He'd gone completely bald since his White House days and this actually gave him more gravitas than when the mousy grayish brown thinning hair sprouted from his scalp. But the voice and childish self-centeredness betrayed this newfound illusion of dignity.

"You didn't bring yours?" Ruth snapped, then, in a softer tone, "Don't worry, Warren. I'll let you use mine if you need it." She looked up, flashed her eyes around the table riveting everyone's attention, and the meeting came to order.

"So what we have here are basically only two possibilities." It was Hendrian, voice pitched lower with assumed authority, startling me and, it seemed everyone else around the table, including Ruth, who glanced his way and quickly back to her iPad, allowing a twitch at the corner of her mouth to signal amused resignation. Hendrian obviously had interpreted her eye contact as permission to lead the discussion. Too bad Adele Schwammel wasn't there, I mused, to put him in his place with one of her deliciously derisive

SACRIFICE

snorts.

Hendrian continued, "Something's either happened to her or she's gone over to the dark side. We must take both possibilities seriously."

"She was abducted," Pink said evenly. He stared at Hendrian with a blank face but with eyes that appeared to be trying to burn holes in the bald man's head. "She would not betray us. She would not betray me," he added with the same emotionless voice.

"Hey, looks like Love Potion Number 14 works pretty good," said Hendrian, his obvious effort to win a laugh coming out a sneer. When no laugh was won, he went on, "I know you're seething inside, Pinkerton. Frankly I'd rather have you shout at me than talk like a robot. Did I say, frankly? I meant to. Be frank, that is."

His face had reddened and as he opened his mouth as if to say something more, Ruth cut him off. "Oh for chrissake, Warren, shut up! For a man as brilliant as you, you sure as hell should be able to control your ego. Maybe you should try a little Vulcana. You're positively embarrassing at times."

"I don't need any help getting an erection," he snapped, but his face had turned crimson and his eyes were locked on his blank yellow pad.

"I'll take your word for it." She turned abruptly from her former National Security Advisor to Cromwell. "Anthony, what do we know for sure?"

Cromwell recapped what Pink had told us, including Pink's insistence he and I be the one to contact Gladys's mother. He added his disapproval of this plan, arguing it was a job that needed professionals.

Ruth turned to Pink. "We can't risk having you out there, Pink. We don't know what happened. If someone abducted Gladys they could simply be using her for bait to get to you. You're the one they want."

"Gladys knows everything I know. They don't need me."

"Maybe not, but if they get you to show yourself they can take you out of the game. They can kill you, Pink."

"Gladys would never cooperate with them. Never. I know her better than anybody."

Ruth pondered, made some doodles on her yellow pad. She sighed. Looked up again at Pink. "I hate to question your intuition here, Pink, as I know yours is more highly developed than mine or anyone else we know. You're in a class by yourself. But as a practical matter we can't assume -- we, and I don't expect you will agree -- that Gladys, for one reason or another, has not betrayed you and us. It can happen to anyone. It can happen for reasons we may never have suspected and may never know.

"What if they abducted her mother? Does she have anyone else in her family they might have taken or threatened? Anyone in Nigeria? She could still love you and still be betraying us."

Pink stared at her, silently and without expression, his eyes bulging with consternation. Finally he nodded, one time, a concession to Ruth's argument. "Yeah. Could be," he said.

Ruth quickly decided on a course of action and issued her orders. Pink and I and Joan Stonebraker would drive to Leicester, Virginia, to find, if possible, Gladys's mother. Joan would maintain a constant link with Ruth via a secure satellite routing system. Two of Cromwell's security ground teams would be on alert 24/7, with additional helicopter teams maintaining constant visual contact with our car. We were to leave within the hour.

SACRIFICE

DANGER AHEAD

Anyone expecting to find clues here that might help pin down The Cottage's location will be disappointed. I've already revealed that Gladys's mother was living about two hours away in Leicester County, Virginia, which might or might not be precisely accurate but is not vital to security at this point. To give you anything more specific, in words comedian Dana Carvey once used in his impressions of then-President George H. W. Bush, "wouldn't be prudent. Not gonna do it."

Our ride was what appeared to be a new dark metallic blue Buick Enclave.

"I know what you're thinking," said Joan when she noticed my surprise. She had brought the SUV around from an underground garage to the exit facing the circular drive at the edge of the extensive woods that buffered us from casual prying eyes. "The government drives black. Well, we're working undercover today, you might say. Besides, I prefer the blue."

She handed each of us a leather folder that concealed an official looking photo ID and a sparkling gold badge.

"Treasury agents," she said as I squinted to get a closer look at the writing on the ID and badge. "I suggest you put your regular identification documents at the bottom of your overnight bags. Can't you read that, Al? You're Doug Chesnic for this little mission. Pink, you're Frank Horrigan. You're both agents of the U.S. Treasury Department. Don't ask."

"Joan, for chrissake, I'm on parole. I can't get caught with this!"

"You won't get caught with it, Al. Neither will you, Pink. These credentials are for you to flash if we have to question people who get suspicious, if we can't find Mrs. Alabi -- neighbors, landlord, that sort of thing. If these badges don't do the trick and somebody calls the police -- which they won't, but if they do -- and I can't talk our way out of any trouble our security team will be on us like a flies on a meadow muffin. OK?"

"But what about you, Joan? You're sticking your neck way out here. Giving us these phony credentials." I extended my arm and waved the leather case at her, hoping she'd come to her senses and take it back. She waved me off.

"I keep these with me at all times," she said. "These are from the old days for the kinds of situation where we needed at least the appearance of backup. Like the posses in the Old West. You're my deputies now, boys, and you had damned well better not screw up, you hear?"

"But, Joan..."

"But what?" she snapped.

"Look, you know I trust you implicitly, even though you did scare the hell out of me when I thought you were dead, but I understand now why you had to do that, I think. What I don't understand is how were you able to get our faces on these plastic ID cards so fast? You didn't -- we didn't -- know about this until this morning."

She laughed. "Al, look at your buddy, Special Agent Horrigan." I turned and saw that Pink was grinning widely.

"In the lab, Al," he said. "I can do anything in my lab."

When I turned back to Joan she was holding a black, short-barreled revolver out to me. She had another in her other hand. "Put this in your pocket. I'll show you how to do it so it won't show through your pants and so you can get it out in a hurry without an accidental discharge." She handed the other one to Pink, who seemed dumbfounded, holding it as if it were about to explode.

"Look, the chance of you having to use those things is next to zero, like winning the lottery. OK? They're strictly a last-ditch survival weapon in an absolute worst-case scenario, like if something happens to me. You don't need any skill to operate

SACRIFICE

them. Just point them at whoever is trying to kill you and pull the trigger. Simple as that. OK?"

"Alright, so we get there and Mrs. Alabi's not home. What are the neighbors gonna think when three Secret Service agents start combing the neighborhood?" I fought back a smirk, knowing I'd just laid four aces on the table. After all, I was a former governor of Iowa. I'm supposed to win one now and again. Of course Joan took the pot with her royal flush. This consisted of a plastic scroll she unrolled and stuck to the driver's side door. Publishers Clearing House proclaimed the large glossy letters.

"One for each side," she said, smiling brightly. "Everybody loves a winner. They'll trip over each other cooperating with us. Just remember to smile." She detached the magnetic sign from her door and rolled it back up. "We'll wait until we're there. Wouldn't wanna cause an accident on the way."

By the time we rolled out of the woods onto the nearest road the sun had slipped below the horizon. Pink had the back seat to himself, as Joan wanted me riding shotgun.

"We're old friends," she told Pink.

"No problem," he said. "I'll just stretch out and take a catnap."

MATHEW PAUST

ROAD WARRIORS

I settled back in the soft leather seat, enjoying its acquiescence to my body as if designed for my comfort alone. The muted whoosh of its yielding cushions released a heady aromatic ambience that spoke of newness and stylish luxury. This, in the muted azure cockpit glow of the dash display, seduced me into a composure I knew better than to try to exploit, despite Joan's reassuring presence in the driver's seat beside me where I watched her adept manipulation of levers and buttons to adjust the positions of her seat and then the mirrors and dashboard light level.

I had implicit confidence in Joan, in her integrity as a person and in her professionalism. She never gave me reason to doubt her during the White House days leading up to her unexplained "death." I accepted the story then and I accepted now that the intent of her complicity was innocent. I trusted her, despite harboring fundamental questions about that and our present situations. Yet, I held my tongue while we undulated on soft springs down the several-miles of private gravel road past rigid sentries of cedars and pines until we reached the highway, except to note what seemed to be a lack of security in the vicinity.

She tilted her head toward me. The start of a smile had nudged a ripple in the part of her cheek showing through the veil of gray-streaked brown hair that reached to her shoulders. "The trees have eyes," she said, keeping her voice soft in deference to Pink, whose snoring had already begun behind us. "Ears, too." She nodded at a saluting uniformed guard who emerged from a barely visible shack set back among the trees where the road met the highway.

"No gate. What good is he?"

Braking the SUV at the intersection she turned her face toward me with a full smile. "Electromagnetic pulse, Al. He touches a

SACRIFICE

button and anything within a hundred yards that needs electricity to run shuts down instantly. Oh, and there's more than one guard on duty here at a time. You must not have seen the other shacks along the road."

I hadn't, and I was impressed if not surprised considering the other sophisticated and even exotic defense measures Wilde Labs had deployed to protect this project. What did surprise me was Joan's smile, the likes of which I had never before seen on her face. The rather flat yet nicely featured face now animated by the play of muscles with a mystery of highlights reflecting the cabin's interior glow struck me as beautiful.

Until that moment I had not associated beauty with Joan. I don't recall her sexuality previously registering with my libido and this might have been partly because of her position and her professional bearing and a sense in the back of my mind, although I had no particular reason to think so, that she might be a lesbian or, if provoked by, say, overt flirtation, a combative feminist. She'd worn baggy suits that concealed her most obvious female features, and much of the time hid with sunglasses her most prominent charm, large pretty brown eyes. These were sparkling tonight, and her comfortable-fit jeans and the pullover knit jersey she wore under a light windbreaker did, without flaunting, reveal enough of her gender's charms that I enjoyed an unexpected stirring in my loins.

"You know something, Joan," I said after she launched us onto the highway and accelerated to a precise five miles per hour over the speed limit, "a lot of what happened before and what's happening now still bothers me. Bothers me quite a bit, in fact, and I hope we can talk about it tonight." We had the road pretty much to ourselves at the moment. There were no lights behind us and only an occasional oncoming vehicle. The night was clear enough that I saw the blinking red lights of an aircraft overhead. It seemed to be going in our direction. "Is that our escort?" I pointed.

"Could be, Al. Probably. What's on your mind?"

"Quite a bit, actually, but I want to say something first before we get into the stuff that's bothering me. I want you to know that of all the revelations, and there have been a lot of them...they seem to be ganging up on me since you got me out of prison...but of all of this new stuff about the drug and keeping me in the dark and the mission you all have for me and how we're going to save the world and all and on and on, the one thing that means the most to me – and I mean this completely, no bullshit, Joan, I mean it – was finding out that you were still alive. It was like waking up from a horrible nightmare and finding out that's all it was, just a goddam nightmare.

"I'm just so glad you're alive, Joan." I wanted to go on with more about how I felt, because the relief of saying what I'd said was making me giddy, but gushing isn't my thing and I knew I'd already gone too far. I don't handle embarrassment well, and I was too aware I'd just embarrassed us both. I tried to think of something to say to conclude, or to put it more eloquently or at least more intelligently but I was afraid I'd just keep gushing. I took a deep breath and let it out. Snuck a look at her. She was staring straight ahead. I noticed a small glass screen on the dash was dark. I reached forward and tapped it with my index finger.

"This a little TV?" My voice was croaky, like a high school freshman's asking a girl to the prom.

"GPS screen."

"Is it broke?" I was glad for the darkness. My cheeks were aflame.

"Don't need it, Al. Anyway, it's not secure. We won't get lost."

"Oh. Yeah."

We drove in silence, the only sound was the hum of the tires on asphalt and Pink's snoring. I felt like humming a tune or pretending to sleep, but sanity intervened and I merely swallowed and rested my head against the seat and tried to think of some way to break the conversational impasse I'd created.

"Al?" Uh oh.

"Yeah, Joan."

SACRIFICE

"That was a sweet thing to say. If it's any comfort, I hated having to do it."

"You mean..."

"Pretending to be dead. It seemed stupid."

"What was the point?

"They wanted to stress you out, push you as far as they could to see if you would snap. They figured it would be better if you snapped in a controlled environment than, say, in public or on TV or God knows where. I argued for them to let you in on it, ask you how you felt and if you wanted to see a doctor, so you would know what was up. I told them I thought it was more dangerous for them to use you as a guinea pig, which is what they were doing."

"Who were 'they,' Joan?"

"Ultimately it was Ruth's decision."

"I know, but who all was part of the discussion?"

"I'm still working for Ruth, Al. I'm sorry."

"Yeah, I know. That's cool. But I'm still on the hot seat. I need some help thinking this through. I can still tell you all to go to hell, you know, if I don't believe in what you're doing. You know that, Joan."

"I'll talk with you about the mission, what I know of it. I'll tell you what I can and what I think. OK?"

"I trust you, Joan."

MATHEW PAUST

DUELING BLACK BIRDS

Joan might have seen the lights the same time I did, but I mentioned them first.

"Are there two helicopters escorting us?"

She spoke without me seeing her glance up, her eyes seemingly focused on the road ahead. "Not together. Probly something else. Airliner, maybe. Hard to tell from the ground what level they're flying at."

"I don't think so, Joan. These guys are flying side by side. They're going in the same direction."

I watched the tandem flashing lights move parallel to the highway ahead of us. They seemed to weave effortlessly through a field of stars and planets and probably galaxies that were visible in patches between occasional cloud clumps that had started arriving in our sky that afternoon.

"No, Joan, they're together," I said, watching one of the flashing red lights suddenly expand into a bloom of white, orange and dark red many times its original size. Joan joined the conversation with interest now as the fireball arced away from the road in a parabolic plunge toward the ground dragging a tail of flaming debris in a pretty fair impression of a comet: "Oh, shit!"

She followed this outburst with some crisp undecipherable questions I realized she was addressing to the tiny lapel microphone attached to the earpiece she seemed to wear whenever she was on duty, which, for all I know might have been 24/7. I made out a few numbers and words, among them: "Is that us?"

Then another "Oh, shit" with less drama and, after a pause, "Oh, well that's good at least."

SACRIFICE

"What's" good? I got the "what's" out but it vanished in the spectacle of the fireball's meteoric impact with the ground. The actual impact was screened by trees, but I still found myself reflexively throwing my arms in front of my face. The shock wave from a powerful WHUMP rattled me and underlined the sensation of closeness, which Joan quickly contradicted, although in a tense, no-time-for-bullshit voice.

"At least a mile away. We're OK," she snapped while the grounded fireball expanded further, billowing voraciously up over the treetops and outward as smaller explosions hurled showers of sparks toward the blackened sky. Seeing this in front of me jump-started the panic a recurring dream has brought on since childhood in which I'm watching Vesuvius erupt over Pompeii. I'm struggling to escape as the monster cloud of black volcanic ash and dark red burning gases looms nearer and larger, but my feet can barely move through what I imagine is ash that's already fallen and that I sense is burying the city and that I won't be able to get away from it in time. I've always managed to wake before the worst happens, but now I know I'm not going to wake from this...

"Al! Al! It's OK! It's too far to reach us!" It was Joan, and I realized I'd been squirming in my seat, pumping my legs, trying to escape Pompeii. I straightened up in the seat, breathed deeply and let it out. She had slowed the SUV and was looking for a place to pull off the road. We were on a stretch with no driveways or fire lanes. It was a dense piney woods and looked to be so at least as far ahead as the crash site, so she rolled us to a stop on the gravel shoulder. She turned off the engine and slumped in her seat, staring through the windshield at the inferno.

"Sorry, Joan," I muttered. "A little flashback there. What the hell's going on?"

"We're under attack," came a calm voice from the back seat.

"It might have been an accident, Pink," I said, hoping to hell I was right.

"No, Pink's right. Our security's been breached. You were right,

Al, that was another helicopter you saw and it wasn't one of ours."

"Another helicopter?" Pink again.

"Our monitoring station identified it as an AH-6. No markings, no response."

"Killer Egg," Pink said.

Joan had turned in her seat. "You two get out of here," she said, keeping her voice surprisingly conversational.

"Say what?" Me.

"Look. We don't know who sent that other helicopter. We don't know if they know about us or were just responding to our helicopter. We don't even know if the other helicopter went down, too. Maybe it was an accident. Maybe they collided. But the other was the AH, the attack version. Ours was the MH version, unarmed, for surveillance. We just don't know.

"But if they've spotted this vehicle, you two cannot be in it, you cannot be near it anymore. So get the hell out and hide in the forest. I'll take the SUV away from here, dump it, find something else to drive and come back for you. I should be back here in another couple of hours. So hop out, boys. We've had a change of plans."

"But..."

"Don't argue, Pink." If they found us they have Gladys. Simple as that. We figure out what to do later. Right now, you guys need to stay out of sight until I get back. Al, do you have your transponder with you?"

"My what?"

"That remote Ruth gave you at The Cottage to use on the birds."

"I don't, Joan. I didn't think we'd run into any birds out here."

"Well, looks like we just did, huh. Here, take this." She handed me another plastic device identical to the one I'd left in my room. She explained how to use it to communicate with her. It would be our lifeline until she returned. She leaned forward and gave me a quick sisterly peck on the cheek, the scent of her shampoo for a moment blocking out the dread welling in my stomach. Then she pushed on my shoulder. "Out. Stay out of sight. I'll be back."

"I'll be baaack," snarked Pink in a perfect impression of the Schwarzenegger line as we stood in the grass next to the tree line and turned away from the spray of gravel the SUV's tires hurled at us as it rocketed back onto the road and headed toward the crash site.

MATHEW PAUST

IS THAT A BANJO I HEAR?

Awkward. I strongly suspect there's a better word beyond my immediate grasp to capture all or most of the emotions churning within me as I stood in calf-high weeds on a chilly cloudy night with a crashed and burning helicopter a mile up the road and the leading winds of a likely approaching thunderstorm carrying into my nose the disaster's oily stench along with a reminder there was probably another helicopter circling overhead looking to wreak evil upon me and my companion of the moment, a strange, brilliant bird who called himself Pink.

The more I think about it I know there must be another, more appropriate word, because shock surely figured into the equation. I was either in shock or partially in shock – a sort of half-conscious suspension of conditioned motor reflexes while attempting to sort out priorities from the abrupt onset of a cluster of completely unexpected urgencies – or else I was stunned by fearing the approach of the kind of near total shut-down of function severe trauma induces, physical or emotional, which can end in death or at best an impermanent catatonia. In lieu therefore of something more definitive or precise I shall go with "awkward" in describing my indeterminate hesitancy to attempt assertive thought as an alternative to blubbering panic.

"Sir. Al. Mr. Geddes, sir..." I became aware of Pink's voice amid the throaty social chatter of frogs, the whistle of stench-bearing wind gusts through the pine branches and the distant squeal of first-responder sirens.

"Uh, sorry, Pink. Look, so far so good, OK? I'm guessing the helicopter thing was an accident, pure and simple. Accidents happen. Joan will be back before we know it. OK?" I stopped when even I became annoyed by my babbling.

"Sir..."

SACRIFICE

"Al. Please. I'm a convicted felon, for chrissake. I'm no sir."

"Yes, sir, Al. Sorry, it's a habit. We should get back from the road. You know, just in case." He took my arm and tugged me toward the trees behind us. "We'll find a log in there to sit on. C'mon." As if summoned by Pink the headlights of a vehicle appeared around a curve, heading in the same direction as Joan. I lurched backward and stepped into a shallow ditch, damned near spraining my ankle. Pink helped me get behind the tree line where we both instinctively turned our faces away from the road and froze until the vehicle, tires hissing on the pavement, had passed. The sweep of its headlights had illuminated a deadfallen tree trunk further back about ten yards, but I couldn't make it out in the dark.

"You have a flashlight?" I asked.

"Yessir I do. Never without it. Lucky us, huh." He produced something no larger than a Bic lighter from his pants pocket, flicked it on and illuminated a surprisingly wide swath. We made our way gingerly through a tangle of vines, ferns, prickly greenbriar and smaller dead branches that littered the way to the log we'd seen in the headlights. Pink switched his flashlight off after we'd arranged ourselves on the log. "No spare batteries. Gotta save these guys," he said.

With it dark once again the frogs picked up their conversations after it seemed they'd held their tongues during our invasion of their domain. In fact I doubt they paid us any heed at all, as is the way with impassioned courtiers, and suspect it was merely my attention to more pressing matters that "silenced" their love songs in my mind.

Once situated on the log I fished around in my jacket pockets until I found the transponder Joan had given me. Its screen came alight with the touch of a finger. It seemed much brighter in the dark of the woods than it had in the SUV. I studied the screen, trying to remember Joan's instructions.

"I wouldn't call her yet," Pink said. "In fact we might should forget using that thing at all. If security's been breached then that thing could lead them straight to us."

"Joan said..."

"Joan didn't know. If she finds out this communication net's still OK she'll call us. I think we should wait for that to happen."

"Good idea," I said, feeling sluggish that I hadn't thought of it myself.

"How long do you think it'll take her?"

"I don't know, Pink. We might hafta sleep here tonight."

"You're shitting me. We don't have anything. No sleeping bags. Nothing."

"We can scrape some clear spots behind this log. The trees should protect us a little if we get rain. If we had some dope we could get stoned. That would help, huh."

I waited, hoping Pink would whip out some rolling papers and a baggie. He didn't. Annoyed by the dark and by gusts of wind that swept through more and more frequently, blasting our faces with dust and dead leaves, we uprooted weeds and pulled away layers of nature's detritus until we'd cleared an area of soil that was surprisingly soft and yielded the muted pungent odor of humus and gave way fairly easily to our scraping until we had depressions that fit our hips, which I had learned as a Boy Scout were the tenderest body parts when trying to get to sleep on bare ground. We piled the soil from these depressions into earthen pillows. I covered mine with my T-shirt and used my jacket as a blanket. We made these sleeping spots so both were parallel to the log, which was situated so it served fairly well as a barricade to the wind that was growing more intrusive by the minute. We had just managed to finish our labors when the first salvos of thunder crashed through the clouds. I lay on my back and watched through the canopy of trees as lightning danced maniacally above the intricate network of branches. A hard rain began to fall, crackling at first like popcorn through the trees and soon peppering us with its icy persistence. I rolled onto my side and pulled my jacket over my head.

"You OK, Pink?" These were the last words I remember saying.

SACRIFICE

"Good as can be," I think he grumbled.

I slept some, I think, but not easily.

The rain was letting up when dawn broke and the storm's electrical accompaniment had passed over. We could hear its occasional rumbling in the distance. I couldn't stop shivering with cold. Soaked to the bone we mechanically pulled branches over our makeshift beds, which the rain had converted to mud baths. My intent was to obliterate any sign of our having been there, although I knew it was unlikely anybody would be coming this way for at least another day, if ever. At least these motions helped us warm up a tad and feel diligent before we started what I considered would be a tortuous death march deeper into the trees. I was tempted at first to creep back to the highway to see what intelligence if any we could gather from the crash site, but that temptation quickly fled when a breeze brought the first stinging whiff of burned petroleum to my nostrils. That scent of danger was all I needed to accept with deep relief that we were where we were and that we had the advantage of sanctuary ahead of us the further we penetrated the forest's embrace.

It was an exercise in masochism at first, with natural obstacles and torture devices impeding our every step. Joan had given me a map of the area and I started studying it for navigational signs that might lead us to a village that wasn't near any major highway. Our misery eased some when we stumbled onto a deer trail that was relatively clear of underbrush. We followed this until we came to a small clearing and sat on another fallen tree trunk to rest.

We were hungry. We'd slaked our thirst with rainwater wrung out of our shirts directly into our mouths. I was at the point where I was willing to betray whatever secrets anybody wanted from me for a damned Wendy's Bacon Cheeseburger. I started to confide this to Pink in an attempt to make a joke, but I saw that his face had a strange look. A look of alarm. He held a hand up to keep me from speaking.

"You two dudes stand still. Do not move. I have you in the sights of a rifle." The voice was male. It was calm. It was nearby but came from behind some bushes. I held my hands up and away from my body. Pink did the same.

"Don't shoot," I said. "We're harmless." Not sure why I said that, but it provoked a low chuckle from behind the bushes. The man was still chuckling when, with a sudden movement that shook a spray of rainwater off the leaves of one of the bushes, he stepped onto the trail in front of us. He was about my age, with wild snow-white hair and a weathered face blurred by a stubble of white beard. My first impression shouted, Unibomber!!! He looked sturdy, dry and alert, and was pointing a lever-action carbine in our direction. In a confident, resonant voice he ordered us onto the ground, face down. He patted us down and relieved us of the leather cases containing our fake badges and IDs, he took our wallets and my transponder and he took our revolvers.

"So you boys are harmless, eh? Treasury agents? You here because of my delinquent taxes?" We grunted but no intelligible words came out. He chuckled again. "Sorry boys, I'm afraid your luck has run out here, because you're completely out of your jurisdiction. This here is the Republic of Tax Freedonia and you are looking at its president.

I tried to speak again, but was able to muster only the same unintelligible grunt.

"I may have to execute you boys, you know, for having entered my country without a visa. In Tax Freedonia this constitutes espionage. The penalty, of course, is death. We can hold the trial right now if you like. You may speak in your defense."

I rolled onto my side and pushed myself to my knees. Suddenly too weak to stand, I rolled back onto my ass and sat staring up at our captor. Pink had managed to get to his feet.

"We're not really agents," he said. "We're not government at all. We're hiding from somebody and we respectively seek asylum in your country."

"Yeah? How do I know you're not jerking my chain? You were armed. Why should I believe you?"

"Check our driver's licenses. The names are different than the ones with the badges. We're fugitives. We don't give a shit what you're doing here. We slept all night in the rain and we're starving. For chrissake, man, cut us some slack!"

The stranger stared intently at Pink during this appeal, then he turned his face to me and his expression seemed to soften. He waved the rifle upward.

"OK. Get up. I may be crazier than usual to believe you but at least for now I do. Besides, I have all the firearms. You guys look like hell. I was just fixing breakfast. Let's go eat.

"By the way, I'm Randy. Some people call me President Newgate." He held out his free hand. We shook and mumbled our real names and expressed our sincere gratitude.

MATHEW PAUST

OUT OF THE FRYING PAN

Our captor stared at us so intensely it seemed imprudent for me and Pink to try to communicate with each other. At one point, moments after the man calling himself Randy Newgate told us he would feed us breakfast, I started to turn my head enough to try to catch Pink's eye, but felt Newgate's glare and turned instead to him. His ruddy, weathered face offered no expression but his attention seemed focused with an intent that was impervious to distraction. I stared back, waiting for him to indicate our next move. I assumed his camp or tent or the headquarters of his government or whatever the hell he wanted us to believe was somewhere further along the trail we'd come up. I expected him to swing his rifle barrel, movie style, in the direction he wanted us to go. Instead he just stood and stared at me, giving me an uneasy sensation that something in the dynamic had shifted. Either he had changed his mind about the offer of hospitality and decided to shoot us on the spot, or, more likely, he was stoned, fuguing with indecision.

"Where to?" I asked, hoping to keep him on the preferred task.

Now he swung the rifle barrel, toward the bush he'd been hiding behind. "You see where I came out?" he said, the words arched in a snarl, "That's where you go in." This did not look good. It occurred to me that as soon as I had gotten a few feet into the woods, behind the bush he'd pointed at, I might be able to elude a bullet or two if I ran like hell, assuming there was room to do so. I knew that once in the dense undergrowth it would be harder to move, but it might also be easier to hide or at least duck behind cover whenever it seemed he was about to fire. His rifle had a lever action, like a cowboy carbine. You had to crank the lever under the trigger guard down and back up to eject the fired cartridge casing and push a new round into the chamber. I remembered Chuck Connors as The Rifleman on TV shooting one

SACRIFICE

of these rapidfire, working the lever up and down so fast you could hardly see it move. But that was fantasy. Hard to fire accurately that way especially if the target was ducking and dodging through a woods. Plus Newgate would have two targets to worry about. I knew I had to signal to Pink somehow that when we were off the trail we should run in separate directions. I decided that at the last second I'd point away from me and yell, "RUN!!"

Which is what I did. Turned my head until I saw Pink at my periphery, extended my arm, finger pointing away from me, and shouted "RUN!!" as I launched myself in a straight-ahead dash through the underbrush. Within half a dozen steps a lurking greenbriar vine, nature's inspiration for razor wire, coiled itself around my left ankle and wrestled me face down into a nest of plants, twigs, small branches and other organic matter, some with stabbing skills that did a number on my arms and the front of my body and my face. I undoubtedly yelled something along the lines of SHIT at the moment of impact. I heard shouting voices and what might have been the sounds of elephants crashing through underbrush as I struggled to untangle myself or at least maneuver so I was facing skyward rather than nose down on the ground.

Comforted only by realizing I had yet to hear gunfire I considered the possibility I might be able to use the ground cover for concealment, squirm into some godforsaken thicket of sadistic vines and bushes and hope Newgate might also trip and fall in his haste or maybe it would rain again and disrupt the bastard's search and give me time to slow my breathing and think. These incipient schemes evaporated instantaneously with my success in fighting through the torturing greens unto my back only to behold, standing over me, glaring down, a gun-wielding Randy Newgate, his dirty jeans and slick gray rain jacket silhouetted black against the cloud-streaked morning sky. I decided to continue the assertive mindset I'd assumed with the decision moments earlier to escape, albeit reduced as I was to immobilized prey with attitude my only remaining weapon. At this point the only remaining stake, in my mind, was dignity.

"Where's Pink?" I said, trying my own authoritative snarl.

Newgate laughed.

"Who? You mean your buddy? Throckmorton Moynihan Pinkerton?"

"What?"

"I'm not going to try to say that again. That's the name on his Wilde Laboratories Ltd. ID. Can't say I blame you for calling him 'Pink.' Where is he? I don't know, Alfred Pierce Geddes III. He might be getting away. I don't care one way or the other. You're the one I want."

Oh, shit. "Want? What do you want me for? Who am I to you?"

"You know, Alfred Pierce Geddes III, I may look like a ragged old hermit nutcase living in the woods like the Unibomber. That's probly what you think. Know what? I don't give a rat's ass what you think. I may be a descendant of Edward Teach, better known as Blackbeard, and I may be crazy as a fucking loon. Probly am, truth be known. But I know who you are. I know who you were. I even read your fucking book."

"Oh, shit."

"It wasn't that bad. Little too much paranoia. Self pity. Got you in a little trouble, too, I see. You haven't served very long, though. What'd you do, escape? Haha. No. You were a big shot. No way they're gonna keep you in the prison population very long. Too many horny dicks be wanting to try some nice soft big-shot ass, huh? Anybody try you yet? They take numbers, big shot?"

"Fuck you, asshole! I"ll tell you one thing, Newgate, if you try to do what it sounds like you're getting ready to do you won't be hearing me squeal like any pig. You might hear me fart like one. I have a really bad case of diarrhea. Projectile diarrhea, and I'll shit all over your dick and your face if you get too close. Hear me? Go ahead. Let's get it on, asshole."

It surprised me to hear my voice saying this. Without any quaver or hint of irony. I sounded really mad dog pissed. I stared up into his face and tried to work my right leg free of the brambles so I could get in a good kick to a knee or his crotch or even his face if

SACRIFICE

he started trying to mount me. I knew he'd have to put the rifle down. I knew he had at least to be guessing after that little speech of mine that I wasn't afraid of being shot. I really don't think at that moment I was, either. I figured if I got a good kick into his balls or throat or face and he went down I'd have an even chance at getting my hands on the rifle. That was my plan. Deciding on it gave me a much-needed burst of energy.

MATHEW PAUST

WE'RE NOT AFTER YOUR STILL

I lay on my back squirming in a rain-soaked briar patch and staring up at a nutcase who glared down at me with mal-intent and a rifle. The perception that time had slowed to a glacial pace alerted me that the most primitive regions of my brain were quite aware of being on the cusp of what could be my imminent demise. These words were not the ones most likely scrambling in my head then, but they best describe the bigger picture of the neurological overdrive the crisis had summoned.

I have a vague recollection that a swarm of internal voices had begun vying for supremacy in these fateful seconds. The prevailing voice reminded me the drug Vulcana had rearranged my cognitive priorities so that in an instance like this, with enough extra time to evaluate instincts and conditioned reflexes, paying heed to the more rational choices was the safer bet. Recognizing this advantage had a narcotic effect on the fronds of hysteria burgeoning in my abdomen. Relief descended like Superman's cape, cooling the nerves and encouraging an almost arrogant calm. Thus, I now had on top of the surge of energy from my decision to act, the poise of a warrior mentally equipped to avail myself of whatever tactical edge might appear. At the moment, this consisted of marshaling all of my intent and will into my face. I wanted him to see the face of a man willing to kill to live, yet not afraid to die if it came to that.

Was I? Willing to kill and not afraid to die? At the moment I truly believed I was both. Now? I don't know. I am at peace, relatively speaking. What I do know is that should I ever again find myself in a similar situation where my life is at stake and it's either I kill or expect to be killed, I feel confident I can summon the same mindset I did then writhing on my back in the wet underbrush bleeding in a tangle of greenbriar and staring up at a delusional hermit who had the muzzle of a .30-30 deer rifle pointed my way.

SACRIFICE

At the same time I still had no idea what really was going on in Newgate's head. He hadn't said a word since my threat to propel liquid feces on him if he tried to pull a Deliverance on me. He'd made no further move toward me, either, but I suspected my racing mind had greatly slowed its time perception, and possibly only a second's fraction of real time had passed since my shouted threat. He stood over me as if transfixed. It occurred to me to say something more, to taunt him, distract him in some way from my effort to untangle the leg with which I hoped to disable him.

All that came to mind, though, was some Hollywood crap like Hey, asshole, put the gun down and fight me man to man. Whatsamatter, you chicken bukbukbukbuk? Huh? Huh? Chick chick chiiiii-ken bukbukbukbuk. I sensed this might get me kicked in the groin or clubbed in the mouth with the rifle butt. Or shot then and there. I abandoned these wispy thoughts and concentrated on directing my willful stare through his eyes into the back of his screwball cranium.

At least I think I only thought those silly taunts. You'd think I'd remember if I actually said them out loud. Maybe I started to, although I'm pretty sure I had a better grip on my faculties. The reason I'm now second guessing is because of what I distinctly remember happening next. Newgate moved. He seemed to be starting to raise the rifle to his shoulder. His head swiveled. Then came the screech: YEEEEEEEEEEEHAAAAAAAAA!!!!!!!

I jerked my head toward the sound and saw a large shadowy form swoop screaming through the air straight at us. I tried to duck my head, banging it on something sharp, as the flying object passed directly over us and crashed into the branches of a nearby pine tree. A quick glance back at Newgate told me my opportunity had arrived. In ducking, he'd lost his balance and was staggering. More importantly his rifle was pointed away from me. I'd freed my leg by then and launched a kick at his nearest knee. The kick fell short, hitting his shin but with enough force to knock him further off balance. He crashed to the ground, and I was on him with a desperate vengeance. We wrestled. He was stronger and quicker, and before I realized what was happening he'd jerked my arms roughly behind me and clasped something metallic around my wrists with a loud click.

"Handcuffs?" I shouted.

"You goddamned right, you dumb shit!" He was shouting, too. Then immediately started laughing. He grabbed my collar and pulled me up to see what had caught his fancy. Then I started laughing, too.

"Stop laughing and get me down, goddammit! I can't move!" Pink howled. He was trapped among the branches of the pine tree, still clutching some kind of vine he'd evidently used to swing from another tree in a valiant effort to rescue me from our captor. Letting me drop, Newgate clambered over to the tree, but Pink was too high to reach from the ground. Newgate came back to me and undid the handcuffs.

"All right, goddam you," he said. "If you want to get your buddy Throckmorton down from that tree..." He collapsed into laughter, slapping his thigh, bent over, laughing harder than I'd seen anybody do since my dad watching Jonathan Winters lose it on the Carson show. This continued with Newgate awhile. He'd try to tell me what he expected me to do, and then would break up again. I started to get concerned, then I looked up at Pink again and started laughing again myself.

"Hey," Pink shouted finally. "Get me the hell down before you laugh me to death. I could die up here."

SACRIFICE

CAT UP A TREE

Confusion. Surprises leading to confusion leading to more surprises leading to... My state at the moment as Newgate charged off through the underbrush to find a ladder to get "another goddam cat down from a tree," was near paralysis from a combination of embarrassment and the pain from my scratches and bruises. My only consolation was that Newgate seemed not to be what I had most feared. He demonstrated this by removing the handcuffs when Pink started yelling for help. Too, he'd left the rifle leaning against the tree Pink was stuck in when he headed away for the rope.

It was possible he was simply addled by drugs or mental illness, but, even so, his compassion was evident with his unblinking willingness to take pains and risk leaving me unattended, and with access to his rifle, to help get Pink out of the tree. I lost sight of him yet could hear him crashing through the thick foliage and tree debris. At one point his voice carried back with shouted encouragement: "Hang on, dammit! Gimme a minute!"

My concern at this point was for Pink, too. He had stopped hollering and looked as if he might be unconscious, wedged as he was between two branches. He was slumped, unmoving, leaning inward against the trunk.

"Pink!" I called up to him. "You still with us, bubba?" Getting no response, either vocal or physical, I moved over to the tree and stood directly beneath him. I called his name again. Nothing. Something dropped from where he was, barely missing hitting me. I hunkered to see what it was and found several quarter-size splotches of blood. Another fell while I was hunkering. It splashed on a root knee and several droplets bounced up onto a cuff of my jeans. "Pink!" I yelled louder. "Say something! You're bleeding! Speak to me!" Nothing.

The nearest branch that would support my weight was out of reach, but it occurred to me that with Newgate here one of us could boost the other up. I shouted in the direction he'd headed, telling him to hurry. No response from him, either. I turned my view back up to Pink and saw an arm move, then a leg. I could see that his arms were draped over the limbs he was wedged between, and now I worried he might be slipping. I moved directly under him so that in case he fell I could try to break his fall.

"Hang on, Pink. We're getting a ladder!" I thought I heard him start to mumble something, but couldn't make anything out. His voice sounded drugged. No sign of Newgate with or without a ladder. I shouted again in the direction he'd gone. Suddenly something landed heavily on my shoulder, sending a paralyzing jolt through my body. "Hey!" I shouted and jerked my head up to see that Pink had planted one of his sneaker-clad feet next to my neck. His other foot was swinging just above me evidently looking to alight on the other shoulder. I reached up and grabbed the ankle on my shoulder and then reached for the other until I had a firm grip on it, as well. Pink's elbows were locked around a branch, pulling him over and hiking his shoulders in a frozen shrug.

"I'm gonna steady your feet now so you can ease down and grip that branch with both hands and lower yourself to where you'll be only a few feet from the ground. Then you can let go and you'll drop straight down. I'll keep you upright and make sure you land on your feet. OK?"

Pink mumbled some more and did as I'd suggested. He landed awkwardly and lost his balance, but I held him steady and eased him to a sitting position on the ground. His mouth was bloody and a nasty bruise on his forehead had raised a tennis-ball-size lump that was turning dark red. His cheeks, nose and chin were bleeding from scratches and blood had soaked through the right leg of his jeans just below the knee. I sat down beside him. He smelled of stale sweat, pine sap and blood.

"That was a pretty brave thing you did there, Pink. It took balls."

SACRIFICE

His face twisted as if he were trying to smile. I added, "But as it turns out I think this guy Newgate is OK. He set his rifle against the tree over there when he went off for a ladder to help get you down. I guess we misjudged him."

Pink tried to speak, but it was clear the injury to his mouth, which appeared to be a cut and bruised lip and maybe a couple of broken teeth was preventing coherency. He nodded his head vigorously up and down and tried to smile again as if he understood and seemed as relieved as I was that we were out of immediate danger.

I heard rustling in the underbrush and turned my head in that direction. Newgate appeared through a thicket of bushes. He was dragging what looked like a rope ladder. He walked up to us, dropped the rope and sat down across from us.

"Don't know what I'm gonna do with you guys," he said. His voice sounded weary. He looked weary.

MATHEW PAUST

HOBBLING IN THE HOGAN

Despite his apparent weariness Newgate seemed nervous or anxious about something. It was clear he wasn't comfortable. He seemed more than casually concerned about Pink's injuries. His eyes squinted, furrowing his brow, as he peered at the bleeding scientist. He leaned forward to get a closer look.

"Your ankle's swollen, Pinkerton. It's either sprained or broken. We need to get you back to the hogan," he said.

"Hogan?" I said.

Newgate stood. "It's not far. See that green mound?" He pointed back the way he'd come with the rope.

All I saw that could be said to resemble a mound was a dense clump of bushes about as far from us as the width of a city street. "You mean the bushes?" I said.

He shook his head and his face relaxed into a half smile. "Good to know the camouflage still works. C'mon let's get him in there. You up for a little walk, Mr. Pinkerton?"

Pink's bloodied face registered little more than dazed confusion. He raised his head enough to make eye contact with me and nodded once, then twice, but looked as if he were about to pass out. He tried to speak but his words were slurred and incomprehensible. I stood, too, feeling wobbly and sore but well enough to help Newgate support a badly limping Pink along a footpath through the underbrush to what now was easily recognizable as a man-made structure covered with camouflage netting into which plants and small bushes were anchored. An olive-brown Army blanket hung across an opening. Newgate lifted the blanket to one side and the three of us entered.

The interior of what he called a "hogan" was roomier than it

SACRIFICE

appeared from the outside. Holding to the dome shape of its exterior, its construction looked to be simple, consisting of some kind of fabric skin stretched over a framework of parallel poles that radiated outward and down from an anchoring ring at the top, creating the effect of a squat teepee. When I stood in the very center the top cleared my head by a couple of feet and the arc from that point outward enabled me to walk upright along a radius of three to four feet before I had to start stooping to avoid bumping my head on the frame.

The predominant odor was a mix of pine lumber, synthetic tent fabric and the more domestic scents from cooked food and worn clothing. There were no windows, but there was a small air conditioner protruding from an opening in the timber frame. Newgate had attached two rows of LED track lights on opposite sides near the top. Both tracks were lit when we entered, providing adequate illumination. A floor of machined boards was sturdy enough to indicate the dwelling rested on a solid foundation. Furniture was simple - small folding desk, folding camp chair and a table that held a hot plate and some cooking utensils and dishes. There was a cot with a pillow and blankets against the opposite wall. Newgate nodded toward the cot and we helped Pink over to it and eased him down onto the thin mattress.

"We should check him over quickly before he lies down," Newgate said. "I have some first aid stuff here but we may need to get him some help if it's more than we can handle." He unlaced and removed the sneaker from Pink's injured foot and pulled down the white cotton athletic sock. The ankle was grotesquely swollen. "Pink, I'm going to be pressing a little on your ankle to try and make sure it isn't broken. It's gonna hurt a little." He motioned for me to hold Pink's shoulders. Mr. Geddes is going to hold you steady while I check you out, OK?"

Pink said nothing. His face was blank, and showed no recognition of what Newgate had just said. I was starting to worry Pink was slipping into shock. I mouthed the word "shock" to Newgate, raised my eyebrows inquiringly and tilted my head toward Pink. Newgate shrugged. Pink startled both of us then when he spoke.

"I'm not in shock. My ankle hurts like hell, though. Do what you have to do and get it over with. I'd like to lie down here awhile and just rest."

"OK, then. Here goes," Newgate said and began squeezing on the ankle, working up to the shin and back down to the top of the foot. Pink's face remained impassive, although several times his eyelids blinked rapidly and he breathed deeply. "Hurt?" Newgate asked.

"Yeah, a little."

"If it's any help, I was a medic in 'Nam. I should be able to tell if anything's broken. I don't feel any bones sticking out or anything giving way too much when I push on it. If a bone is broken and I push on it you won't be able to sit still and handle the pain like you are."

"I'm pretty good with pain," Pink said quietly.

"OK, then. How about standing up and putting your full weight on that foot. If you can walk from here to the desk over there and back without screaming like a banshee I think we can safely assume all you have is a sprain. A bad sprain, but something that will heal without needing a doctor." Pink nodded assent, and Newgate and I helped him to his feet. Newgate reached under the cot and pulled out a stout stick about four feet long with a knob at one end. He handed it to Pink. "Here you go, bubba. Use this, but it won't do you much good if your ankle's broken."

Pink gripped the stick at the knob, leaned his weight on it and stepped off toward the desk across the room. After two halting hobbles he stopped, took a deep breath and looked around at me. "Hurts like hell," he said, "What are we gonna do if the damned thing's broke?"

"Mr. Pinkerton, let's cross that bridge if we come to it," Newgate said. "Your ankle feels worse now because the shock is wearing off. You always have some shock at first at the point of injury. Keep walking. You haven't hollered yet. That's a good sign."

Pink commenced his thumping hobble, a little faster now as if the

SACRIFICE

faster he went the sooner the agony would be over. He made it to the desk where he slumped, then leaned against it with both hands after leaning the stick against the chair.

"Shit. You have a laptop here. You have electric lights, A/C, hot plate and the gods only know what all. In a damned teepee. You're not the typical hermit, Newgate," Pink said. "I mean, Mr. President."

"Nothing's as it seems, anymore, Mr. Pinkerton. C'mon back here. I'll give you a couple Vicodin so you can get some rest. I'll fry us some eggs and bacon. Coffee's already hot." When Pink remained slumped against the desk, Newgate added. "You boys have something to do with that killer egg that went down last night over there, don't you." He nodded in the direction we'd come from.

"That's a rhetorical question. I just want you to know I'm not some dumb ass hiding out in the woods with post traumatic stress disorder. There's video of the crash on CNN. Mr. Pinkerton, you may return to the cot."

MATHEW PAUST

TWO FIRES

It was early afternoon before Newgate went to his desk and powered up his laptop. The deliberate way he approached it, standing for three or four seconds and gazing at it as if debating with himself and then moving resolutely to the flimsy chair and lowering himself carefully onto its webbing, had a ritualistic air to it, as if he were hesitant to observe the rite in front of strangers.

The morning had been busy for him. A quick and efficient short-order cook, he whipped up a batch of scrambled eggs, bacon and toast, which, with the freshly brewed coffee, helped ease me toward a minor sense of comfort from the clammy dread that had been leaching from my pancreas since daybreak. After breakfast he replaced the skillet with a steel pot and soon had a stew of vegetables and a ham bone simmering on the hot plate. The aroma from the pot further lightened my spirits. At around noon he gave us steaming bowls of stew, which we ate with pieces of what tasted like a fairly fresh baguette he'd taken from a small black refrigerator I hadn't noticed until then. Newgate grinned and responded with an exaggerated Gallic shrug when I asked him where he'd gotten the bread.

I gradually became aware of a quiet good humor in this strange man, who, soon as we'd finished breakfast, went to work examining our injuries. Besides a few bruises and scratches, I was fine. Pink's bleeding, except for his mouth, had stopped by the time we get him into the hogan. His punctures and scratches looked worse than mine, contrasting starkly with his pale skin, but Newgate assured us they were superficial. He gave us paper towels soaked in hydrogen peroxide to wipe down the scratches. He gave Pink a small glass of peroxide as a rinse for his mouth. He fished an elastic bandage from a footlocker next to the cot and wrapped Pink's swollen ankle, instructing him to put as much weight on it as he could stand as soon as possible.

SACRIFICE

"The sooner you start using it the sooner it'll heal," he explained.

"Can I keep this stick?" Pink still mumbled, not yet used to the bloody gap left when he lost the two or three teeth smashing into the tree. I almost laughed, remembering a song we used to hear on the radio when I was a kid, sung in a sibilant, whistley falsetto, called All I Want for Christmas is My Two Front Teeth. I think we had the record. Spike Jones, I think. I shot a glance at Newgate, who lifted a corner of his mouth in acknowledgment.

"It's yours, Mr. Pinkerton. That's a piece of blackthorn my grandfather gave me as a kid when we were deer hunting once. Said I could use it as a shillelagh when I joined the force."

"Did you?" Pink lisped.

"Yes, sir. Followed in grandpa's footsteps. Kept the shillelagh in my trunk for good luck. Never used it, though, as it was intended."

"So you're Irish then?" Decided it was my turn to join the chat.

"Not from my name, Mr. Geddes. On the maternal side. My mother's mother's side were O'Learys. Everyone else was English. Used to have some real donnybrooks at family get-togethers."

"I'll bet," I said. "You were joking when said you were descended from Blackbeard, right?"

"Oh, no, sir. I never joke about family. My mother's maiden name was Teach. Ring a bell?"

"It does. I'm impressed." I grinned. Newgate chuckled. I wanted to keep the conversation going. He seemed to be opening up. "So did your fellow officers know you were from pirate stock?"

"Oh, yes. I caught a lot of ribbing. The chief wanted me to work narcotics, go undercover, grow a beard, put gunpowder fuses into it and fire them up when we did a raid."

"Did you?"

He shook his head and laughed. "Our insurance wouldn't cover it if I got burned. I thought about it, even asked the city's risk manager. He looked at me like I was nuts." Newgate's face grew serious. He lowered his chin and aimed a level gaze at me. "So, gentlemen, how about I get a turn with the questions? What the hell you doing out here? What's the deal with that killer egg?"

I started to speak, my mind frantically scrambling to come up with some kind of bullshit story, wondering at the same time what difference would it make if I told him the truth. I had a feeling he was pretty good at ferreting out the truth no matter what stories people might try on him and that we might be better off not arousing his suspicions any more than they already were. I'd decided to take this course, and had gotten out, "Mr. Newgate, we could be in a lot of trouble..." when Pink interrupted.

"You could be in danger if we told you what we think is going on. The less you know the better." His voice was strong, the lisp barely noticeable. He'd pushed himself up into a sitting position on the cot.

Newgate wasn't fazed. "You could be in more danger than you think, gentlemen, if you don't lay your cards on the table." His voice was stronger than Pink's. No lisp. "Remember who's in charge here now."

Pink wasn't backing down. "No disrespect intended, but I think whoever shot down that helicopter was after us. They're still after us. They would kill you without thinking twice if you were in the way. And if we're gone and they find you and suspect we were here...am I getting through, Mr. Newgate?"

This was not the Pink I thought I knew. Hard even to remember the rapidfire geek talk with the heeheehee punctuations. My head was swimming. I watched Newgate's face turn back and forth between mine and Pink's. I was looking back and forth between the two of them. Were we getting somewhere or were we slipping deeper into the quicksand?

Newgate remained unfazed. His voice had calmed when he next spoke: "All the more reason for you to tell me what you know, fellas. I'd rather some bastards shoot me dead than be tortured. I know torture. The Vietnamese taught me torture, OK? Tell me

SACRIFICE

what the fuck you know!"

"So you can rat us out? Go to hell, Blackbeard!" This was me.

"I'll make that decision, on my terms, when the time comes. I'd like it not to come to that. I think maybe you and I, without knowing, are on the same side down the line. Don't ask me to explain what I mean by that. But right now you are either going to come clean with me or you've had the last of my hospitality. And don't ask what I mean by that, either. Are you catching my drift, Mr. Pinkerton?"

This volleying back and forth eventually petered out when the stew was ready. We agreed to a time-out for lunch. Pink and I exchanged glances that told me we might be about to enjoy our final lunch. But we'd worked up an appetite and the stew smelled good. We ate ravenously, although Pink had some trouble with the hot liquid on exposed nerves where his teeth had been. The slurping sounds were almost comical. Nobody registered amusement. We'd stashed the dishes and were sipping water Newgate kept in the little refrigerator when he told us it was time to go online.

"Gentlemen, take a look at this," he said, his voice projecting a guarded alarm. I helped Pink limp over to the desk. We leaned over and stared at the screen. Newgate had called up the CNN website. He punched the start button on a video of the helicopter crash site, showing the billowing flames and oily black smoke erupting into the sky. Then I saw something that froze my blood. As the camera panned back from the site a smaller fire came into the picture. It was a car, totally engulfed in flames. No, it was a van, an SUV. It was our Enclave.

MATHEW PAUST

TROUBLE AHEAD, TROUBLE BEHIND

I was sure enough it was our Enclave that the sight of it ablaze on the video sent me into a minor fugue state, a complete withdrawal from my immediate circumstances into an internal emergency conference. I most likely looked dazed to Newgate as my ramped-up cerebrum began to quickly sketch out questions and options, acknowledging the likelihood that a sea change had occurred yet again and that I just might now be facing the worst predicament of my life.

Of most immediate concern was that the burning vehicle was indeed the Enclave. If so, it would mean Joan Stonebraker was either dead, badly injured or a captive. This would mean our link to Wilde Labs was severed, that we were in effect adrift with no tether to the mother ship. This led to the question of who had done this, caused our helicopter escort to crash and subsequently the SUV to be destroyed. A competitor? Who else could even know what was going on? If a competitor then maybe Pink was safe, at least from murder. Torture would be a distinct possibility if he refused to cooperate. Who else could it be? The government? What government, ours or some other country's? Did it really matter so far as what we had to do next, which was to avoid detection? Would there be a reward? Could a reward entice Newgate to betray us? Might he betray us anyway, just to get us out of his hair? My fugue was quickly pushing toward an inverted hysteria. I sensed I might be on the verge of a catatonic episode. I forced myself to look up, turn my head and meet Newgate's eyes. Instantly I knew I'd made a mistake.

"That's your vehicle, isn't it," Newgate said. It wasn't a question. I looked at Pink and saw that he also was struggling. A slight nod of his head told me he was deferring to me to answer.

"I don't know. I can't be sure," I muttered. I didn't fool Newgate.

SACRIFICE

"You're scared."

"I prefer uncertain."

"You're scared. And now I'm thinking maybe I should get you two the hell out of here. I don't like being around scared."

"We don't either, Newgate," Pink piped up. "And we're not. Al said 'uncertain,' and that goes for me, too. That might be our ride in the video. If it is it would be a setback, for sure. But we're not the panicky type. Are you?"

Newgate allowed a small grin. He nodded at Pink. "I like your attitude, son. Are you a refugee from the White House, too? I don't remember you in the book, or are you using an alias?"

Pink stared at Newgate, not returning the grin, and kept his focus on the other man until the grin went away. Then he said, "The helicopter that crashed was our escort. We don't know what happened, but I saw another helicopter flying next to it just before it blew up.

"We're in danger, all right, but so are you. If they can find us they can find you. Getting rid of us won't do you any good. They might have tracked us right here to this hogan, sending teams in at this moment. You said something about maybe we were on the same side. I don't know how that could be, but let's just say for the sake of argument that we are. And in one respect we are. Both on the same side. Al and I are fugitives, and now so are you. Problem is we don't know who from."

Pink was surprising me by the minute. I shifted my eyes back and forth between him and Newgate. Pink was calm and deliberate. Newgate nodded several times, following intently. When Pink finished the two stared at each other briefly, then Newgate nodded again and turned to me.

"Let's see what CNN has on it." He turned back to his laptop.

Pink said, "I read it. They don't know much. The helicopter was a drone. Ours. No mention of the other one."

Newgate wasn't paying attention. His eyes were fixed on a small blinking red flag in a corner of the screen. He tapped a key, opening another window. It contained one word: northeast. "Intruder," he said, his voice taut. He moved swiftly to the hogan opening, grabbing the rifle propped next to it and pulling back the blanket. "Mr. Geddes, come with me. Mr. Pinkerton, don't make a sound. If they don't know exactly where we are they might not see the hogan."

"You have another gun?" I asked. He pulled one of our revolvers from a pocket and handed it to me. He pulled out the other one and tossed it to Pink.

"Not a sound, Mr. Pinkerton," he said as we stepped outside. It had warmed considerably. The sun was out, sparkling off the remaining droplets of moisture on the leaves. A grand day for a picnic, I thought, almost laughing at the incongruency. I followed Newgate along a virtually invisible footpath that ran parallel to the more obvious one we'd taken coming in. The only noticeable evidence it was passable through the undergrowth and briars was the chopped-off ends of briared vines that otherwise would have reached across like strands of barbed wire. Someone, undoubtedly Newgate, had been through with a machete, something I wished I'd had at that moment. We reached a grove of sumac. Newgate motioned with the flat of his hand for us to stop behind the curtain of palmetto-like leaves. He knelt, and motioned that I do the same. I wasn't in a position to argue, so, stiff and aching in every joint, I creaked down into a hunker, then lowered my butt onto the still wet, cold ground. Newgate frowned at me so I rocked forward onto my knees, bracing myself with my hands.

Fifteen or twenty minutes passed with no sound but an occasional argument among some birds, the rustling of a rabbit scurrying through nearby underbrush or the belated distant racket of jet engines laboring so high all I could see was a silver glint at the head of a wispy tail of white vapor miles in front of where the sound seemed to emanate. When we heard the intruder there was no mistaking something large and awkward was approaching, crashing along the trail. Newgate was on his feet in a flash, moving so quickly the little noise he made had ended likely before

SACRIFICE

it could register with whatever was out there. He motioned for me to stay down as he stepped around the grove and stood, crouched slightly, his rifle pointed up the trail.

"Hold it! Hold it right there," he barked. Peering through the leaves I saw a pair of jeans. The stance of the legs wearing them looked vaguely familiar. I leaned forward to get a better look. I shouted.

"Newgate! It's OK. She's OK! She's with us!" It was Joan.

BOX OF RAIN

Not much was said on the way back to the hogan. After a tense introduction, Newgate allowed Joan to keep her sidearm. He seemed flustered at first.

"I wondered how much of the book was real," he said, "But I didn't think it would have real people dying who were still alive."

Joan crinkled her brow, looked at him, then at me. "Executive Pink. We haven't talked about it yet," I said. She shook her head, asked only where we were going. "Shelter," I said. She followed Newgate and I followed her. She smiled broadly and sighed with relief to find Pink in the hogan.

"Anybody want to tell me what's going on?" she asked after sitting on the cot next to Pink while Newgate poured her a cup of coffee.

"You first, Joan," I said. "We saw a video of the Enclave inside a ball of fire. I thought we'd lost you...for real."

"Almost did. I pulled onto the shoulder when I got to the crash site. Not sure why I did that but I guess I was hoping I could learn something. Almost the instant I stopped I was nearly blinded by a green light coming through the windshield. I knew it was a laser because I saw the beam. If it had hit me directly in the eyes I'd be blind. The windshield broke it up enough, but I knew what was coming next...well, I didn't know what but my brain was screaming to get out of the damned vehicle. I pushed the door open and rolled out into the ditch, got up and ran as fast as I could into the field. It was corn so I wasn't as visible in among the dried stalks. I got about six or so steps into the corn when CLANK WHOOMP! Whatever it was hit the metal first. Some kind of missile, I guess.

"I laid down between the rows for a while. I thought I'd be too

SACRIFICE

easy to see if I ran. That damned little black bird kept circling. I expected to see the green laser come at me again, even in the corn, but after first responders started arriving the bird flew off and I got up and walked to the woods. I backtracked to where I let you out and hoped you'd still be fairly near. I kept a lookout for the damned bird but it must have gone back to its daddy."

"Did you try to contact us with your transponder?" This was Pink.

"I lost it, Pink. I think I took it out and set it on the seat in case I saw something to call in. Do you still have yours?"

"I have them," Newgate said. "But I wouldn't trust them now for anything. Someone's breached your security big time."

"That they have," Joan said, her voice mournful.

We filled the next few days with talk. I didn't say much, serving more as a focal point for glances and grins as the two experienced interrogators went at each other. Pink was technical adviser. As our host, Newgate led off impressing us with his understanding of my book and extracting the updates. He flashed me a quick grin when Vulcana came up as Pink explained its propensity to induce erections that lasted as long as the mind wished them to.

"That's all it was at first," he said. "It was an improvement over the other ED drugs, which simply increase blood flow. Vulcana stimulates the neocortex, giving it dominion over the libido and the circulatory system."

"At first?" Newgate surprised me with his acuity.

"We've improved it. Giving empathy more say in decisions."

"Whoa..."

"Mitigating the monster, we call it. The new generation Vulcana tickles those regions of the cortex that help you understand the intentions behind certain gestures. Integrates the other person's ego with yours in forming perceptions. Cuts away a lot of misunderstanding while you feel what the other person feels." Pink was getting a tad excited here and I started worrying he'd slip back into his machinegun patter with the heeheehees that could blow his credibility. I needn't have worried. He had it controlled, and Newgate stayed with him, nodding briskly, his eyes widening as the implications began to grow.

"No wonder people want you dead," he said when Pink paused to take a breath. "The erection thing alone could overturn our entire neuroses-based economy. Men buy stuff so they'll get laid, women buy stuff so men will want them. Do you have something like this for women?"

"Primrose Lane." Joan said this and immediately blushed.

"That good, huh?"

She retained her composure. "With PL women don't need men, at least not as much." Her voice, while softer than moments earlier, betrayed little emotion.

"What about the empathy thing? I suppose you'll say women are naturally more empathetic, but I know some..."

Pink jumped back in. "As a general rule, yes. Our theory is that with men no longer anxious about performance they can relax and enjoy less competitive pursuits. Women won't feel the stress of competing as much, either, especially with PL taking their edge off, so to speak. "Do I have it right, Joan?"

"That's the theory."

"You have doubts?" Newgate said.

"It's unrealistic to hope for one-size-fits-all in anything except...with pharmaceuticals," Mr. Newgate. "There will always be exceptions, maybe many exceptions. All we're hoping for is that in general people will have better self-esteem and be kinder to each other. That would be an important breakthrough. A very important breakthrough," she said.

Newgate, leaning forward in his camp chair, followed the conversation with his eyes as the import of what he was learning sank in and presumably stretched his imagination a tad. He surprised me at one point with an exhale of breath reminiscent of days long past when one only reluctantly released a reverse gasp

SACRIFICE

of rare and mighty fine illegal smoke the kind politicians might eventually no longer be required to describe as having entered the lungs unintentionally.

"It would be revolutionary," he said, his voice hushed with awe. He looked up at Pink, a ripple of worry tensing his face. "You've tested this?"

"With generation one. Al took it by accident and the volunteer test subject panicked when his erection persisted. He went to a hospital. That's how word of the project leaked out, we're pretty sure."

"How about the new version?"

"It works on mice."

"Mice?"

"Both aspects. The empathy part was overpowering."

"No humans?"

"One. Me."

MATHEW PAUST

SEE WHAT TOMORROW BRINGS

In her turn with the questions Joan made it clear she was more than casually curious about Newgate's background and circumstances. Where did the electric power come from. Who owned the property he was squatting on. Where had he been a cop. Where did he get his food. She laid them out in a package as if making polite conversation, which softened the process from sounding like what it was.

"Tell us about yourself, Mr. Newgate..." Using his last name to convey respect and emphasize her seriousness while avoiding the too obvious psychological ploy of feigning informality. Interrogation lite. Newgate smiled. He knew the drill. He answered her questions with a friendly directness that seemed genuine.

He revealed, with a minimum of sparring, that he'd been a cop in Newport News for 11 years before retiring officially on disability but essentially "for rocking the boat.

"I cooperated with an FBI investigation of corruption. Nothing came of it. Local politics. In New York they'd have set me up like they did Frank Serpico. Here they put me on the curb with a pension. I haven't collected a penny of it."

"You're set up pretty nicely here, Randy," Joan said, sensing correctly it was OK now to drop the formality a notch. "You must have saved some money."

"A little, but I don't use banks. I'm completely off the grid. The only people who know where I am are people I want to know where I am."

"No wife, I take it. Kids?"

Newgate's mouth twitched into the semblance of a one-sided

smile but his eyes shifted to a focus somewhere over Joan's shoulder. When it became obvious he intended not to respond further, she asked who owned the land he was squatting on. "Nature Conservancy," he answered.

"They must know you're here?"

"Oh, yes. It was part of the agreement we reached when I donated the land." This brought his three guests to heightened attention. Joan lifted an eyebrow.

"I inherited it from an uncle. On my mother's side."

"Teach?"

"That's the family legend. There's no historical evidence. I traced the title back to the Civil War when a lot of court records were burned. The earliest plat I found, dated March 27,1869, shows 1,278 acres in the names of Oliver and Priscilla Thatch, which was a common variation of Teach. According to the plat the land came to the Thatch family as a royal grant, but no date is given as to when this took place. I have found nothing earlier on either Priscilla or Oliver, but a great aunt claimed she had written proof in the form of a pardon of an Edward Teach signed by the North Carolina governor. I have never seen this pardon nor have any idea where it might be, if it exists or ever existed, but that's the family story."

When Newgate paused then, the only sounds in the hogan were of our breaths exhaling. Joan and I looked at each other. Her unusually widened eyes told me she was as rapt as I was by our host's implications. I decided to spell her for at least one question.

"Do you think you're Blackbeard's descendant, Randy?" I studied his face, trying to picture a younger version of it, the unkempt gray hair and beard stubble black as night, pale blue eyes less pensive, fierce now as a fearsome pirate's. His amused smile banished this image.

"I don't know, truthfully. Could be. There are some in the family convinced of it. We'll probably never find undeniable proof one way or the other. Anyway, I'm the custodian of record of the property. It's posted. The only hunting allowed here is along a 90-acre strip at the south edge and that's restricted to a hunt club. Occasionally their dogs will run a deer up this way, which is why I wear a half-assed uniform during hunting season. Never had any trouble with the boys. I'd rather they didn't hunt at all, but it's a tradition that dates back to before I was born. I know some of the club members.

"You're wondering about the power. Solar panels. Fifty yards away. Pretty well camouflaged. I found some non-reflective material that's barely visible from an airplane and I have it well concealed at ground level. Water's piped in from an artesian well not far, either. I have a shed next to the hogan that's as hard to detect as this. Tank in there for showers and even a flush toilet. I put a lot of work into this, getting it livable for the long haul."

"How long?"

"Long as necessary. I could live here the rest of my life."

"How long have you been here?" Joan was back in charge.

"Oh, let's see. Six years? Yeah, I think so. A little over six years. Time flies when you're not paying attention."

"So, Randy, I'm really very curious. If you don't mind. Why?"

"Why?

"Yes. You don't strike me as the stereotype of the disgruntled veteran who turns his back on society, who can't readjust to the demands and details of civilian life after being at war. For whatever reason. Emotional or psychological problems. They just can't or don't want to have to cope anymore. You're...You..."

"I'm normal?"

Joan laughed, politely. "Randy. No, I can't say I would consider you normal. Not from what little I know of you. But, then, who would I consider to be normal? No, I consider you eccentric, for sure. You're an interesting man. Intelligent. Rational. You seem well-balanced. You don't seem to lack ordinary social skills, yet

SACRIFICE

here you are. Avoiding society. Do you ever leave here? Go to town for mail? Supplies? To, ah..."

"Socialize?" Newgate's turn to laugh. It came out calm, good-natured.

Joan and I laughed. Pink was grinning.

"I have a vintage Indian motorcycle in the shed, if that answers your question."

The exchange of information wound down after the motorcycle revelation. Newgate heated a pot of vegetable soup and fixed some cheddar sandwiches for our supper. While we ate he went to the shack and returned with an armload of air mattresses and sleeping bags, inflating the mattresses with an electric pump and arranging them around the cot, which he made clear was Pink's.

The sun was low in the sky and the temperature was chilling when Newgate suggested we turn in for the night. No one argued. My sleeping bag smelled of pine and some kind of chemical, probably a bug repellent. My jacket had dried in front of the small electric space heater Newgate turned on earlier. I folded it into a pillow and arranged the bag. The air mattress was inflated just enough to keep me off the floor, but not so much that I might roll off while asleep.

Newgate approached me as I was about to zip up the bag. "We'll talk more tomorrow," he said, handing me a small, pale blue pill. "Imodium. For diarrhea," he said. The shared irony flicked between us without a sound, leaving only a trace of amusement on his face. I grinned a foolish grin, stashed the pill in my shirt pocket, zipped the bag and was soon asleep.

MATHEW PAUST

THE DIE IS SHAKEN

I awoke after a couple of hours and had to pee. A cacophonous blitz of snoring disoriented me at first, especially after I opened my eyes and saw the dark shapes of other sleepers around me. Then I remembered the night before, and it all came back to me. It seemed considerably colder in the hogan than it had even during the storm, despite the space heater and body heat from the others. I had no intention of trying to find my way to the shed and its plumbing. I would slip away a few steps from the hogan, take care of business and return to my sleeping bag without disturbing the others. That was the plan I developed while groping in the dark for my sneakers.

The snoring was getting louder. It sounded distressed, as if someone were strangling. I sat up and knew immediately it was Pink. I climbed out of my bag and moved closer to the cot. He was lying on his side with his mouth hanging open. I didn't recall him snoring the night before, but we'd been in the open and the thunder and rain might have drowned out the sounds. I was thinking now it might be because of his injuries. Maybe he broke his nose smacking into the tree. It could explain the tortured breathing. I was surprised he could sleep at all and that the noise apparently had not roused anyone else.

The hogan's chilly interior morphed to sauna heat in contrast to the wind gust that cut through my clothes and slapped me fully awake when I stepped past the blanket into the night. The sky was still bright with stars and a full moon but the sudden plunge in temperature had silenced the frogs that had entertained us with their mating songs the previous night. I decided to get my business finished pronto. I walked to the nearest tree for concealment and directed my stream downwind. The small pleasure from relieving that pressure vanished like the steam from my urine as the day's bruises and strained muscles

SACRIFICE

reasserted their complaints. I had turned to head back to my sleeping bag when a sharp green light near the other side of the hogan entrance froze me in place.

Bouncing like one of those balls that mark the subtitled words to a song on a movie screen, the green light was working its way toward the hogan entrance. I responded without a thought, running toward the light with my fists balled and ready to do whatever I could to prevent an attack on the people inside. I had taken no more than four or five steps when the light flared up so brightly it blinded me and forced me to stop.

Joan's description of the laser that found her SUV moments before it blew up immediately shrieked in my head hurling me to the ground. I crashed into some more prickly bushes and tall Johnson grass already wet with dew and braced myself for whatever was next on my attacker's agenda.

"What the fuck? Hold it right there!" The voice was muted but familiar.

"Randy?" I cowered in the underbrush almost hoping it was somebody else.

"Al! What are you doing out here?"

"Shit! Had to pee. What's with the green laser, and why are you out here?"

"Had to pee. It's not a laser. Just a green flashlight. Easier on the night vision than white light. You didn't poop your pants, did you?"

"No, I don't think so, no thanks to you." I was afraid our noise might have awakened the others and that Pink or Joan would come stumbling out with a gun and freak seeing Newgate's green flashlight. Evidently not. They were either sleeping too soundly to notice or were simply stealthily awaiting further developments. We entered cautiously, Newgate first, to no reception other than Pink's raucous snoring.

The comfort of crawling into the sleeping bag was sensually reassuring, although I had trouble getting back to sleep. Grateful as I was for Newgate's hospitality, I knew we couldn't stay much longer and I wondered where in hell we would go. What would we, could we, do next? Those thoughts were still drifting in and out of my half-consciousness when morning arrived. Newgate was already up making pancakes and Joan was not in her sleeping bag.

"She's in the shed. There should be enough warm water in the tank for showers for you and Pinkerton if you don't overdo it," he said.

"Overdo it?" I wasn't sure I'd heard him clearly.

"Turn the water off when you soap up. It's a trick I learned in 'Nam. I have plenty of water from the spring, but it's an old tank. Heater's not as fast as the newer ones."

"I'm surprised, Newgate. I thought you'd have only the newest and best."

"Fuck you, Geddes. What's the deal with Joan? She like men?"

"Fuck you, Newgate. Give her a try if you need to know."

"I just might do that."

The smell of frying pancakes and bacon had already lured Pink awake by the time Joan returned from the shed. She looked fresh and rested. The hot shower and cold trek between shed and hogan had given her face a healthy flush. She'd wrapped a small towel like a turban around her hair and brought with her into the hogan a soapy smell that mingled with the breakfast aromas.

"Feel better, Joan?" Newgate said, his voice carrying more life than when he'd spoken to me. "You hungry?" She'd walked over to the hotplate and was murmuring something to Newgate as I left the hogan for my turn in the shed.

"Damn. That's all we need," I muttered to myself, slogging along the path, not certain what I meant by it beyond a vague sense of concern for whatever chemistry might or might not be brewing between Joan and Newgate.

SACRIFICE

WE PLAY FOR LIFE

Soon after Pink turned down breakfast we decided he needed to see a doctor. Bruised and swollen, his face looked as if he'd gone a couple rounds with Rocky Marciano. His breathing was still labored, and he said his head felt like it was going to explode. Newgate's gentle probing with fingertips around Pink's nose elicited a heart-rending yelp of pain.

"Broken," Newgate pronounced. "I might've been able to set it yesterday, but the way it's swollen now I wouldn't wanna try. It could be a multiple fracture." He noted that he'd broken his nose while playing high school football, and was back in the game after a ten-minute rest on the bench.

"Coach grabbed my nose between his fingers and jerked it back into place. It bled a little, so he stuffed a cotton ball into each nostril. That was before the helmets had facemasks. It still hurts like hell if I touch it the wrong way. Gotta take care when I blow it."

Tempers flared a tad when Newgate said he would take Pink to a doctor friend in Newport News. They would take the motorcycle.

"Afraid I can't allow that, Randy." Joan said, her words garbled from a mouthful of pancakes. She swallowed and took a sip of coffee, setting her cup on the floor beside her. "This is a secure operation. Pink's safety is critical."

"Pink's safety is already compromised, Joan. He's running a fever. Needs medical help as soon as possible." Newgate's demeanor was calm, but firm.

"Can't you bring the doctor out here?" This was my contribution. They both looked at me. Newgate shook his head.

"Why not?" from Joan.

"I trust Doc Bot, but I don't bring anybody out here. You are my first visitors in six years, and I'm not happy about it."

"C'mon, Newgate," I said between bites of the delicious pancakes he'd made for us, "we respect your right to privacy here. I personally respect you for your service to our country and to your community as a police officer. I mean this sincerely. In the short time we've been here I feel as though I can trust you. I think you're an honest man..."

He held a hand up as if stopping traffic. "You don't need to finish. You were going to tell me how important your mission is and how this is a chance for me to stick my neck out once again as a patriot and good citizen blah blah blah.

"Believe it or not, I haven't written off society out here in my hogan. I might live like a hermit, but I have not withdrawn into some kind of cocoon, which I'm sure you're thinking. Believe it or not, I, too, am part of an important mission. In fact, I think my mission may just be more important than yours. Believe it or not."

As he spoke, Newgate had alternated his steady gaze between Joan and me as our eyes were locked on him. This continued after he finished and the three of us sipped our coffee. When neither Joan nor I spoke – I was too busy thinking to speak – Newgate continued: "Speaking honestly, with no personal disrespect intended, I think your plan to save humanity with some damned pill that gives men better erections and bigger hearts is, if you will pardon the word, ridiculous."

This aroused Pink, who started to sit up on his cot. He lay back down with an awful groan, evidently in pain too great for the effort, which convinced me he was in no shape to ride on the back of a motorcyle. The back of an ambulance was the only conveyance I could see for Pink at that point.

Newgate glanced at Pink, then turned back to us. "As I said, no disrespect intended. I think your pill would be a great commercial success, but the potential for corruption in the human species is too deeply rooted. Can you imagine what your pill might have

SACRIFICE

done to, say, Adolf Hitler? Or Al Capone? Or Ivan the Terrible? Don't you think the drug that drove those guys — unchecked power — wouldn't roll right over the stuff you're talking about?

"But, look, I'm not gonna argue with you about theories. You think your drug will save humanity, I say that's a crock. OK? Let's agree to disagree, at least for now. What I'm going to do is show a little good faith on my part because I believe you are sincere and I believe you are taking a great risk for your faith in this drug and I believe you are being hunted by some very dangerous people. Right now that's enough for me to want to do all I can to help you. I'm going to call Doc Bot and see if I can persuade him to come out here. Mr. Pinkerton needs medical help as soon as he can get it, and I'm going to do everything I can to see that he does. OK?"

Joan and I looked at each other. Her face was composed but she lifted her eyebrows slightly, which I answered with a slight nod. I turned to Newgate. "We're indebted to you, Randy. Thank you."

Newgate was already moving to the foot locker next to the cot. He tugged the lid up, reached under some clothing until his hand rattled some harder items further down. He pulled out an old-fashioned cellphone.

"It's a throwaway," he said, gesturing with the small, flip-up device. "No way my call can be traced. I call Doc, if I get his voicemail, which I probably will, I leave a short, coded message, he'll call back with a short, coded message and then I toss the phone. I have a few more for emergencies. That's all they're for."

He made the call, spoke briefly and flipped the phone shut.

"I got him. He was getting ready to go fishing. I'll take the Indian, we'll meet somewhere" - he winked - "and I'll bring him back here. Gimme two hours, OK?"

We were still eating his pancakes and bacon when we heard the motorcycle fire up and roar away.

MATHEW PAUST

THE WHEEL IS TURNING

Dr. Botticelli, or "Doc Bot," as Newgate introduced him to us, was a small man with white curly hair that crowned the back of his head. The first impression he made on me was of a grumpy toad. This came partly from the shape of his head, a horizontal ovoid with a thick white mustache over lips stretched so wide they seemed to force his cheeks into parentheses. And this was sans smile. In keeping with the toad resemblance the physician's eyes protruded, giving him a perpetual look of emotional excess, either of fright, intense focus or ferocity depending, I imagined, on circumstances.

I've seen other people with bulbous eyes who exuded a gentle, even joyous, understanding of the ironies around them. The same bulging of eyeballs as Bot's but with a subtle configuration of facial musculature and skin creases that signaled merriment. No hint of such with Bot, although in either extreme, I mused at the time, the facial expressions, as with those of the newly born, might plausibly be attributable to gas.

"Uh huh, OK," Bot muttered, nodding abruptly when Newgate introduced us. He did look me in the eye, which dispelled any impression he might be shy. His expression gave nothing away, but conveyed a subtle suggestion he was annoyed to have been taken away from his fishing trip and, further, that he would tolerate no bullshit from anybody, except maybe Newgate. Lugging the traditional doctor's black bag in one hand, he marched briskly to the cot and muttered something to Pink before setting the bag down with a muffled clinking of its contents.

"Chair please," he ordered, prompting Newgate to bring him the folding chair from his desk. Soon as he sat, Bot opened the bag and began removing the tools of his trade. I recognized a stethoscope and the kind of flashlight doctors use to peer into

SACRIFICE

small spaces, such as ear canals. Bot ignored us once he went to work on Pink, checking his pulse, listening to his lungs and, finally moving to the swollen nose. Newgate motioned for us to follow him outside, which I was more than happy to do.

"Doc's bedside manner is...I guess you could say, lacking?" he waited for the laugh. I just smiled and shook my head, didn't see how Joan responded but imagine her face was composed and non-revealing. She said nothing. "I just wanted to reassure you that he was one of the best emergency room physicians I've ever seen."

"Was?" Me.

"Oh, he's retired, er, semi-retired. Takes a few patients in a little office he's set up in his house. We grew up in the same neighborhood and were medics together in 'Nam. He went to med school when we got out. Best friend I have. Trust him with my life."

Not much I could think of to say after this revelation, although I couldn't help but wonder why he had to take us outside just for that. I turned back to the hogan, thinking Newgate was finished. I saw Joan looking that way, too. I think we both were starting to grow concerned about Pink and the situation we'd found ourselves in – above and beyond the obvious accumulation of dangers. What if Doc Bot were to insist that Pink be hospitalized? I knew Newgate would oppose the idea of a medivac helicopter landing near his hideout. He didn't even want his best friend out there, the man he said he trusted with his life.

"I hope your friend can take care of Pink right here," said Joan, giving voice to my own worries. Newgate frowned at her as if he hadn't quite understood what she'd said. She added, "We can't take him to any hospital. That would be impossible."

"Don't worry," he said. "There's no way I would allow anyone else to come here and it would take a medivac chopper to get him out, anyway. But to answer your first concern, Doc will do whatever has to be done. Your friend could not be in any better hands."

Before either of us could respond, Newgate continued, "I was pretty worried myself until I got back here. I left in such a hurry I forgot to explain my detection system to you, in case another...an intruder happened along, you know."

"I kept an eye on your computer screen, Newgate. I saw that little window pop up before, when Joan was coming down the trail. The only window I saw while you were gone was when you rode up, and I heard the motorcycle before I saw anything on the computer." This won a few positive nods and a relieved grin. "Good," he said and waved a hand toward the hogan. He started back, and we followed.

Doc Bot's toad face creased with irritation when he saw us enter. "Com'ere," he growled. "Hold him down." When I didn't move fast enough he raised his voice, "Grab hold of his legs and keep him from flopping around. This is gonna hurt!" He nodded at the others and motioned them into position, Newgate on one arm and shoulder, Joan on the other. Pink's eyes were half closed, so I assumed he was sedated. It puzzled me that so much restraint was needed for whatever Bot intended to do, but his authoritarian manner precluded any contrary thoughts.

I did as ordered, clamped down on each leg just below the knee. With everybody in position, Bot leaned over grabbed hold of Pink's nose and gave it a quick brutal jerk. I flinched from the sound of bone snapping, and then froze when that sound was followed immediately by a shriek so sustained and powerful I thought the hogan had been struck by some kind of missile.

The shriek stayed in my head half a minute after it had actually stopped, but then my full attention was required on those legs I was assigned to keep from thrashing about. And they were trying, and they were strong. I leaned into the job, gripping the shins as hard as I could and using my not inconsiderable upper body weight as backup insurance. I could see Joan and Newgate struggling similarly as Pink had gone feral in his pain and was using every muscle at his disposal to hurl his oppressors off. A spray of warm blood strafed my face, neck and arms, and I saw the dark red droplets had covered the others, as well. I was struck by the fleeting thought that I hoped he didn't have AIDS, but that notion

SACRIFICE

was instantly supplanted by the more urgent requirement to simply keep him still, keep him from breaking loose.

And then suddenly the struggle ended. I hadn't noticed Bot return to his patient after he'd stepped back quickly from the nose maneuver, but now I saw him straighten up. He was holding a hypodermic needle.

"He'll sleep awhile now. I didn't give him this before because I didn't want him to swallow his tongue. Some reflexes operate differently when you're unconscious," he explained. Bot seemed more relaxed, too. I felt like collapsing on the floor. In fact, that's what I did. Joan took the chair Bot offered her, while Newgate was back at his hotplate heating up a pot of coffee.

"Will he be alright?" Joan asked.

Bot waited a good part of a minute before answering. He seemed to be deep in thought. When he finally spoke, he sounded weary, cautious: "We'll know in twenty-four hours. I gave him an antibiotic for the infection. If the swelling goes down he should be out of the woods. If not..."

"Can you stay here?" Joan again.

Bot looked up at Newgate and waited until his friend turned and saw him. "She wants me to see this through. You good with that?"

"Stay as long as you like, Botman. Unless you're afraid the fish will miss you."

"Fort Rucker," the doctor said. It seemed his mustache twitched a little at each end before it relaxed back to its default scowl.

MATHEW PAUST

CLOUDS OF DELUSION

It took two days before Doc Bot pronounced Pink "out of the woods," with the infection and fever gone and the healing of his face progressing satisfactorily. You couldn't have known this from looking at it. The nightmarish swelling was gone but I winced every time I saw the bruising that took its place with its core of blackened subdermal blood feathering outward in vectored purplish shades to a sickly yellow corona. Most importantly, Pink was able to breathe without laboring. The snoring that had made sleep in the hogan difficult for all was reduced to an occasional gasp or snort that I, being an ordinarily light sleeper, might have been the only one to notice.

The tension between Newgate and us that had existed from the first and then ramped up in the discussion about the need to bring Doc Bot to the hogan, continued to simmer despite our distractions over Pink's condition. Once Pink was out of danger and Newgate left again to take Bot back to Newport News the three of us hashed out a strategy for our next moves.

"So what now?" I asked as Joan and I sat on the floor in front of Pink's cot. Pink was feeling rather chipper – in the pink, sorry – and was sitting up on the cot munching on a bacon and cheese sandwich he'd put together with leftovers from the breakfast Newgate fixed for us before he and Bot rode off on the motorcycle.

Joan looked hard at each of us, then bowed her head and stared between her knees at the floor, meditating. Slowly her head rotated from side to side and she sighed deeply. "We need to get out of here." When she looked up I saw a familiar intensity in her eyes. They met mine, but seemed focused on something distant. It was a look I'd seen before, often, at a time when our duties were officially designated, when we both answered directly to

SACRIFICE

the President. We still answered to her and we still called her Ms. President occasionally but our situations – all three of them – no longer carried the imprimatur of the presidential seal.

"Something about this guy just doesn't add up," she said. "All my antennae are tingling – and, no jokes, Al, please. I'm seriously worried."

"He saved my life," This from Pink in a matter-of-fact voice that carried no spin. When no response came he added, "He could've shot us and buried us out here. Who would ever know?"

"Pink's got a point, Joan," I said. "The guy's gone out of his way to help us."

"Al, the guy's too good to be true. That alone sends up flags. Out here in the woods? Six years? Living in a grass hut? Al, he has..." She sprang up from the camp chair and headed for the hogan entrance. "C'mon, guys. Take a look at this!" She pulled the blanket aside and was gone before we were across the room.

Outside we followed her down the trail that led to the shed. Before reaching the shed she veered away down another path I'd not seen earlier. This led us to the solar panels and what appeared to be a smaller shed, also hidden under carefully place bushes. She stopped by this shed and pointed up at the top of a sweet gum tree. "Check that out." A blazing sun forced me to squint and scan the upper branches until I spotted what looked like a satellite dish. Pink saw it, too.

"Parabolic antenna," he said. He inhaled deeply through his mouth, let it out in a rush and added, "What the fuck."

"A guy who's trying to hide shouldn't have something so easy to detect," Joan said. "If nothing else, his Internet provider knows where he is."

"Unless he built it all himself. Maybe he's a genius, like me." We ignored Pink's half-hearted try at humor.

"Maybe the answer's in here," Joan said. She stooped to examine the front of the outhouse-size shed. "Padlocked. Out here in the woods? Isn't that strange." We trudged back to the hogan after agreeing it was indeed time for us to separate ourselves from this mysterious hermit, although we also agreed we had no idea where we would go or what we should do once we were out of what we'd come to call "Newgate's Woods."

In the hogan I opened the discussion: "I say we confront him. He might have a reasonable explanation for everything."

"What if he's been leading us on?" Joan countered. "We don't know what he's up to. With that dish he could be talking to China. Or worse, with some terrorist group that would love to hold us for ransom. He wants us to trust him so we'll stay put until his friends get here."

"He saved my life for the terrorists. Oh, boy. Out of the frying pan, huh?"

"Who knows, Pink? Joan makes a good point. We could well be under house arrest. I still think we should ask him what the deal is. If he has sold us out we wouldn't get very far anyway, even if we started right now."

We agreed to confront Newgate when he got back, which we did after first casually suggesting we were ready to mosey on along. Joan did the talking. She didn't fool Newgate one little bit, but he was good-natured about it.

"I know my accommodations aren't the best, folks, but I'm afraid you'll have to remain my prisoners awhile longer." Pause for reaction. Stunned attention. "Hey, I guess you didn't find the bug I didn't forget to turn on when I left, huh." He reached under the computer desk and showed us a micro-transmitter the size of a Zippo lighter. He laughed. "Don't worry. I'd have been disappointed if you hadn't found my satellite dish. I'd have been extremely disappointed if you accepted me and everything here at face value.

"You keep forgetting I read your book, Al. I believe in you folks, what you've done and what you hope to do. I'm skeptical of what your miracle drug can do, Mr. Pinkerton, but I believe your intentions are righteous. I haven't been very good at persuading you of my intentions, I'm afraid, but now that we're putting all our cards on the table, I suppose this is as good a time as any." He pulled the chair back over to the desk, sat and tapped a few keys on his laptop. A video window opened and filled the screen with what looked like a couple of lights – one red, flashing, and other a steady white - moving against a dark background toward the camera.

I soon realized the video had been shot at night from an aircraft and that the lights approaching the camera were attached to a small helicopter.

"Oh my god," Joan murmured, about the same time Pink blurted, "Oh, shit!" We were about to view the destruction of our escort helicopter by the one upon which the camera was mounted. A streak of green light shot out from under the camera and splashed against the side of the other helicopter, which was now so near I could make out the insignia of American Enterprises under the cockpit bubble.

The screen went dark. Newgate had switched off the video.

"We didn't shoot it down," Newgate said quietly. "We don't have the capability yet to hack their controls. We merely audited." He quickly added. "They were both drones. That much I know."

MATHEW PAUST

TRAILED BY TWENTY HOUNDS

Joan's reaction to Newgate's little demonstration was to harden into the icy, unwavering police-mode she so often had exhibited during our White House days. I recognized this subtle withdrawal of feminine warmth before she spoke. It might have seemed to someone who didn't know what to look for that she had gone into a trance, as she became perfectly still. Yet, there was nothing overtly rigid or slack in her posture as she stood beside the desk still staring at the computer screen, which now displayed its desktop image of what appeared to be a photo of a cosmic black hole, one of those deep space drains around which entire galaxies swirl in a vortex to...

"Who are they?" she said, her voice compressed to its interrogation room timbre.

"Chesapeake Security."

Newgate's utterance of these two words produced a black hole of sound in the hogan. Not even Pink's raspy breathing was audible. Joan rotated her head slowly from the computer screen to meet Newgate's face. Standing slightly behind and to the side of Newgate, I could see her eyes flashing dangerously.

"Zombie killers," said Pink, breaking the silence. Newgate nodded, his eyes still locked with Joan's. Joan and I knew of Chesapeake Security, the shadowy company that trained and deployed mercenaries, often under government contract, in hotspots worldwide. I had not heard the term "zombie killers," but assumed, with Newgate's silent acknowledgment, the term was familiar to him. Without need of a prompt, he filled us in.

"My son was an IT supervisor with them when they got into the drone phase. They brought in these kids, teenagers who were hooked on video games. Recruited them at competitions. I guess

SACRIFICE

one of the popular games involved shooting zombies or some such. Anyway, somebody put up a zombie killers decal and that caught on and it's what they've been ever since.

"These kids operate – or did operate; they've probably moved by now – out of an old boat barn at a marina Chesapeake bought when they started getting big. All they do is sit at computers, day and night, running Chesapeake's drone fleet. It's mostly those small black helicopters like yours that got shot down. They have a few of the really tiny drones, like birds, and Chris said one even looks like a bumble bee.

"They're mostly for surveillance, but we know drones can be lethal, too. The kids who push the shoot button wouldn't have a clue what they were shooting at unless they watched the news, which they don't. They just kill images on a computer screen. Zombies."

"Guns for hire?" I asked. I'd heard of them, but knew little beyond what I read in an occasional news story.

"If you can afford them. Most of their clients are corporate."

Joan snapped, "Who hired them to shoot down our helicopter?"

"I don't know. I can look into it. It could be they just challenged the bird and shot it down when they didn't like the response. They routinely patrol this corridor, mostly I assume for the government."

"Just shot it down? Just like that?" Me again.

"They would have determined it was a drone. They're more careful with manned aircraft."

"Not so with womaned SUV's huh." Joan.

"Point taken. I'll see what we have on their databases. That's not my area, but I'm sure we have access, or could get access if need be." Newgate's manner had become more formal, presumably as he now appreciated the gravity of what we were up against and that he was now involved.

"So what is your area?" Joan.

"Monitoring flight patterns. I'm like the radio spotters on the South Pacific islands in World War II. You could say this is World War III if you wanted the drama."

"I'd just as soon stick to our immediate problem. If we're going to trust you, Newgate, I have to know who this 'we' is you keep referring to. Who are you working with?"

"If you're going to trust me, Joan? Looks to me like you're in a tad too deep already to be saying 'if.'"

"I'm still a federal officer, Newgate."

"What are you gonna do, arrest me?"

"I hope it wouldn't come to that. Why won't you tell me who you're working for?"

"Why do you need to know?"

"Wouldn't you? Want to know?"

"I would. And I'd tell you, if I knew."

"Newgate, cut the shit. You monitor flight patterns for somebody. You communicate with somebody. You said you would ask somebody to see who hired these zombie killers to blow up my SUV. Now, who is this somebody?"

"I can give you the next email address I'll contact, Joan, but that's a one-time thing. It's a different address for each contact. Same with the cellphone numbers. Nothing's the same. I'd love to know who I'm working with...well, I take that back. Supposedly none of us knows any of the others. We share a purpose and that's all. Harder to catch us that way. Impossible, I hope."

"Anonymous," Pink blurted.

"That's one way to put it," Newgate said.

Joan wasn't giving up so easily. "How did you hook up with these anonymous hackers in the first place? You had to know somebody?"

"That is true, Joan. That is true."

SACRIFICE

"Your son?"

"That is true."

"Can we meet him?"

"Nope."

"Because?"

Newgate turned his back to us and walked slowly to the hogan entrance. He answered without turning around. "He's dead, Joan." Then he pulled the blanket aside and stepped outside. Joan called after him, "I'm sorry," but the blanket had already flapped back in place.

MATHEW PAUST

THE DIE MUST FALL

Joan started after Newgate, scolding, "Oh dammit great job Stonebraker somebody kick my ass goddammit to hell...," but I stopped her before she reached the blanket.

"Joan! No! Let him go!" She stopped and turned her head back toward me, neck-length brown hair whipping impatiently across her face.

"I was wrong to push him like that, Al. He's given us no reason to mistrust him. I was just..."

"We're all stressed, Joan. You were doing your job. Newgate understands that. He was a cop. Besides, we need a moment to talk." I motioned to Pink to check the microtransmitter Newgate kept under his desk. Pink found it, held it up and shook his head to indicate it wasn't on. I nodded, and he slipped it back into its bracket out of sight.

Joan turned to face us but stayed by the entrance, as if to block Newgate if he returned too soon. "So talk," she said, then, "Sorry, guys. I didn't mean to snap."

I suggested we needed to decide on our next objective. Would we shift our priority to finding out who hired Chesapeake or continue to Leicester?

"We've got find out what happened to Gladys," said Pink. "Newgate said the Zombie Killer helicopter was just patrolling the corridor."

"What about our SUV?" I said. "That was deliberate. There aren't any SUV drones yet, that I know of."

"Coulda been an accident," Pink said, his tone testy.

"With me being the collateral damage? I don't think so, Pink.

SACRIFICE

That was deliberate. We need to find out who's behind this. And when we do we'll find Gladys."

"I wanna talk to her mother, Joan. I'll go by myself if I have to. Gladys might have left something with her mother that can help, or told her something."

"Pink, Gladys might never have gotten to Leicester. And we don't know where her loyalties are right now," I said. My intent was to derail what appeared to be a developing stalemate between Pink and Joan. Not my smartest impulse, but I've learned that doing anything is usually better than doing nothing.

"Gladys didn't sell out, Al! I'd bet my life on it!"

I started to speak, but Joan beat me to it. "We can't have you betting your life on anything, Pink. Or ours."

"You don't understand," Pink said. "We love each other. I know that sounds silly to both of you, but I don't care. I know Gladys better than either of you do, better than you ever possibly could. I love Gladys and she loves me. End of argument."

"This doesn't have to be an argument, Pink," Joan said. Her severe tone had softened, but I knew she was still thinking and speaking as a cop. "We need to work together, for our own sake and for Gladys's. We don't know what happened to her. We'll go to Leicester and talk to her mother. We'll start out today. But please keep an open mind on this. Things are happening fast now. Each moment has the potential for an unpleasant surprise. A lot may depend on whether Newgate can tell us who hired these people, and if so, who they are."

"I should have that for you by tonight." Newgate said this as he pulled the blanket aside and stepped into the hogan. "I know you want to get going and I don't blame you. I'll give you one of my throwaway cellphones and call you as soon as I know something."

We spent the rest of the morning getting ready for the road. Newgate made some ham and cheese sandwiches and packed them and three apples in a small day pack along with several plastic bottles of water. He gave Pink a vial of pain pills and returned the revolvers and transponders to me and Pink.

Before we left he handed me two of the cellphones with instructions they could be used only once, either to call or to take a call.

"Stomp on them when you're done using them. Smash them to pieces and then spread the pieces in different places. No telling what the tech guys can do with that stuff these days.

"My advice on which way to go? I know you didn't ask, but here it is anyway: Don't go back the way you came. The highway is crawling with black SUVs and suits. They're scouring the incident scene, forward and back. Probably already have photos of you, Joan, if you left anything behind that didn't burn up. If they ID you that should keep your face off the TV for a little while anyway. But sooner or later word will get back to somebody and then you'll have to go to ground.

"Doc Bot can give you a lift to anywhere you like. I suggest taking the trail I used with the Indian. It's no more than a dozen miles to a county road that doesn't see much traffic. I've taped Doc's number to one of the phones. Call him when you reach the road. He knows where the trail comes out. Remember to destroy the phone as soon as you're finished with it. If you get Doc's answering service, leave this message: Hey, bubba, the fish are tired of waiting. Get your ass out here.

"Can you remember that? No names, OK? Just that message, those exact words." We nodded affirmation. Then Newgate smiled, reached in a pocket of his cargo pants and pulled out our ID folders.

"Here you are, Agent Chesnic. Give Shirley my best," he said with a wink, handing me mine. To Pink he said, the smile exchanged for a grim glare, "Agent Horrigan, you made my day." Joan erupted in an embarrassing burst of guffaws.

"What the fuck?" from me. Pink just looked clueless.

"Movies, guys. Inside joke. Nicholas Cage played Agent Doug Chesnic in Guarding Tess. Frank Horrigan? Well, you would know

SACRIFICE

him better as Dirty Harry. In the Line of Fire. Sorry. We had these lying around in the office. I couldn't resist."

Pink shrugged, still looking clueless. I did my d'oh, ya got me grin, cocked my thumb and shot Newgate with my finger. We stuck the folders in our pants, though. Good souvenirs if we got out of this alive.

As a parting gift Newgate handed me a machete.

"Damned briars grow pretty fast out here. You can leave it with Doc."

With that, we were off.

MATHEW PAUST

RUN THROUGH THE JUNGLE

It was mid-morning when we started out. The air was warming from the cool spell after the last storm as a bank of grayish clouds inched up from the southwest horizon bringing another. Our goal was to reach the road before the next one hit, which the Weather Channel was forecasting for late afternoon. Fecund aromas rising from the forest floor to greet this prospect corroborated other harbingers, most noticeably that of the birds. A pair of cardinals, several mockingbirds and a tribe of chickadees darted among the trees heralding the arrival of nature's gift with their excited chatter.

We need to hustle. Don't wanna get caught out here in the storm," I said after explaining an infantry patrol tactic we would use to minimize detection from any more helicopter drones. We would stretch out, one moving ahead, then stopping, then the next catching up and stopping and finally the third coming to the others. We would repeat this leapfrog progression over and over until we reached the road, the theory being that one object in sporadic motion is less noticeable than three moving steadily, simultaneously. Not foolproof, but it would lower the risk.

I decided to lead off, partly to demonstrate and also to avoid distracting Pink with concerns Joan and I were talking behind his back. I knew his fixation on Gladys was the only thing keeping Pink from realizing the awful truth we faced. Joan and I had not acknowledged it to each other but I figured she must have quickly grasped the significance of the drone destroying our SUV, which had to be considered deliberate. There was little chance whoever was operating the drone would have known all three of us were not in the SUV at the time. Our slipping out and into the woods was in the dark of night at a time when the drone would still have been occupied with making sure its first target was neutralized. We were out of that van and out of sight within seconds. This

SACRIFICE

meant whoever ordered the kill meant to kill Pink. And this could only mean Gladys was still alive and cooperating with those who wanted us dead.

Once Pink came to this logical realization, which could happen at any moment, he could come unglued, most likely insisting it was all the more important to rescue Gladys, as the only way she would cooperate with anyone but him would be under torture or believing he was already dead. Clearly she was a brilliant scientist and could undoubtedly carry on alone with the research on Vulcana, but could she be misled into believing she was doing so with her dead lover's blessing? Pink would believe so. I leaned more toward the theory she was was ditching Pink for a promised bigger piece of the profit pie. My cynicism was grounded, alas, in hard-won experience.

"Who goes next?" Pink shouted after me as I started down the trail, wielding the machete for any greenbriar bogies at ten or two o'clock.

"You," I shouted back. "Joan likes to watch you walk." I immediately had second thoughts about that last, which was impulsive, but figured anything to lighten the mood was a good thing. My plan was to send Joan ahead next and then back to me. I would explain to Pink, if he asked, that his safety was more important than either of ours and that it was best to keep him between us. I was hoping he would protest and ask to be given a chance in the rotation. This would give Joan and me a moment to compare notes without arousing his suspicion. This happened, to my relief, about an hour into the hike.

She surprised me by bringing it up as soon as Pink was out of earshot: "They must know by now he wasn't in the SUV." She had leaned close to practically whisper in my ear. The scent of her breath and hair distracted me, but I still knew what she was saying.

"It's almost ominous they're not combing the area with those damned helicopters," I said. "You don't suppose Newgate's with them? Sending us straight to the cattle car?"

"I guess we'll know when he calls us. If he calls us."

Bringing our trust in Newgate into doubt was unsettling. Coincidental as it was to run into him, ostensibly a member of a popularly rumored mysterious insurgency, it also made sense he would not necessarily sympathize with what we were doing. He'd read my book. This I believed. Executive Pink provided a look at our government, but from the inside. Even if he was what he said he was, a rebel helping a group of computer hackers opposed to big government and its corporate controllers, what's to say he didn't consider Wilde Laboratories part of the problem? He'd made it clear he doubted Vulcana was worth the risks we were taking.

Suppose he'd written us off as deluded fools and was merely humoring us, getting us out of his hair now? Suppose he wanted us dead to keep us from blowing his cover, fools that we were? He could have his hacker network anonymously tip off Chesapeake Security and a Zombie Killer drone could be waiting for us up the trail a bit – far enough away from his hogan to keep any snoops from wandering back the way we'd come. Or, better yet, wait until we made it to the road and zap us before Doc Bot could get there, if the good doctor even bothered to show.

Who would have trusted the Unibomber in a similar situation, despite maybe sympathizing completely with his cause? His insanity made him unpredictable. He recognized no authority. What was it Newgate had said when we first stumbled unto his place? Something about a tax free zone or nation and he was the president? I thought then we were in the hands of a nut case. He'd quickly persuaded us differently, but some nut cases can do that, seem perfectly rational and charming if it served their purpose. What if...

"Al!" Joan tugged on the sleeve of my jacket. "It's Pink. He's stopped. Who's going next?"

I looked down the trail and saw the blaze-orange kerchief waving back and forth. Pink had reached the end of his leg. I looked at Joan. She shrugged. She had gone last time, before Pink demanded a turn at walking point. She didn't seem tired, but I

SACRIFICE

sensed she wanted me to go next. I smiled and patted her arm.

"I'm off"

MATHEW PAUST

JUNGLE BUNGLE

We were about halfway from the hogan when the helicopter appeared. My ears picked it up first, the wupwupwupwup of the rotorblades drawing near. My first reaction was to freeze. Joan and Pink were up ahead and I was awaiting the blaze-orange signal for me to do my leg before the next point took off. I hadn't seen the flag yet, which meant Pink had not yet gotten to Joan.

"Get down! Chopper coming," I shouted and dropped to the ground. I heard Pink's distant "What?" answered immediately by Joan's sharp "Get on the ground and lie still!" By then the copter was close enough that I felt its thundering concussive beat on air grown heavy with humidity. The deadly mechanical bird was swooping in from the direction we were heading. It was moving so fast that before I saw anything I knew it was directly overhead. Its powerful blades whipped the tops of the trees as it passed, and, rotating my head to one side, I caught a flash of sunlight strobing off the tail rotor. The black bird was gone as suddenly as it had arrived, but I remained frozen, my ear pressed into the trail, hands clutching some kind of bushes as if to keep me from being sucked into the sky.

"Stay down!" I shouted, knowing the rule was to send at least two birds on missions, each serving as backup in case the other went down. But this wasn't hostile country. No reason to expect groundfire from these woods. I took several deep breaths and released them slowly, calming my nerves and making up for the oxygen deficit I'd incurred unconsciously holding my breath. Hearing nothing but the rapidly diminishing sound of the copter that had buzzed us, no new mechanical sound to suggest the approach of another, I struggled to my feet. I brushed off a reconnaissance patrol of ants, the advance units having reached nearly to my throat.

SACRIFICE

"Hello!" I shouted down the trail. "You guys OK?" It took two hails before I saw a flash of blaze orange, and then Joan appeared. She was walking toward me. I headed toward her as fast I as could move my sore stiffened legs. She covered more ground than I did before we met.

"We need to rest. Pink is exhausted," she said. She wobbled then and swayed as if about to fall. I grabbed her and pulled her against me, then arched back so I could look at her. She pushed lightly but firmly with both hands and I released her. She took a backward step, a glint of annoyance flitting across her face. "Sorry. Ankle fell asleep back there."

It was about 2:30 and I wanted to get to the road before sundown, which was when the storm was supposed to hit. The billowing, darkening front had reached up to cover about a third of the sky, about to swallow the sun. Knowing the margin of error allowed by meteorologists, I figured the storm could be upon us a good two hours ahead of the last forecast we'd seen before leaving the hogan – well before we reached the road. And once the sun slipped behind the cloud bank our progress would be slowed by diminished visibility. I could tell Joan wanted a rest break for Pink but she, too, knew the downside of too long a delay.

Before we could share our thoughts, the earth shook in synchronization with a powerful, sickening WHUMP that triggered my reflexes to grab Joan, who was already moving toward me. I wrapped my arms around her and cringed, expecting another blast like the first, but after a wait of fifteen seconds or so without another violent sound, I relaxed my grip on her. She was turned toward the way we'd come, face tilted upward and looking over my shoulder. I saw her expression change from thoughtful to wide-eyed alarm before her voice erupted.

"Al!" she said and raised an arm, finger pointed skyward. I pivoted in time to see a ball of angry black smoke with a dark red fiery center lift above the tree line and boil into the sky atop a trailing plume. It was several miles away but its location touched off a fireball of horror in my intestines that I could see reflected in

Joan, in her face and in the coiled tension of her body. We uttered the same word almost simultaneously: "Newgate." It came out of both our mouths sounding like a prayer.

"We can't go back there. We need to get to the road," I said without thinking. I figured Newgate was dead and that the helicopter might have been manned and might have landed to make sure. If it was a drone it surely would hover awhile and scour the immediate area. No sense making it easy for them by walking into camp.

"I'll go back, Al. He might have found out who hired this zombie squad. We need to know. You go ahead with Pink. We'll figure out a way to link up later."

"You're right. But I should go. You need to stay with Pink. If you get to the road and have to wait for Doc Bot, or if he doesn't show, a man and a woman look more natural together."

She thought for moment, then nodded abruptly. "Good. Be careful. You have that revolver?" I nodded. She turned to go, then turned back, took a quick step forward, raised up on her toes and gave me a quick peck on the cheek. She was smiling. "Be careful," she said again, more gently. She turned and trotted back toward where Pink was waiting. In less than half a minute I saw the flash of blaze orange, saw it wave back and forth twice, and knew she'd found Pink. I took a deep breath and started up the trail toward the hogan.

SACRIFICE

HARD RAIN

I felt the epiphany coming the instant I started back up the trail. The sensation was akin to the vertigo I get with the approach of a headache but with a greater sense of urgency, a dire need to bring coalescence to a myriad of notions of varying shapes and strengths grappling for dominance. I imagine were I fowl this sensation might approximate the relentless stress that compels a hen to seek a safe place for her egg to land once she's squeezed it out. I had no such luxury and would have to squeeze out my fully formed idea whenever and wherever it appeared along the trail. And not a single cackle could be risked.

My first inkling a metaphorical egg was nearing the vent came as I sorted through my immediate options among the constants and variables facing me. It would take three hours at best to reach Newgate's hogan, about the same time Joan and Pink would need to reach the road at the other end of the trail. These times would be extended if the storm hit before we reached our destinations. In fact, the darkness alone once the storm front engulfed the sun would slow us.

My time alone now was in effect my nest. I do my best thinking either under the pneumatic stress of a deadline or while walking alone undisturbed by present concerns for another human sensibility. The only place I've been able to find this essential solitude is in a woods, incommunicado. I'd left both of Newgate's disposable cellphones with Joan. My thinking was that if I found Newgate alive and if he had learned who hired Chesapeake Security or if he left something, a clue or fragment or code of some kind, something that could help us solve the mystery, and I could find another cellphone in the rubble of the hogan, I would pass whatever I found along to Joan. I had memorized the phone's number. If worse came to worst and Newgate's camp was gone I would try to find my way safely to a convenience store and buy a new throwaway phone just to check in with her.

I moved at an uneven pace, with occasional stops to both rest and break up any pattern that might be discerned by someone monitoring the trail. I figured now that Newgate's camp had been identified and taken out perhaps whoever had done it would use satellite surveillance to attempt to pick up any movement in the vicinity. The storm front would provide cover from this but I decided I'd rather risk detection in the meantime than wait until the storm brought its full brunt to bear.

What struck me first, and was the catalyst for the mental scrum that gave me a temporary reprieve from my external tribulations, was the realization I was in active mode for the first time since my conviction on what I now know to have been trumped up felony charges of prosecutorial misconduct. I'd assumed I merely made a wrong turn politically and found myself in a murderous neighborhood, with no recourse but to ride out the consequences and hope a switch of wind direction would restore me to liberty, chastened but with a greater attraction on the speakers' circuit than before. Accepting my fate thusly enabled me to switch out of the usual, for me, frantic survival mode into a lower-key almost relaxed mindset that required little more than a reliance on patience and a will to abide. Virtually no thinking required.

With what I learned subsequently this was unnatural for me beyond the fact I was no longer paid to think, and in fact could expect only additional troubles for doing so. My inadvertent ingestion of the drug Vulcana supposedly ginned up my logical thinking capability. One would expect, then, a higher degree of frustration at not being challenged intellectually. I tried to ameliorate this predicament by spending as much time as I could in the prison library, but reading is passive compared with the problem-solving exercise I had daily in the White House and, although to a much lesser degree, as Special Prosecutor.

My release on parole and assignment to the Vulcana project had plunged me deeper into the morass of reaction. (I started to write "reactionary thinking," but I realize I'd been continually behind the curve at every step of the way since landing in Wilde

SACRIFICE

Laboratories' lap.) My brain was reduced to such a go-along-get-along yassahboss reflex that my few efforts at asserting myself, throwing the occasional tantrum, were as impotent as trying to run in a nightmare. Now I was in a real nightmare, a deepening, darkening nightmare, but I was walking freely.

My sense of freedom, precarious though it was, had such power it shook me out of the caution that had stymied me from acknowledging merit in Newgate's skepticism of what Wilde hoped to accomplish with Vulcana. Now I could see I'd been harboring similar concerns all along but felt too compromised to give these thoughts full rein. Better erections and bigger hearts is how he put it. Attractive on the surface, no question. Realistic as a panacea for the descent of civilization into self destruction? Could a better balance among the mental forces vying for dominance reverse the man-made bucket our species was riding to Hell?

Mr. Spock and Sherlock Holmes are all logic and no id. Is that the ideal way to be? Both are fictional characters whose mental predominance hold fast atop their pedestals in our collective imagination. Are they symbols of wistful thinking? Are their attributes realistic? Could their personalities be diagnosed as symptomatic of Asperger's Syndrome, a brain disorder? Does Vulcana push us too close to Asperger's? Is the drug's empathy counterbalance effective? Once I allowed that these questions were not only valid, but, considering the risk I was being groomed to take, that they addressed something vital to us all, I let go of the cerebral inhibitions that had kept my thoughts corralled, the gate swung open and out everything galloped.

CRACKBOOM! A lightning strike so near I could smell the ozone. My reverie of unrestrained cogitation had so completely absorbed me I lost track of the approaching storm, which had blocked the sun and was rumbling its thunder so near now it startled me to recognize it had been providing an intensifying accompaniment of background menace for some time without registering on my consciousness. I glanced up and flinched at a sky bulging with black clouds and alive with lightning both in strobing sheets and the ragged, forked streaks of lethal current that darted among the clouds and reached down to stab the ground. Wind gusts whipped harsh, cold rainsprays through the trees and against me as a taste of the deluge to come. The excited birds, getting their wish, had gone silent.

I plodded onward.

SACRIFICE

FIRE ON THE MOUNTAIN

With the storm upon me my thoughts shifted from pensive to instinctive flashes of survival mode. I dove to the ground when the rainspray morphed into hail, strafing me in horizontal bursts with pea-size pellets that stung like a yellowjacket swarm. The thunder was constant now and lightning bolts danced so frequently around me I began to wonder if they were a new type of drone sent by Chesapeake Security.

I lay in the middle of the trail, fully exposed except for my jeans and the light windbreaker jacket. Windbreaker, uh huh. Nutty impulse to chuckle when my besieged brain tried to amuse me with the notion I should have worn a galebreaker jacket. The hail managed to find me on the ground, curled into a fetal position, knees pulled up as close to my chin as possible and head tucked between my forearms. I was already soaked when a deluge of icy rain joined the hail to keep me pinned down and go for a drowning to boot. This is when my dad appeared to me.

Don't worry. No magical realism here. He did, however, fill the vacancy left by my pre-storm musings and now the survival flashes when I knew there was nothing further to do but stay small and make myself believe Mother Nature really didn't want to kill me, and if Chesapeake Security was doing this, well, then to hell with everything. Dad's suddenly welcome pompous voice interrupted this downward spiral with one of the ubiquitous adages he'd annoy us with back in the day: A hundred years from now it won't make any difference.

Yeah, but if I can't borrow the car tonight she'll go out with Buford and I'll look like the biggest dork in town, I would whine. He wasn't good at repartee, which is odd because he was a lawyer, so, instead of engaging me with a more persuasive argument, such as if having wheels was all that made Buford more attractive to her than me, then they deserved each other. I might come back with more adolescent wheedling, such as it wasn't the wheels themselves so much as the event to which the wheels would carry us, or, her and Buford as the case would be if I couldn't get the car, and he then could parse the situation and apply more wisdom and skillful courtroom logic and, if nothing else, wear me down while still holding my respect. But no, he simply repeated himself, like a tape loop.

A hundred years from now it won't make any difference.

But now, curled up as if in the womb, my thumb close enough to suck should I become that desperate for comfort, helpless amid a deadly assault by forces beyond ordinary reason, I found comfort in those irritating, infuriating words of old. They had become a mantra. Dad had been right, in the narrowest of contexts. While a more sophisticated me might have argued that every act or non-act we're involved with can reverberate down the generations, change whole dynamics of heritage, hell, could alter history, I had no sense of such import at the moment. This despite the irony of my mission with the Vulcana project. I merely wanted comfort, and my dead father was providing it for me with his sad, tired cliché. It was the perfect antidote for the vanity prep I'd been getting that I was to be humanity's savior, point man for a new, smarter, kinder world.

A hundred years from now...CRACKBOOM!!! This time I felt the heat from the strike. Immediately the sound of flames crackling cut through my childish fear and jerked me upright, mentally. I still lay on the ground but I'd pulled my arms away from my head and rolled my face up to see what the hell had just happened. A tree not ten yards away was ablaze, engulfed in a ravenous rush of flames. Its heat was intensifying so rapidly I knew I would roast if I didn't get away, which I did. I rolled onto my knees, pushed myself upright and ran up the trail as fast as I could get my cramped and terrified legs to go.

As I ran I worried about another lightning strike that this time would be a direct hit, frying me where I stood. I also worried that the tree was burning too quickly for having been in two heavy

SACRIFICE

rainstorms within a week. I worried the surrounding dead leaves and twigs would respond the same way and that the kind of forest fire that rages out of control in a windstorm was imminent. I ran with the inspiration of searing heat at my back until I tripped and fell hard, managing to turn my hips just enough in time to take the force of the fall on an upper arm and shoulder instead of my face.

A cushion of decomposing leaves beneath the new growth of vegetation softened the impact, likely saving me from bone breakage. Still, hitting the ground so hard stunned me, nearly knocking the wind out of my lungs. My first reaction was to twist my head so I could face what I assumed would be the roaring wall of fire about to embrace and roast me alive with what I'd always heard was one of the very least pleasant deaths. To my relative joy, this expectation suffered express disappointment. There was no fiery wall coming toward me. There was the burning tree and it was still a sight to behold, with flames leaping high above its top as it consumed branches and trunk, shooting out occasional bursts of sparks the wind immediately whipped away and smothered along with incinerated leaves, which, caught in their green adolescence, left white protesting trails of smoke as they fought against flight in the superheated turbulence.

Hypnotic. The fire and the maelstrom that brought it, leaving me with nothing to do but lie on my organic bed pelted by hail and wind-whipped icy rain, stare at the immolation, now about thirty yards away, and surrender again to my father's admonition that what was happening didn't matter in the grand scheme and if the worst were to come then so be it because there wasn't a damned thing, not one damned possible thing, I could do to stop it.

It was then, as I began negotiating a new surrender, I heard my father's voice once again.

MATHEW PAUST

OLD MAN DOWN THE ROAD

I felt his presence before I heard him speak. It was his stare. Political writers called it "The Look" and rarely failed to mention it when referring to his outsized influence in the senate, especially at the pinnacle of that influence when he parlayed it into an unsuccessful bid for president. My sister and I dreaded The Look. It said so much more than words. It was the granite face of the judge about to pronounce sentence. People on the receiving end usually knew what it meant for them, and if they did The Look was all they needed. Words would be redundant. For those who were new to Big Al's wrath the redundant words quickly brought them up to speed. The combination of Look and words was enough for them to make it a point to remember not to make the same mistake again. Many who incurred Big Al's tectonic rage swore thereafter they could feel his disgusted eyes upon them with their backs turned even if they had no idea he was present. Some claimed they hadn't a clue how they might have provoked his anger. If they'd known him like I did they'd have known it could have been something as simple as an overheard remark that reached him second or third hand.

I knew what it was this time as I lay shivering violently on a spongy bed of organic debris over a trail fast becoming an endless mud bog within scorching range of an inferno in a deluge of hail, rain and lethal voltage. Big Al's Look was conveying his paternal shame that a son of his would cower helplessly under any circumstances, especially while taking comfort from a bullshit line he'd used as a catchall on us kids to distract us from our petty concerns. The Look, just as potent if not more so for residing in sense instead of person, now carried burning scorn that trivialized the inflamed tree and reduced the lightning and hail to nuisances. Get up, it said, but not before you answer a few questions, you plodding feeble-minded ee-dyit. His favorite insult.

SACRIFICE

No need to be redundant, Dad, I might have muttered at the intrusive familiarity that presided as a psychic chilblain, which I knew no mantra or incantation could dispel. I felt an impulse to insult this specter of authority as I do in stressful dreams when some conjured opponent has me at a critical disadvantage and I'm aware at a crucial point that I'm dreaming and can vanquish the foe with a mere show of contempt. I knew this was different. Death, my death, was too near for me to be fencing with an old ghost. This was a solemn moment. Big Al evidently agreed, as he ignored my chickenshit riposte. How can you let them make such a fucking fool out of you?

They have me by the balls, Dad, I shouted, sounding off "like [I] had a pair" before he could insult me with that old Army basic-training chestnut.

Balls? What balls? That boss of yours has got you pussywhipped. You're pathetic, Junior. I'm rolling in my grave.

The stuff works, Dad. I saw a mouse fuck a rat to death and then die from remorse.

Jeezuz, Junior, I would laugh my ass off at you if I wasn't so ashamed. You believe that shit? What'd they do, give you some LSD and lead you around by your feeble fucking mind?

You know, Dad, I never thought of that. It's possible, but I don't think so. I've done a lot of LSD and I know when I'm stoned. I wasn't stoned, Dad.

You don't think so? Holy shit. You're even dumber than I thought. They make drugs, right? So they made some LSD so good you couldn't tell you were stoned. You suppose that is possible?

Goddammit, Dad, why are you so sure this stuff doesn't work? How would you know? What if it does work? Either way, wouldn't it be worth trying to find out?

Sixty-four thousand dollar question, Junior: Why you? What's so important about having you be the one to take the risk?

Access. Gallston knows me. He owes me.

You're on parole, for chrissake. Gallstone isn't gonna give you the time of day. You're a fuckin' politician. You at least know the only influence you have anymore is how much you can get in speaking fees.

Don't worry, Dad. He'll see me.

Got something on old Gallstone, eh? Good for you. That's my boy. But really, Son, so the fuck what? You give him this shit, he changes, and what? Just because he can get a hard-on whenever he wants to and suddenly gets all touchy feely and says "elementary, dear Watson" or "your illogical approach to chess does have its advantages on occasion, Captain," what's to keep him from doing the Devil's business same as he always has? He'll just be happier doing it. He'll rationalize his greed just like everybody else. It's the human curse.

OK, let's say you're right. Just for the sake of argument. So why, assuming Wilde is just cynically using me, why go through all the hooplah? Why not just promote Vulcana like any other drug? Why test it on the unsuspecting public? They could send me back to prison. They could send Ruth to prison. What's the point?

Ruth will never go to prison, Junior. You know better than to suggest something like that even in a hypothetical argument. Ex-presidents don't go to prison. You will undoubtedly go back to prison no matter what happens. Wanna know what I think is going on here?

Please!

Does the hard-on part work for you?

Yes, Dad.

Good. Glad to hear that. How about the touchy-feely and the brainiac shit? You smarter and sweeter?

Hard to tell, Dad. I've always been pretty quick on my feet and I think I have a kindly nature. I got the prototype formula. Pink says they've improved it considerably. So what do you think's really going on here?

SACRIFICE

Publicity. Big adventure, big stink, drone helicopters shooting other drone helicopters and empty SUVs — not that they'd give a shit about...what do they call it now? Collateral damage? Anyway, it's alllll about publicity. Don't care what you say about me, just spell my name right. Remember how they got Primrose Lane off the ground? That's right. Damned near brought down the presidency. You were there. Ringside seat. Hottest stuff going now, isn't it. Worth billions and growing. Enhanced orgasms. Now they got enhanced erections. They're using you, son. Trust me for once.

Dunno, Dad. Seems like a lotta trouble just to promote something that's not even available on the market yet.

Trust me, son. Get the hell out while you can.

MATHEW PAUST

WHO'LL STOP THE RAIN

The worst of the storm's fury abated in concert with the departure of my dad's essence as if the old man dead still exercised more natural influence than most living men. Not quite enough to stop the rain, though, which fell in a steady downpour as I pushed up out of the mud, brushed off clinging debris and renewed my slog up the trail. The rain did extinguish most of the fire, leaving charred branches with glowing patches that sent white smoke rising in vertical contrails to feed a spreading ghostly strata through which the rain passed without noticeable disturbance. Now that I knew there was no longer a danger of being burned alive, I found the musty, acrid smell oddly pleasant, reminding me of my childhood and our family bonfire celebrations that followed a day of raking leaves.

Yet this respiteful whiff of nostalgia did little to supplant the unease stirred by my strange encounter. Questions continued to sputter long after my dad's spectral appearance like fuel vapor dieseling in a heated engine. What if I am in fact playing the sap, as Bogart tells Mary Astor he won't in The Maltese Falcon? A sacrifice bunt to get the product buzz on first base? Anything's possible, of course. That's something I learned in politics early on. I learned it vicariously watching Dad play the game and I experienced it first-hand when I started playing. The trick was to play with confidence without ever forgetting to expect the unexpected. Thus far in this outing about all we'd had were unexpecteds. Whatever was up, I knew I was in too deep to quit without a well-devised escape plan.

Not a good time at the moment for devising anything. Just to think about escape was unthinkable, stuck as I was with more immediate survival priorities – for me and my companions, and even Newgate, assuming he was alive. This made getting back to the hogan, or what might be left of it, a no brainer. Newgate

SACRIFICE

alive could have information, or know how to get it, that could save my life and Joan's and Pink's. Even if Newgate were dead he might have left information that could tell us who wanted us dead. Maybe even tell us who killed him, assuming the two murdering entities were not the same. I didn't see any reason why all four of us would be targeted by the same executioners. Unless...

Unless Ruth was right. Could word have reached Wall Street strategists that Vulcana's implications bode ill for an economy based on neurotic consumption? Did they snatch or lure Gladys Alabi into a position to learn first-hand the pharmaceutical's effects? Are they now persuaded that if primitive fears of inadequacy were replaced by smarter, sweeter, more vigorous dispositions the lures of greed and power would diminish and with them the desire for irrational acquisition and domination of others? A most perplexing prospect for the ideological capitalist. A most frightening one for his practical counterpart. More dangerous than political revolution. Deadlier to the ruling elite than an outbreak of plague. Were I on that side of the divide, the Devil's side, I'd be a fool not to at least consider the option of murdering anyone with the motive and means to bring such catastrophe to the socioeconomic hierarchy.

This would mean even if Gladys cooperated willingly they'd want her dead once she had demonstrated Vulcana's effectiveness. Pink would be on their hit list, too. Applying a tactic organized crime has used effectively for generations the corporate assassins might try to lure him out of hiding by bribing or coercing someone close to him to betray him. Gladys could fill that bill better than any of us. All the more reason to focus on finding her as our first order of business, which, as it happened, is what we were doing.

I leaned toward this theory of our adversaries if only because the plausibility of being the butt of a marketing stunt was too harsh to contemplate, made even more irritating by the strategic proximity of my old foe Warren Hendrian. We hadn't always been at odds. Teammates during Ruth's run for the presidency, I'd met them both at a governor's conference. Hendrian was already working for her, having taken a sabbatical from Yale during her first run for the New Jersey governorship. I was two years into my term as Iowa's governor and Ruth had just begun her second in the Garden State. Hendrian was still on her staff.

I knew them both by reputation. Ruth stunned the political world in her first campaign by running on a platform that included a call to legalize marijuana. Hendrian had been gaining recognition as a history professor who called his one course The Death Rattle of Western Civilization. I had read his book, Fatal Appetites, which made a persuasive argument that western societies were too preoccupied with creature comforts, too spoiled to survive.

He lacked charm and was physically unattractive – dumpy and awkward - yet we'd hit it off at first, the three of us sitting on the floor in Ruth's hotel suite getting stoned on Hendrian's pot as we got acquainted. The animosity that grew between us didn't start until later that year after I resigned the governorship and joined Ruth's presidential campaign full time. I've always assumed he was jealous of the rapport I developed with Ruth, which led to her naming me chief of staff once we were in the White House. Hendrian, as domestic affairs adviser, had to go through me to get to her.

So, yes, the tables were now turned and Hendrian towered over me as a top executive of Wilde Labs, and, yes, he was enjoying the turnabout and was certainly not above the nastiest sort of payback either of us could imagine. I'd tried to get a grand jury to indict him for dereliction of duty during the Rose Garden sting. He'd responded by getting me sent to prison for malicious prosecution. We both felt righteously justified doing what we did. We were bratty kids on a playground. Was this another payback from the little weasel? Would Ruth go along with such shenanigans or was she being sucked into it, too? I couldn't get my head around that. Hendrian adored Ruth too much to splash any mud on her just to get at me. No, this was not the scenario. Sorry, Dad, I shouted to myself, you're wrong!

SACRIFICE

NO SIMPLE HIGHWAY

The rain had let up to a drizzle long before I drew near Newgate's camp. Still no light, though, as cloud cover screened the heavenly bodies from view. Fortunately the trail was navigable in the dark, and I had my pocket flashlight for moments of uncertainty at several locations where the trail split into forks. Without the machete, which I'd left with Joan and Pink, briars snagged my arms and legs along the way so that by the time I was near enough to smell the acrid consequences of the helicopter's bombardment I was not only soaked, shivering from chill, aching in every joint and so exhausted I was drifting in and out of sleep, I trickled blood from nasty scratches on all four limbs.

The sound of a voice brought me fully awake. Human or animal, whichever, its feral tenor rippled the hairs on the back of my neck to quivering attention. I froze, afraid to move, unable to breathe and then consciously holding my breath afraid of gasping when I had to. Just when I did fill my desperate lungs the voice cried again. It seemed no nearer but I had a better sense of its direction. I was about to round a curve in the trail, one I knew would bring me out into Newgate's campsite, and the cry had come from there. My head suddenly swarming with thoughts, I crept slowly forward.

If the cries were human they would be Newgate's, meaning he was alive but likely in bad shape. If something else, I was guessing coyotes, which I had read were migrating into the area. Coyotes hunt in packs. The sounds of a pack would be terrifying, I assumed, snarling and yelping as they tore Newgate asunder and fought over the pieces. If the two cries I'd heard were coyote it could mean a scout had discovered dinner and was calling the pack, or it could mean Newgate had wounded one and its cries were from pain. Either way, Newgate likely was still alive and perhaps seriously injured, bracing himself for a savage fight to the death when the other coyotes arrived.

I reached into my side jeans pocket and found comfort when my fingers touched the revolver I'd stashed there before leaving the hogan. I'd put it out of mind on the trail, remembering it just now when it occurred to me it might have fallen out during my thrashing about on the ground during the height of the storm. I tugged it out and looked it over, surprised now that I was considering using it how light it felt compared with the .45 I'd carried in the Army. With its aluminum frame and short barrel, loaded with a mere five rounds of .38 Special ammunition, the little revolver seemed hardly potent enough to stop any living creature larger than a squirrel. I knew the caliber was adequate against men, and Joan had explained that the rounds she'd provided were superior ballistically to more conventional ammunition. The bullets were hollow and made of copper. While they weighed less than the commonly used lead, she said, the copper slugs traveled faster, penetrated flesh more deeply and expanded inside the body to tear a larger wound channel.

"They don't recoil as much as lead, either," she'd said, smiling. "Easier on the wrist."

I'd not fired such a small revolver, but the handguns I was familiar with had never given me any trouble with recoil. That was years back, though. My gun skills no doubt had gone soft. Yet I was wishing now my armament was something heavier and more powerful, whatever its kick. Better a sore wrist than a coyote's meal.

I moved forward in a crouch, holding the revolver in my right hand and my flashlight in the other with my thumb on the tail switch so I could turn it on in an instant. I took several steps and then stopped and listened. The rustling of my movements through the brush and rain-soaked leaves on the trail was inevitable, and I strained to hear any movement ahead that might be reacting to me. Nothing. Several more steps. Stopped and listened. Still nothing. I repeated this two or three more times, rounding the curve and seeing where the hogan would be, although despite pupils fully dilated to accommodate the dark I saw nothing but

SACRIFICE

shapeless shades of black. It was while I studied this amorphous visage that I heard the other sound, low-pitched, as if a small turbine were starting up. Instinct quickly corrected this perception as I again responded with the tingling hairs and adrenalin rush that signaled imminent peril.

A flick of the flashlight showed me what I was hearing, as the two embers of reflected light stared directly at me from a distance of about twenty yards. They vanished and then reappeared several feet to the left. All this while the turbine sound increased in volume until it was unmistakable I was facing off with a feral beast that was not happy to see me. Fearing a shot at the creature might miss and penetrate the hogan walls, although I had not yet determined the dwelling's precise location, I fired into the air in the hope my adversary would take the hint and hightail it to a different venue. A blue and orange flame erupted six inches from the snubby's barrel, accompanying a fierce BANG that surely would have accomplished my intended purpose, I assumed, assuming wrong.

The growling increased and seemed closer. I turned the flashlight on in time to see the eyes growing in size at an alarming rate. Lowering the revolver's barrel I squeezed off another round, producing a second piercing blast and fiery tongue. The flash blinded me temporarily and I instinctively stepped to one side, as would a matador to escape the horns of a charging bull. My reflex was nick of time. I felt the brush of rough hair against my abdomen. A powerful gamey odor joined the burnt propellent gases from the fired cartridges as I felt and heard the thud of a heavy body land beside me and begin thrashing in what I presumed were its death throes. Oddly, the growling had ceased after one sharp yelp of pain when my bullet struck the animal at almost point blank range.

I turned my flashlight on the dying coyote and watched its spasms gradually slow until they eventually stopped. I had continued backing away from it, heading in the hogan's direction, but tripped and fell, striking something hard and discharging another round from the revolver I was still gripping, finger on the trigger. At some point in gathering my wits and my person from the ground, I discovered I had fallen against the hogan. No matter what lay ahead I knew there was only one course of action in my immediate future: get myself into the hogan, find something soft to lie on and crash.

And this, no longer concerned the dead coyote's pack might be closing in, I did.

SACRIFICE

SAYING GOODBYE

Sleep was fitful. I felt drugged from the pain and fatigue, yet bothered by my encounter with the coyote, the close call, shooting, and I wondered what had happened to Newgate, especially considering the hogan seemed not to have been damaged by the helicopter attack. Too many notions competing for mind time and too little energy to sort them out. I wanted desperately to sleep, but found that last dip into unconsciousness maddeningly elusive. As it turned out, I did sleep. Apparently the thoughts tormenting me were subconscious. Like a fever delirium. I was dreaming, badly. When I finally awoke I felt worse than when I'd stumbled into the hogan. But now there was no mistaking my state. I was awake, whether or not I wanted to be.

"Who the fuck are you?" The snarling voice ordered me out of sleep. It was still dark in the hogan but I saw pearl gray morning light sneaking in around the silhouette of a human figure standing in the doorway. The light found and glistened off the rifle barrel pointing at me in front of the black featureless figure. Before I could think of anything to say a brighter, blinding light found my face. This light stayed unwavering on me until the voice spoke again, "Geddes? Jesus Christ, what are you doing here?"

I sat up despite a sensation my abdomen was breaking in half. Still soaking wet, I'd begun trembling violently the instant I knew I was awake. I knew if I tried to speak the trembling would render my voice comical, if at all coherent. I tried anyway.

"Roger, you're OK! We saw that helicopter and heard the bomb. What happened?"

"Shot out my solar panels. Where're the others?"

"They kept going. We're out of touch. Why didn't you call us?"

"I did. Last night. No one answered."

"Oh, shit."

"Yeah. You OK?"

"Far as I know. Sore as hell." He had moved closer as we talked. I could see he was limping, badly. He used the rifle as a cane. "What happened to you?"

"Broke my ankle, I think. Concussion knocked me over. I fell wrong." He hobbled to the cot, which I hadn't seen when I stumbled in, and lowered himself onto its webbing.

"Who was it? Any idea?"

"Random flyover, I'm guessing. Saw the panels, not on their list, took 'em out. Freak thing. My camouflage was pretty good."

"Won't they be back to check out the area?"

"No doubt. Figured it was safe to spend the night, that they'd wait until after the storm. We need to get the hell out of here ASAP."

"How, Roger, you can barely walk?"

"The bike's OK. We'll ride out. You know how to operate an Indian?"

"I've ridden an old Suzuki slingshot. Never seen an Indian."

He sighed heavily. "OK, look, my ankle is shot. Good thing you have long legs because you're gonna have to reach your foot up and press the clutch when I yell clutch, and let it up when I'm done shifting. I'll do the hand controls. It'll be one helluva bumpy ride. You up for it?"

"Doesn't look like I have any choice. I'll do what I can."

Newgate started stuffing things into a backpack, including his laptop and a handful of cellphones from the trunk next to his cot.

"We need to torch this place when we leave, Al. There's too much stuff in here can identify me. They might miss the hogan, depending on how hard they search, but I can't count on it."

"What about the outhouse?"

SACRIFICE

"No intelligence in there of any use to anybody. They'll find my satellite dish and they'll know there was something serious here, but they won't get a lead on me for at least a week, if ever. Too big a backup at their lab for them to get excited about some eccentric living in the woods with satellite wi fi. I'll leave the outhouse in case some wayfaring bumblers happen upon it on their way to Oz." He looked up from the trunk, flashed me a grin and then turned serious.

"That's where I spent the night. Figured it was safer than the hogan, harder to find. So what were you shooting at last night?"

"Coyote. Next to the hogan. Don't worry, I killed it."

Newgate straightened and turned to face me. An expression of incomprehension twisted his features. "Coyote? Did you say coyote?" I nodded. His face twisted again, this time into a stricken expression of surprise and pain. "Mickey!" he shouted and began hobbling as fast as he could toward the entrance.

I ran to help him, took his arm. He shook it off. "Get the fuck away from me!" I followed him outside and ran to where I'd left the body of the creature that had attacked me. It was still there. Newgate arrived on my heels and pushed me away, shouting the name "Mickey" several times and then repeating it in a softer voice as he knelt beside the body, threw himself upon it and wrapped his arms around its neck.

I waited until he'd regained his composure and was struggling to get to his feet before I spoke. At the same time I walked back over and lent him a hand. This time he didn't resist. He seemed crushed with grief. "I'm sorry, Roger," I said. "He was attacking me. He sounded like a coyote."

"Half coyote, I think." he said, his voice so low I had to strain to hear him. "More shepherd, though. He'd come and go. I fed him. Never brought a mate or a pack around. Just him. I called him Mickey. He knew his name. He was here last night to...guard me." He started back to the hogan, then stopped and turned around. "We don't have time to bury him. Help me drag him into the hogan, Al."

I did. The dog in fact looked like photos of coyotes I'd seen. Had the long ears and the pointy muzzle. Otherwise his markings were shepherd. We pulled him inside and Newgate covered him with the blanket from his cot. Then he hobbled back to the smaller shed and came back with a red galvanized gasoline can, soaked the blanket over Mickey and sprinkled the rest of the fuel around the hogan. He motioned me to follow him back to the shed for the Indian. We wheeled it out into the cold misty morning as a couple of crows began calling each other from somewhere nearby.

Newgate mounted the motorcycle and I climbed up behind him on a seat that was smaller and harder than I remembered from the Suzuki. Newgate showed me where the clutch lever was and told me to press it in. When I did, he stomped his foot down on the other side and cranked the engine to life. I let up the clutch and we rolled up the path to the hogan. "Clutch," Newgate yelled again as we stopped in front of the entrance. He'd removed the blanket covering the door and I could see an oil lamp burning next to the cot. Newgate raised the rifle he'd been carrying across the seat in front of him, clicked off the thumb safety, took aim at the oil lamp and fired. The bullet smashed the glass lamp, releasing a blue flame that quickly ignited the gasoline. He tossed the rifle through the entrance into the hogan.

"Bye, Mick," he said softly. To me, "Let's roll."

SACRIFICE

IF YOU WANT TO BE A BIRD

Within half an hour of our launch we were one rider. The motorcycle rhythms re-emerged from my decades-old muscle memory so that once I picked up the clutch nuances my leg became Newgate's, knowing when a shift was coming and synchronizing my timing precisely with his. He'd wrapped a towel around the foot bar so he could rest his ankle horizontally and avoid the constant jarring against the bottom of his foot, which would have rocketed up the leg bringing hellish pain into the torn nerves.

We started out slowly, learning the necessary adjustments to accommodate his injury and my rustiness. Newgate's makeshift traction was only partially effective. "Christ!" he shouted, hunching reflexively after the first jolt, which startled me as well, kicking my ass like a leather piston. In less than a mile we had things sorted out and were rolling at a fair clip. The occasional briar tentacle managed to reach far enough onto the trail to taunt us with its stickers, but bounced harmlessly off the leather jackets Newgate had dug out of his trunk before we left.

Serving as clutch man on this ride kept me from feeling like just another passive rider, something to be avoided in the hyper-masculine motorcycle context. The notion of passivity nonetheless lingered as we flew along the trail through a narrow winding chute of blurred browns and greens. Our sense of speed, amplified by the continual visual streaming on either side, pulled my thoughts in faster sequence than usual, tugging me from one momentary stop to the next with barely time enough at each to register a conclusion worth bringing forward. I now suspect passivity was able to bridge these mental pit stops as an overriding theme partly because there were no anticipated outside distractions, no threat of intrusion. A reinforcing companion of this internal theme was the constant potential of devastation from whomever wanted either or both of us dead. A quintessential passivity, being kept at the mercy of forces beyond our knowledge and control. Rats scurrying from one hiding place to the next.

I began to notice a connection between the trail bumps and the brain farts. Each bump punctuated with its ass kick my recognition of another step in the progression of passive situations in which I'd found myself over the years. Went to law school because that's what my lawyer dad expected – BUMP. Married a feisty law school classmate, who picked me and eventually tired of being the initiator – BUMP. Got into politics because that's what my politician dad expected – BUMP. Successful because of my name and because I did what the party expected of me – BUMP. Gave up the governorship to follow a feisty woman to the White House – BUMP. Tried something on my own as Special Prosecutor after leaving the White House and ended up in prison – BUMP. Now following the feisty former president who's led me into a fucking nightmare in which I am now bumping along a woodsy trail on a motorcycle running from disaster to I know not what, carried along by events beyond my ken without even the option to bail out. Prisoner of my consequences. Slave of the whims of unknowable fate...BUMP!

"Holy shit, what was that?" I shouted as Newgate skidded the bike to a stop.

"Dunno, pothole I guess. Christ, my ankle! I need to rest, man." He said. I slid off the back and planted my feet to help steady the bike while he climbed off, cursing again when he bumped his heel as he swung his leg over the seat. He helped hold the bike up while I lowered the kickstand and then we both collapsed on the trail. It seemed as if my entire lower body was sore, but Newgate clearly suffered. He tried to examine his ankle but quickly gave up and rolled onto one side, knees pulled up, muttering to himself. I looked around for whatever we hit that almost threw me off the bike.

What I found was a deceptively shallow depression filled with foot-high grass. When I moved next to it I saw the real culprit: a

SACRIFICE

lateral root along the lip of the hole that acted as a solid tripwire. I probed with my toe, which slipped easily under the inch-diameter root. It made a trap that could give a nasty fall to someone running along the trail. Might even break a foot. That thought was still presiding when a metallic gleam caught my eye. I bent down, painfully, and retrieved a cell phone from under the grass. I quickly scanned the area for anything else Joan and Pink might have left behind. Nada, but that was enough. I showed the phone to Newgate.

"That's it alright. It's on, too. Must've fallen out of her pocket. Where was it?"

"In the hole. I'm guessing one of them took a spill. It's a deep hole with a root across one end. We could've lost the bike."

"We?" He tried to smile through the grimace on his face.

"You know what I mean, Newgate."

"Oh, yes, Geddes, of course. We ride as one!" He said it with the pompous strained Spanish accent of Romanian-born Duncan Renaldo playing the Cisco Kid.

"Do you have the number of the other one?"

He pulled a small spiral notebook from a shirt pocket. "They're all in here." He handed me the book. "I marked it for Doc. You sure you wanna risk a call?"

"I need to know if they're OK. One of them might have gotten hurt tripping in that damned hole." I found the number, flipped open the phone and punched in the call. It rang three times."

"Hello?" It was Joan.

MATHEW PAUST

TIGHTWIRE TALK

I heard noise in the background. It might have been from the phone brushing against something. "Joan?"

"Yes." Her voice was flat, subdued. I considered identifying myself, but thought better. If she hadn't recognized my voice she'd assume it was either me or Newgate, and if neither she could hang up without having given anything away.

"You guys OK?" I heard her breathing now. It seemed a tad labored. Her response came a couple of beats later than I would have expected.

"Yes. You?"

Not sure yet if somehow someone was listening to this conversation in person, at her end, or if she was merely thinking of the potential for electronic eavesdropping. Whichever, staying in character, passively, I kept it cryptic, too. "We have the Indian."

She snickered, a first for me. "Woowoowoowoowoowoo." She did this quietly, but it was so out of character, what I knew of her character, that I found myself suddenly hyper alert for code. I knew she'd picked up on the "we," but I wasn't sure she'd remember what kind of motorcycle Newgate had. I decided to keep the game in play a tad longer.

"Brrum Brrum Brummm," was my move.

"How close?" Thank you.

"Halfway." I waited a beat, then added, "You two alone?"

Another beat, another, another... Lost the connection. I started reflexively to redial but realized that if Joan and Pink were not alone, if somebody else was listening in, the connection might have been deliberately broken. I flipped the phone shut.

SACRIFICE

"Maybe that's all she needed to know," Newgate offered. He was sitting up. Seemed to have the pain under control.

"Yeah, maybe. Anyway, if somebody was there with them listening they'll hear us coming a mile away."

"Not that far. The woods'll suck up the sound. You can hop off a couple hundred yards back and walk the rest of the way. I'll stay with the bike and come charging up if you need some cavalry."

"What about the clutch?"

"If it comes to that I can do the clutch. You all'll hear the engine roar and me screamin' Geronimo. Still got that .38?"

"That's affirmative."

"Shit, you sound like a cop. How many rounds left?"

"Two."

"No extras?"

"Didn't figure we were going to war."

"Al, if you're gonna carry you need backup. Either a reload or another piece. I'm disappointed."

"Fuck you, Geddes, I'm no cop."

"Not you, bubba. Joan's a cop. She should know better."

"Ammo's expensive. She's a prudent government employee."

"Prudent's OK for paperclips. Not with lives at stake." He struggled to his feet, stretched his arms, arched his back groaning, then hobbled to the bike.

"Pink and Joan are armed," I said.

"Not anymore, worst case scenario. When you get near, try to get a fix on them before they make you. If there's more than one, stay hidden and fire a shot, in the air."

"That'll leave me with only one."

"One's all you'll need when I come roaring up. Confuse the hell out of 'em. Joan will know what to do in the confusion. Wish I had my rifle. But, look, you can't try to take anyone out if you don't know who they are. OK? They might be locals. Police, anybody, you just won't know. You shoot in the air and we'll take our chances."

"What if there's only one, or even two?"

"One you might be able to handle. Just walk nonchalantly out of the woods like you been hiking. Keep that .38 out of sight. Joan will know how to play it. She won't know you, you won't know her. Got it?"

"What if it's nothing? They're just hanging out waiting for Doc Bot?"

"Then you come back and get me and we do the two-man boogie and ride the rest of the way."

"What? No Geronimo?" Newgate shook his head, waved me off and grabbed the handlebars. He swung his gimp leg over, this time clearing the seat by a hair or two. I kicked up the stand, climbed on behind, punched the clutch and we brought the Indian roaring to life.

The mid-morning sun had burned away the storm's wispy trailing clouds and was warming the air, pulling moisture from the greenery in curtains of rising steam. Newgate twisted the throttle and revved us up and we rolled forward through the barely visible on our course to confront the barely fathomable.

SACRIFICE

TRIBULATION TIME

I heard the theme from High Noon soon as I started walking up the trail toward the road, where I expected to find Joan and Pink and possibly – very probably – some hostiles. It wasn't Tex Ritter singing "Do not forsake me, oh, my darrrrr-lin'," though. It was Newgate, leaning against his Indian, wearing a grin and pretending to strum an imaginary guitar. I curled my lower lip out and gave him a Gary Cooper glower, cocked a finger and mimed a shot at him. The damned tune accompanied me in my head the rest of the way, its beat thumping in time with my cautious steps...on this our wed-ding dayyyaaa...until I saw what looked like someone standing at one side of the trail when I rounded a curve. The mist had burned off by then but if what I saw was human its form was partially obscured by overgrowth in my line of sight. I moved to the same side as the figure and crept forward, slipping my hand into the pocket where I kept the revolver.

Without warning something rustled the bushes in front of me. I jerked backward but a hand appeared and grabbed my arm as it tried to withdraw the .38. Joan stepped out. Her other hand held the pistol she'd brought from The Cottage.

"What happened? Where's Newgate?" She released my arm but continued holding the pistol.

"Not far. He's with the Indian. We were being cautious."

"We weren't cautious enough."

"Where's Pink?"

She nodded toward the woods. "He's with one of them." I stared at her. Her face glistened with sweat, clothes were soaked, hair a tangled mess. No sign of injury, though. Her mouth twitched into the beginning of a smile. "We're OK, Al. Three men jumped us. Two are dead." She slipped her pistol back into the holster on her belt and started walking. I followed.

A couple of steps off the trail I saw what appeared to be a small black mound. The mound came into focus as two black-clad bodies. Several more steps and we were in a small clearing. Pink and a man dressed in black tactical clothes were seated on the ground. Pink was murmuring to the man, whose face seemed frozen in a grimace of sheer terror.

"I'll get Newgate," I said and headed back to the trail.

"I hope you brought a shovel," Joan said, nodding toward the bodies. "It's warming up out here."

Newgate in fact had packed a small folding camp shovel, which Joan and I took turns using to dig a grave just deep enough to keep the buzzards from spotting anything delicious. We dragged the two, both dark and with features suggesting a Mideastern descent, to the shallow hole and pushed them in. Each had a hole in his forehead, filled with clotted blood that had turned nearly as black as their clothes, and the backs of their heads, hair trimmed military short, had been blown out by the pressure of the expanded copper bullets. The odor of fresh feces presaged more repugnant scents already in the making. We rolled a rotting log from nearby to compress and further conceal.

As we worked, Joan explained that as soon as she had seen something black emerge from the bushes she kicked Pink's legs out from under him and fell atop him while drawing her pistol. The morning fog still obscured clear vision at this point, but Joan could see well enough to get her shots off before her attackers even had a fix on her position. They'd set up an ambush with two on one side of the trail and the third across from them.

"I got the two I could see," she told me. "I think one of them shot the third one by mistake. He's the one Pink's interrogating."

Newgate was stretched out on his side tending to his own misery while Pink continued talking quietly to his captive. The man's hands had been fastened behind him with plastic cuffs. Someone had tied a tourniquet around one of his legs above the knee. The tourniquet had once been white, probably a T-shirt, but was now

SACRIFICE

a deep red. Blood from the tourniquet on down the leg had turned the color of the man's black cargo pants to a dark maroon. Pink never acknowledged me or Newgate, his attention riveted to the man seated in front of him. Pink's voice was so muted I had trouble making out what he was saying. The other man was silent.

"Has he spoken at all?" I asked Joan.

"Not a word."

"What is Pink telling him?"

Joan rolled her eyes. She and I were seated against another log on the other side of the small clearing from Newgate, with Pink and the prisoner in the center. "Hard to say," she said. "He's had no training as an interrogator, but he said he knows how to talk to people on Vulcana."

"You gave this guy the drug?"

"Pink gave him an injection. He said the effect at first would be similar to a bad acid trip. The mind is in turmoil as the intellect does battle with the instincts and conditioned reflexes. That's how Pink explained it."

"I don't remember having a bad acid trip in the White House after I took the pill."

"Wait until we get back to The Cottage, if we ever do. You need to see the videos we shot of you then. Read your book, Al. You got a little wiggy there trying to figure out what was happening."

She was right. I did think I was losing my mind.

"How long will it take?"

"Hard to tell. Pink says it's different for everybody. Depends on your background, your nature, your circumstances."

"How long with this guy? Pink have any idea?"

"No way of knowing, but if he doesn't come out of it in a good way, we leave him here."

"Leave him here to die? Isn't Doc coming?"

"We haven't called him yet."   Her face was set, grim, unyielding. She turned and met my eyes. The hazel still shone but had lost its sparkle. Hard as agates. "Al, my assignment is to protect Pink. Period. My assignment does not include taking prisoners. I can't get anyone else involved in this. No Homeland Security, no local cops, nobody.

"If this guy decides to cooperate, help us find out who's behind this, who our enemy is, I'll see he gets medical help. I'll do all I can to help him. If not, he's a liability. He stays here."

I started to speak, but she added, "I'm gonna call Doc now. This guy has until Doc gets here to decide how to play it."

SACRIFICE

TIME IS SHORT

Joan finally reached Doc on the disposable cellphone after getting a busy signal a couple of times and hanging up. When he answered she spoke quickly, giving him the lines she'd memorized from Newgate. She added, without speaking any names, there would be one injured party and possibly two. I took some comfort from this, recoiling inwardly at the prospect of leaving the wounded man behind to die. I knew Joan was right, but I wanted the Vulcana to work. As we waited we watched intently but neither of us interfered with Pink's attempts to bring the prisoner out of his stoic refusal to speak.

Or maybe he was in a kind of shock or catatonic state from the drug. His face was frozen in an expression of extreme discomfort, not something a stoic ordinarily gives away, and his eyes tracked Pink and occasionally registered comprehension of Pink's words. Pink continued speaking softly, but I was able to get the gist of what he was saying. He explained that the injection he'd given the man was not LSD although it might be reacting similarly. He explained that the drug is designed to give a person greater reasoning powers, that this might cause turmoil in some minds that have been operating at more instinctual or conditioned levels.

"Highly trained people like yourself," he added. "You might be experiencing contradictory sensations. Your more immediate concerns conflicting with what you were conditioned to accept as your duty, bringing more weight to the equation. Your sense of duty has been suppressing your survival instinct despite its being the most powerful of all instincts. But now you're gaining the rational strength to enable your survival instinct to prevail, as is meant to be..."

Joan and I looked at each other simultaneously. I suspect my face registered a what the fuck expression as I leaned in and whispered, "Pink can't expect this guy to know what the hell he's talking about. I can barely follow him and I've been hearing this stuff for weeks now."

"He's speaking to the neo-cortex, assuming this guy's hasn't atrophied. No emotion, no threats – although I may jump in here pretty soon and let the guy know his clock is ticking – just an explanation of what's happening to him. Pink's doing a good job. Better than I could do under these circumstances."

Mention of my name interrupted our muted conversation. "Mr. Geddes over there," Pink turned and pointed at me, and the prisoner's eyes followed, meeting mine for an instant that sparked electric as he seemed to size me up in an invasive way that angered me, "was given this drug by mistake. He knows what you're going through. As you can see, he's OK now. The effect does not wear off. It's permanent. It strengthens your reasoning powers for good. I'm the scientist who developed this drug. I've taken it myself. There's really nothing to be afraid of."

Taking this as her cue, Joan abruptly stood and walked over to the two. She leaned forward and peered directly into the prisoner's face. "There is if you don't start talking to us. We have a doctor on his way right now. If you're still sitting there staring at us without speaking when he gets here, we will leave you sitting there staring at whatever the hell you want to stare at when we leave.

"You will bleed to death. And, you wanna know something? Buster, I don't give a fuck how long it takes you to die." She glared at him a couple of seconds longer, then turned her back on him and walked over to where Newgate was still lying on his side, nursing his ankle. She offered him one of the pain pills he'd given her for Pink, but he declined. "Won't help me much, Joan. I can wait 'til Doc gets here. Thanks, anyway."

Distracted from his monologue, Pink stood up, stretched and wandered out of the clearing for what I assumed was a piss break. When he returned he sat down next to me. His face still looked pretty bad, the bandage over his nose filthy, with yellowed bruises

SACRIFICE

radiating out from there.

"How you feeling?" I asked.

"I've been better. You?"

"By comparison I'd have to say great, but I won't."

"You're a gentleman. Vulcana does that to people."

"So is this guy gonna talk?"

"I think he's coming around. Wish I had another hour or so with him."

"Be a shame to waste hi...the opportunity," I looked to see if he'd caught my slip. He gave no sign. Rested his chin in his hands. I noticed the prisoner staring at us, his face still conveying the haunted look, the dread I'd seen in it when we arrived. "At least he's not giving us the stinkeye. You think that means anything?" I asked.

"It does. He sees us as monsters now. Witnesses to the guilt he's experiencing. Condemning judges. He can't bring himself to trust anyone right now. If his chief or his supervisor or whatever were to walk up right now and set him free, it would be the same thing. He feels completely, totally alone right now. You know the feeling."

I nodded. Indeed I did. I still do from time to time, yet I've never felt as alone since as I did those terrible days in the White House when I feared trusting anybody — even myself — with the president's life. A new, harsh voice interrupted these gloomy reminiscences. It was Doc. He'd brought a van fitted out with a couple of cots.

"What about the Indian?" I asked, when Newgate failed to mention it.

"No room. Can you ride?" he asked, looking at me.

"I'd rather not. It's been awhile."

"God dammit. I'll ride the damned thing. I hope you can drive the van." This with a sneer on his mouth to match his voice.

Joan helped Newgate up and supported him on the walk to the van, which Doc had parked on the shoulder of the ill-kept asphalt road. After getting Newgate settled onto one of the cots, she came back to the clearing. All eyes were on the prisoner now. He'd ratcheted the contortions of his face up a notch to where he now looked seriously frightened.

"Leave him," Joan ordered and turned back to the trail. I turned to follow her. Doc and Pink kept staring at the prisoner. The two whispered to each other. Pink called Joan to come back.

"We can take him," he shouted. "He's coming around."

"I don't see any change. He just looks like a man who doesn't want to die," she said.

"Know a better motive for conversion?" This was Doc. "I can keep him alive at least another day or two. He's no good to anybody if we let him die here."

Pink spoke up. "Liz can bring him around. You know, good cop bad cop?"

"Liz, huh? So which one is she? Good cop?"

"He hasn't gotten his erection yet. That'll be her job."

Joan laughed. The harshness gone from her voice. "Well, can't say you didn't try, Pink. OK, bring this specimen along."

It took the three of us to get the prisoner to the van. His pain, as much physical as mental, made it almost more difficult to move him than if he'd deliberately resisted. He didn't, which was another good sign. We waited in the van until Doc came roaring out of the woods on Newgate's Indian. He pulled in front and led the way.

SACRIFICE

OH, NO!

The idea of bringing Dr. Knoe in on the interrogation at first delighted me, for personal reasons as well as the prospect she might be the key to unlocking the mystery of our adversaries. My delight began to fade as I guided the van along the narrow road. My thinking swerved into the lane of suspicion my feverish dialogue with my dead father had opened during the storm. I needed input from the others, but I thought it best to ease into my concern about Wilde Laboratories.

I addressed my question to Pink, who was sitting beside me, but turned my head and spoke loudly enough for Joan to hear, too. "Aren't you concerned about calling her? Isn't it fairly apparent their security's been breached?"

"I'll use one of the disposables. We can meet her somewhere and bring her here. It's a risk but we need to get this guy to talk," Pink said.

"They can pick her up when she leaves. Follow her to where she meets us," I said.

Joan joined the conversation: "I'll talk to her. We have decoy procedures. One of Cromwell's people can bring her and he can send other cars out at the same time. If they wanna follow all of them they'll show their hand and we'll have our own choppers. Armed. They want a goddam fight we'll give 'em one."

I decided to wait awhile longer before lobbing the grenade, that this whole rigmarole might be a PR stunt. I was about to pull the pin when our prisoner let out a long and troubling groan. This to me signaled intense pain, probably emotional as well as from the bullet lodged in his leg, and reminded me that if this was an elaborate promotional stunt it was as cold and ruthless a program as any devised by the maddest Madison Avenue whiz kids in the history of advertising. It meant not only were they quite willing to put mercenaries into mortal danger but that other players, perhaps myself, perhaps everyone in the van, could be expendable.

If found, the dead mercenaries might be traced to a company hired by a cutout, a dummy entity harder to trace. Even if that scheme were to unravel eventually, if some enterprising investigative journalists were to dig out the story, it would be too late for those of us willingly sacrificed to a phony mission, trusting goats slaughtered on the altar of commercialism to embed the name Vulcana into the consciousness of every human being in the technologized world. If we could get this guy to talk, to trust us, to fill us in on what he knew, we might have a chance to expose such an outrageous stunt before it gained momentum . It seemed to me anyone who might not want this man to talk would ensure he didn't live long enough to do so. The list of suspects was vast, including everyone except those of us in the van. And the prisoner's "conversion" by Vulcana would supersede the test I was supposed to undergo. He'd be an even better subject, as I'd already been primed by the Vulcana predecessor. Turning a professional thug into a Renaissance man would be vastly more dramatic evidence of the drug's effectiveness. I'd already scrapped the idea of slipping a dose to the president. My channeled dad was right. I'd never get close enough. And watching what happened to the prisoner convinced me the risk was too great. If something went wrong I would be charged with attempted assassination, or worse.

A public demonstration on a large stage was next logical step, but to what purpose? Which would be the hotter commodity, make Hendrian a billionaire quicker, a drug that could turn everyone into a saint or one that gives men the power to call up an erection at will? Which prospect would be more believable from a marketing point of view? This wouldn't matter if the drug did both. The perfect Father's Day gift, but for women? A question for Dr. Knoe. Pink might know.

"Hey, Pink, you tested Vulcana on women?"

SACRIFICE

"Yes, sir, Al. Most definitely."

"And?"

"How does it affect them? Well, we've had only one test subject so far. Too soon to draw any conclusions."

"I'm not talking about Rhonda Rat here, Pink. I mean a real woman."

"Oh, she's real, alright."

"Pink, let's not be coy, OK? If anybody has a need to know right now it's me."

Pink turned in his seat in what seemed a sly way as if to check out the other passengers. But he stopped when facing me, and stared until I turned and met his eyes. He said quietly, "Just a volunteer test subject. Nobody you would know," and turned back to face front. I took more from him than the words themselves. He'd put slightly more vocal emphasis on the last one and did something with his mouth, as well, as if cuing a lipreader. He'd given me the name of the test subject and for some reason didn't want anyone else in the van to know.

It was Dr. Knoe.

MATHEW PAUST

TOUCH AND GO

Our little motorcade carried us about a dozen miles along the old highway into a small town the name of which I've decided to withhold in the interest of security for our hosts. In this interest also I shall avoid providing much description of the town but will take you straight to the house where we ended up. I'll even vague up my description of the house enough so that...hell, I'll describe it simply as a majestic old Victorian mansion that appeared well-kept on the outside, with neatly maintained grounds. There were a few trimmed shrubs on either side of the front entrance, two or three mature shade trees and a circle of flowers on the lawn about midway between house and sidewalk.

Doc parked the Indian on a concrete pad behind the house. He slipped the motorcycle between a small silver Toyota and a white Ford Ranger pickup, hopped off and motioned for me to bring the van around to the other side of the truck. As we prepared to start hoisting our prisoner out the van's side I became aware of a new presence, initially from a fresher scent than ours, some mix of spice and citrus with a friendly persistence that cut subtly through the merged odors of stale sweat, bad breath and superheated exhaust fumes swirling among us. I looked up and found myself face to face with one of the most startlingly magnetic women I had ever seen.

My first sensation, the one that arrested me, was her serenity. A relaxed composure that started in her face, large wide-set almond eyes that gazed into mine with a sleepy gravity that drew me effortlessly into her countenance. I became aware of my jaw muscles relaxing as I gaped. Her wondrous eyes beckoned from a canvas of perfect ivory skin gently arranged over a rectangular bone structure that allowed a broad forehead and gave her a strong jaw and chin. Full ruby lips under a comely nose dominated the central plane of her face that winged out and up

SACRIFICE

gracefully with just enough cheekbone to give light an interesting playground. Long shiny brown hair, parted at one side, cascaded down past her shoulders and framed her face in a way that suggested an Apache warrior's.

Somewhere in this suspension of volition, mesmerized by the visage before me, I realized that I might wish to say something, but no words came to mind. The woman whose face had captured me seemed to sense my dilemma, as she allowed the merest hint of a smile to tickle one corner of her mouth. This had the effect of unlocking my paralysis, but before I could speak a growl interrupted my little reverie.

"Hey, everybody! This is my daughter Mary Beth. She's a registered nurse. I've briefed her on what we have here. Let's get these boys inside."

Doc's introduction did more damage than interrupt my delighted daze, it reminded me that I was not only old enough to be the woman's father but, plausibly, old enough to be her grandfather. Made it easier for me to smile and nod and say, "Nice to meet you, Mary Beth," but with less mojo in my voice than I'd been hoping to conjure. She smiled mischievously at me then rotated her head and nodded several times as if taking in the others. "Hi, fellas," she said, then noticed Joan and gave her a little finger-wiggling wave and her own "Hi."

It was only then I noticed Mary Beth was dressed in baggy blue scrubs and pushing a wheelchair. Doc and Joan helped the prisoner off his cot and into the wheelchair. By now the man's expression of intense anxiety had diminished to one of fatigue. What worried me more was his pallor, that of a dead man. The leg with the bullet wound was bloodsoaked but evidently the tourniquet had stopped most of the bleeding, as there was no sign of dripping. Mary Beth adjusted a strap affixed to the wheelchair around his upper body, turned the chair around and rolled it up a ramp into the house. I watched them until they disappeared through the door.

Turning back to the van I saw Newgate was already out. Joan had one arm and he was bracing himself against the van with the other. "I'm alright," he croaked. "Just little stiff. Don't need no stinkin' wheelchair. Doc, that daughter of yours is gettin' prettier every day. If I were a little younger I might consider coming out of the woods for good."

This won nothing but another growl from Doc Bot. "Looks to me like you're already out for good. Somebody bombed your place, huh?"

The chatter continued until we were all inside, gathered in a kitchen-size examination room where Doc and his daughter eased the wounded man out of the chair and up onto the steel bed of an examination table, enduring some sharp barks of pain in the process. As Mary Beth began cutting the man's pants away from his leg Doc motioned us to follow him into an adjoining room furnished with cushioned chairs and small wooden sidetables topped with old magazines, clearly a waiting room. He found a footstool in a closet and brought it over to the chair Newgate had settled into. Doc lifted his friend's leg and lowered it gently onto the padded stool.

"You're on deck, Randy. Soon as we get this goofball stabilized you're next," he said.

I found it odd that nobody reached for any of the outdated magazines, and then I realized it would be odd if anybody did. I looked over up at Pink, sitting across from me, face still so bruised and puffy he'd have scared waiting patients in a regular doctor's office.

"Probably wanna wait to make that call, I guess," I said.

"Yeah. Doc's giving him less than fifty-fifty odds to make it. Said he's lost a lot of blood."

"You think she'll be able to get him to talk?"

"She knows the drill. Better than me."

I nodded, suddenly feeling exhausted and sleepy. Must have been about half an hour later when Doc came back from the examination room. "We got him here in the nick of time. I gambled whether to take the time to rig the van up with a plasma

SACRIFICE

drip or hope we could get him here before he bled out.

"I knew it was still dangerous out there for you guys. Figured your safety was my first priority..."

I interrupted, "So will he make it?"

He glared at me. "I said 'nick of time,' if you were listening. No way to know for sure, of course. Lot of things we don't know yet, but I'd say his odds are better." With that he turned and strode back to his patient.

MATHEW PAUST

BEST LAID PLANS

A wee dustup threatened while we discussed bringing Dr. Knoe to the house without detection by hostiles. Joan Stonebraker was the first to use the word "hostiles," and something about the word just then irritated me.

"What if we're the hostiles, Joan?"

Her response was instant, startling. "Inside job? I know. I've thought of that." Pink, who'd been bobbing his head and grinning, as if enjoying some private concert in his head, abruptly stopped the bobbing and lost the grin. We were in the kitchen eating a pizza Mary Beth's boyfriend, Jim, had brought us. Still chewing on a mouthful he'd just taken when he caught the swerve in our conversation, Pink turned on his stool and fixed his eyes on us — first on Joan, then on me, then back to Joan.

"Wha? Nogh Lighh!" he tried to say.

"Swallow your pizza and try again," Joan suggested. He chewed some more, swallowed, drank from a plastic bottle of water and wiped his mouth with his sleeve.

"I trust Liz!" he blurted. "I..." He seemed to choke, drank more water. "...I know her." His emphasis on know had a puzzled tone, as if more for his own benefit, and the intensity of his challenging glare seemed to waver.

"I know her, too, Pink," Joan said, "and I also trust her. But it's personal. We can't afford that luxury just now. And I'm not saying Dr. Knoe can't be trusted. We just have to be cautious."

Narrowing his eyes, Pink nodded slightly and turned back to the pizza in its cardboard box on the kitchen island. He tore off another piece and started it toward his mouth. His hand stopped midway and he turned to look at us again. "OK," he said, "so what

SACRIFICE

do we do? Waterboard her?" His voice was low but the tone sarcastic. Nobody laughed, not even as an excuse to break the tension, but I took advantage of the mood break.

"Joan, if we transfer her to our car – the van, I guess – won't that reduce the risk of anybody tracking her?"

"Unless she's carrying a hound. Somebody could have slipped it in her bag or even in a pocket."

"So we search her?"

"We really have no choice, Al. I wish I had a wand. It'll have to be manual."

"I guess that rules me out, then." My attempt at levity won a head-shake and half-grin from Joan. Pink nodded, deadpan, and returned to his lunch.

We decided I would drive the van, with Joan and Pink along in case we ran into trouble. We would wait until we were ready to roll for Pink to call Liz. Pink would do his teeheehee voice and pretend it was an obscene call, laughing loudly if she tried to speak his name in the hope she'd understand and listen for key words without giving anything away. She would know – everyone at The Cottage would know – that something serious was going on and the call was of vital importance. Pink would mention, cryptically, a place we picked from the state road map, identifying it by a couple of landmarks, and give her a time to meet us there. He said he would know by her reactions if she understood him and would comply. If she seemed completely baffled he would say straight out where to meet us and when. That would be a last resort, and Pink felt certain Liz was sufficiently astute to catch on without the need to go clear.

Either way, we figured once contact had been made we had a window of no more than two hours to get to the rendezvous location before any intelligence that might be picked up by surveillance of the conversation could be converted the into action in time to intercept us.

"The monitor would have to alert somebody up the chain and

then it would go to someone in intelligence for interpretation, if we can keep it cryptic enough," Joan explained. "It would have to be double-checked for any deliberately misleading directions we might have given her, which we can't afford to do because it will be hard enough as it is to get through to her. But they won't know that.

"Then comes the executive decision, maybe requiring a go-ahead from the client before any action is agreed upon. Alternatives: kill us there? Probly not as they won't know who will be with us. Remember, it's Pink they want dead. Track us back to here? Unless their instructions are to kill us if they recognize Pink – Pink, you'll have to wear a disguise – but tracking us back is a better bet for them either way if they can get a fix on us without being made. That would rule out helicopters or obvious pursuit vehicles, which we could shake if we spot them. Of course all this is idle speculation if Wilde Labs is behind this. They'll have Liz bugged or – sorry, Pink – she won't need a bug. We simply cannot afford to rule out any possibility."

Pink sighed. He nodded dejectedly. "That would mean Vulcana doesn't work," he said. "Or she lied to me about taking it."

"Or it might affect women differently," I said.

As it turned out, Dr. Knoe wasn't needed to bring our prisoner around. Doc Bot emerged from the examining room with a odd expression on his usually dour face. We'd been waiting for his word before calling Liz and setting our plan in motion. It made no sense to get Liz until we knew if the prisoner was going to live.

"Mr. Pinkerton," Doc grumbled. "We need you in here."

"Me?" Pink said, jerking his attention back from wherever it had wandered. Doc just stared at him. Pink slid off his stool, looked around and shrugged. "Why me?"

Doc growled again. "First of all, you all should know your prisoner, who tells us his name is Elliot Burke, is stable and fully conscious. Second, he's quite insistent he wants to see the man everyone calls 'Pink'. Third, your Mr. Burke has quite an insistent erection, and, no, his erection was not inspired by my daughter,

SACRIFICE

fortunately for him. It arose only after he started asking for you, Mr. Pinkerton. Get your candy ass in here right now."

MATHEW PAUST

ELLIOT BURKE

Doc Bot led Pink into the examination room, at the prisoner's request, after surprising us with his report that symptoms the prisoner was displaying – a "persistent" erection and confiding his name – indicated the injection of Vulcana he'd gotten before we transported him out of the woods was working. Doc remained with them about ten or so minutes while Joan and I finished the pizza and moved from the kitchen to the lounge area where I must have dozed off, having felt a sudden wave of fatigue once I settled into one of the cushioned chairs. Doc had said his daughter was in another room nearby tending to Newgate, whose ankle Doc still had not examined carefully enough to determine the extent of injury. He'd given his friend a shot of morphine to control the pain Newgate said was becoming steadily worse. Now Doc stuck his head into the lounge and motioned us over. He was smiling, which, with his bushy gray drooping mustache and perpetual grumpy disposition, gave him a grotesque appearance.

"Listen to him in there. The damned fool's telling his life story," he whispered as he led us through a hallway to the examination room door. We stopped just short of entering the room, standing back out of the light. Our prisoner, who called himself Elliot Burke, was sitting up in the hospital bed, waving his hands as he spoke, apparently oblivious of the tubes connecting him to several pieces of equipment including a bottle of something, presumably blood plasma or a nutritional cocktail. The sheet covering his lower body peaked upward as if draped over a small tent pole. Pink was hunched forward in a straight-back chair and appeared to be listening intently. Burke spoke rapidly in a medium-register voice with such little volume it was hard to make out what he was saying. Not that it mattered especially, as it seemed to be a recitation of his experiences in elementary school.

"...and so Mrs. Hanky told me I was supposed to be coloring in the

SACRIFICE

lines but I just couldn't seem to do that and the other kids were getting ahead of me and Priscilla's vegetables were perfect. I mean all her colors were inside the lines and her vegetables looked so real and mine looked so shitty I mean I knew mine were shitty and that Mrs. Hanky was gonna get mad at me and..."

I started to speak, wanting to get Pink's attention, but Joan shushed me and pulled me back from the doorway. If Burke saw us he gave no indication, seemingly intent only on dumping his entire memory on Pink and to hell with anything else.

"Jeezuz, Joan, this could go on forever. What the hell's he doing?" We were back in the lounge. I was flabbergasted.

"It took you two weeks to dump yours," she said quietly, and smiled when I turned to see if she might be joking, although a sudden surge of adrenalin through my abdomen suggested she was telling the truth.

Trying not to betray how shaken I was by this information, I took a deep breath, held it and slowly let it out before saying, "I don't remember anything like that, Joan."

"You wouldn't, Al. Vulcana brings about such drastic changes in your head that none of the test subjects so far has had any memory of this stage. We didn't know what to expect with you, as you were the first human test subject."

"So who sat with me...Jeezuz, what the fuck did I say? I can't believe this!"

Joan patted my arm. "Relax, Al. We took turns. Me and Ruth and Pink. I think Liz even sat with you awhile, too. You just rambled on and on. It's all on tape in case you want to hear it sometime." She was smiling so fully now I couldn't be sure she wasn't pulling my leg.

"Oh, my god. Did I talk about coloring vegetables in kinnygarten, too? Christ! I can't believe this!"

"Hey, buddy, easy does it. You were the..."

"Yeah, I know, the Neil Armstrong of Vulcana."

"More like the Charles Lindberg," Al. "Pink and Gladys have done quite a bit with it since then."

"Speaking of which..."

"I imagine Pink thinks this Elliot Burke character's his best bet to find out what happened to her. He probly is, too. Once he gets through dumping his memory banks we can get to the current stuff. If he lives long enough."

I furrowed my brow at Joan, realizing it was a tad melodramatic, but, hey, I was pretty hyped up from what I'd just learned about my debut with Vulcana or whatever the hell they were calling it when I swallowed a pill thinking it was Ritalin but which was in fact an experimental drug that somehow ended up accidentally in the vial I'd gotten from Wilde Labs when I was White House chief of staff. Allowing the word "accidentally" to be part of this discussion was more and more taking on an edge of sarcasm.

"Doc said he was stable," I said.

"For now. Who knows how long that will last?"

I stood and stretched, then started back toward the examination room. Joan followed. We stopped again at the open doorway. Burke was still gesticulating dramatically and Pink was still hunched on his chair.

"...So Mr. Carleton ratted me out to my mother for what? For talking in his goddam class? What the fuck's with that, Mr. Carleton, you fucking ape asshole? So you fuck me with my mother who has a bad heart and she damn near has a fucking heart attack whupping my ass after fucking Mr. Carleton tells her I was TALKING IN HIS FUCKING CLASS!! I mean, shit, man, what the fuck..."

Joan and I looked at each other. She shrugged. I started to say something. Don't remember what. She shushed me and tapped my lips with her finger. We went back to the lounge.

SACRIFICE

LONG STRANGE TRIP

Elliot Burke's purging lasted nearly three weeks. Pink took periodic breaks so both he and Burke could rest. He said Burke would speak only to him.

"I'm the only one he trusts now but that should change after he evolves more. I feel like I'm trying to babysit something feral, like a wolf."

The strain took its toll on Pink, turning his rust-orange hair white and leaving him weak, with palsied hands and in a daze so worrisome Doc Bot considered having him hospitalized.

"He's not leaving my sight," Joan said. Her voice was calm, yet it held the trademark flat, unyielding tone of her Secret Service authority.

Bot shrugged. He was slumped in a folding chair next to the bed where Pink was hooked to a transfusion of nutrients. Bot look frazzled, too. "Tell you what, Ms. Stonebraker," he growled. "I'm still the doctor here, unless something happened to change that while I was in the can taking a shit. But here I am, still the only one wearing a scope around my neck, so I'm duty bound, just like you in your professional capacity, duty bound to do what I deem in my professional judgment to be the best for my patient."

"You saved Burke's life and set Mr. Newgate's ankle. Didn't need a hospital for that. Why now do you suddenly decide Pink has to go to the hospital?"

"Because I'm not trained as a psychiatrist."

"What? Psychiatrist? There's nothing wrong with Pink that a little rest can't fix," she said. Her voice had risen a couple of decibels.

"Oh, so now you're the doctor! Well, whattaya know!" The words carried sarcasm but his voice croaked wearily.

I felt I should say something at this point, and Joan must have sensed my building tension, as she reach a hand out and patted my forearm. I took this as a signal I should keep my mouth shut. I didn't.

"Doc, goddammit, we know Pink a helluva lot better than you do. Don't you think your hair woulda turned white if you had to sit and listen to that guy tell his life story for three weeks? I know I'd be a basket case.

"We tried to spell Pink, take turns like they did with me, but Burke wouldn't have it. He doesn't know us, any of us. Pink said he'd imprinted on him because Pink was the only one who talked to him in the woods after the shot. The Vulcana."

"Imprinted, huh? Geddes, for chrissake the guy's in love with your Pink. We might have to have a wedding here before this is over. We can do that. Mary Beth's boyfriend is a licensed preacher. He can do the job when he's in town..."

Bot suddenly started laughing, stopped after a couple of guffaws when he saw neither I nor Joan were joining him.

Joan said, "Pink said Burke apologized for the erection. Insisted he's not gay. Pink says it's what happens with males on Vulcana, that eventually you can will it down, or up as needed."

Bot sputtered a half-guffaw. "How old have you gone with your test subjects?"

"You'll have to ask Pink, but Al's taken a prototype. You're about the same age."

Bot turned his hirsute face to me. "Well?"

"It works." I didn't feel like trying to think of anything else to say. Bot coughed and returned to the subject.

"I'll call a psychiatrist friend and have him come here. That OK with you?"

Joan shook her head. "No dice, Doc. No psychiatrist. Pink's no danger to anyone. He's probly smarter than any shrink, anyway."

SACRIFICE

Bot waved us out of the room. Pink called us back.

"Joan!" The voice was weak, higher pitched than usual. He was trying to sit up, reaching with his free hand, but fell back into the pillows when he saw us approaching. "I think Bubby will talk to you now," he said.

"Bubby?"

"Elliot. That's what he's called. Please...please get him to tell you about Gladys."

My turn: "If he wouldn't tell you, Pink, what makes you think he'd tell us?"

Pink reached his hand out, groping at the bedside shelf. "Water?" he croaked. Joan went into an adjoining bathroom, I heard water running. She returned with a paper cup and gave it to Pink. He put the cup to his lips, took a couple of sips and tossed the rest down gulping greedily, and dropped the empty cup on the bed. "He started worrying about me," he said. "Said he was afraid I was too sick to go on." He closed his eyes, seemed to be going to sleep, but a moment later he continued, "He'll talk to you guys now, if Doc will let him. Bubby's pretty weak, too."

I looked at Bot. He nodded and stood. "Let's give it a try," he said.

MATHEW PAUST

I KNOW NOTHING

Somehow Elliot Burke managed to put me at ease soon as we stepped into the room. The eyes were different. The feral glare had morphed into something less threatening, eyes now sparkling with something more complex and human. Most encouraging was the smile, a tad shy, giving the face a look of welcoming relief. The erection was gone.

Joan and I stared at him from the doorway. I tried to think of something to say, hoping Joan might save me the trouble. What might be best? A simple hello? Call him by name? Identify ourselves? Was this to be adversarial or exploratory? A combination of both? What was he like? Burke broke the curtain of ice.

"Come in. Have a seat." His mid-range voice sounded vaguely raspy, a tad hoarse, I suspect, from the marathon monologue he's just concluded with Pink. The tone was pleasant. We walked to the two folding chairs next to the bed. I found myself almost tiptoeing, although Burke appeared fully awake. He was sitting up, resting his back against several pillows. The intravenous tubes had been removed, although a pulse monitor was still taped to a finger. I found it mildly disconcerting that his eyes seemed to have been fixed on mine since we entered the room. After we sat, he shifted his gaze to Joan.

"I guess you have some questions for me," he said, making it a statement rather than a question of his own.

I was still trying to think of something to say, this time hoping for something to set an upbeat climate, when Joan asked, "How do you feel?"

"Exhausted, but fairly comfortable," Burke said.

From Pink's quick summary we knew Burke was a former Army

SACRIFICE

Ranger who mustered out after spending a year in the top secret Joint Special Operations Command. Bored after a couple of years trying to assimilate back into civilian life he signed on with Chesapeake Security. He led the three-man team that ambushed Joan and Pink as they emerged from the woods. After our exchange of pleasantries wound down I decided to go first with the hardball questions.

"So. Who hired you to kill Pink?"

Burke shot me a game face and then let it relax into a cryptic smile. "I can't really say, Mr. Geddes." He watched me as my eyebrows undoubtedly pushed wrinkles into my forehead. It's a gesture I usually employ only half-consciously. There was a time, in my early twenties, when I worked fairly diligently trying to train my face muscles to enable me to lift only one eyebrow, leaving the other grounded. I desired this skill in the interest of projecting a semblance of mature, discerning, superior intelligence. That I failed has ever since nibbled subtly at my self-image despite an understanding the inability stems from a minor lack of motor-skill coordination, of no greater significance than tone deafness, color blindness or math illiteracy. The bounce of his eyes told me my eyebrow jig had registered, leaving the ball in his court. He either wasn't playing or his failure to speak signified an attempt to hijack the rhythm I'd imposed. He out-waited me, which seemed a tad soon considering we were still in the warmup stage. I responded with more boilerplate.

"Can't or won't?" I said with a grim glare, giving voice to a sigh and allowing my face and upper body to sag in accompaniment as if settling in for needless tedium with a stubborn, precocious child.

"Both," he said, conveying a note of surprise that I hadn't anticipated the possibility. He twisted toward us under the sheet. His eyes were wide, his own eyebrows raised, yet not seeming to mock mine. He seemed earnest. As if to emphasize this perception, he continued, "So far as I know I'm still under contract to Chesapeake. In any case our contracts contain standard confidentiality agreements binding for five years after termination of employment.

"But even without that I can't tell you who hired the mission because that wasn't included in my orders. That's standard also. Team leaders routinely do not have a need to know."

Joan joined the conversation: "Who would have that information?"

"Somebody way above my pay grade. Client identities are pretty privileged information. Chesapeake is a tight ship. Very military in structure."

"Anybody besides SS?" Joan was referring to Chesapeake's secretive CEO, Sean Seawell. She knew very few people outside Chesapeake were aware his people called him that. Burke smiled in appreciation.

"Oh, I'm sure," he said, "But not many. Kelleher, maybe." Still smiling, he studied her face. He had named the security company's operations chief, whose identity was known to very few in the intelligence community. The company listed him in its records under a pseudonym.

Joan winced, shook her head and emitted a grunt. "I should hope so," she said.

She tried a new tack: "What can you tell us about Gladys Alabi?"

"Pink has already asked me about her," Burke said.

"And?"

"I told him the truth. I had never heard the name."

SACRIFICE

FALLBACK PLAN

Joan and I took a break after about an hour with Burke without getting anything useful from him. We went to the kitchen and found that someone had brewed a fresh pot of coffee. I poured a cup for each of us, Joan added creamer and sweetener to hers and we carried them into the waiting area and the comfortable chairs.

"He seems cooperative," I said after taking a sip of the hot liquid and waiting long enough to give Joan a chance to speak first. She hadn't seemed eager to say anything.

"He's gaming us."

"How can you tell?"

"Well, what has he given us we can use? Anything?"

"Doesn't mean he's holding out, Joan. He hasn't seemed at all evasive."

"We haven't given him anything to evade. Because all we know is what he told us about himself and that he attacked us in the woods."

"Maybe we're not playing him right."

"Like what? How should we be playing him?" I waited while she took a deep breath, sighed deeply and stretched, reminding me of feminine charms she rarely went out of her way to bring into play. She caught me looking and saw my grin. "Uh oh, this way?" She laughed and dropped her arms. "You're not suggesting..."

"Hey, I didn't say anything. But anything's worth a try, no? Maybe we should bring Pink back in." Joan shook her head. "I mean, just to talk with him, for us to talk with him. Maybe we need to know more about how this drug works. You know?"

"I agree we're probably over our heads with him, Al, but I think we need someone with more insight into where his head is than Pink. I know you and Pink have both taken Vulcana. We didn't seem to notice any difference in you, although you went through some incredible stress. That might have been unprecedented for you so we could only guess how you would have handled yourself had you not taken it. Pink's a research chemist. We need somebody with training in psychology."

"You told Doc Pink was smarter than any psychologist."

"I did, didn't I. What I didn't tell him was I think Pink is smarter than the average psychologist. I didn't want somebody we don't know getting involved in this."

"I'm with you there, Joan. So that leaves only one person I know who fits the right profile."

"Yep. We need to get Liz out here ASAP."

"Back to the trust thing, then. We could be sitting in the crosshairs here." Joan nodded, staring at something on the wall across the room, her face grim, shoulders slumped.

We sipped coffee and mulled the situation, suspending talk. At the time I felt vague disappointment she didn't disagree with my comment about being able to trust Dr. Knoe, because I wasn't sure I wasn't simply being overly cautious. I started wondering if I'd read too many spy novels or watched too many TV series about spies and terrorists and drug dealers and double agents and had simply incorporated those fictional suspense techniques into my expectations.

Realistically if we were being used by Wilde Labs and Dr. Knoe was either in with them or being used, too, unwittingly, we were screwed. If Dr. Knoe was in with them it meant Vulcana's civilizing properties weren't all they were cracked up to be, at least not for females. But what choice did we have? I was thinking myself into a fatalistic acceptance, knowing it might be a fatal mistake but feeling trapped, like a lab rat in a maze with only one way out.

"Let's call her," I said.

SACRIFICE

Joan nodded: "I don't see any alternative."

And so we did, as we'd planned earlier. Pink called, using one of Newgate's disposable cellphones. Pink spoke briefly in what seemed to be a shorthand code. He handed the phone to Joan, who set up the rendezvous site.

"We don't have time for the decoy drill," she said after flipping the phone shut. "C'mon, Al, you drive the van. Pink, you stay here. If things go south I don't want you in harm's way. You'll be safer here."

"Isn't it more dangerous without the decoys?" I said, feeling a tad miffed she hadn't consulted me before deciding.

She looked at me with surprised eyes. "Maybe, maybe not. I've been thinking about what you mentioned before, that Wilde might be behind this thing. It seemed crazy at first, but it's starting to make sense. Not much is known about Vulcana outside Wilde Labs, and what is known is pretty sketchy, more rumor than substance. Certainly not enough to launch so bold an operation. Not yet, anyway. I think you're probably right, Al. Somebody at Wilde has an ulterior agenda. It's the most plausible explanation at the moment."

"No one you can trust on Cromwell's staff?"

"Yeah, he has a couple good people. I trust Anthony, too, but the kind of decoy operation we would need to make it worthwhile would involve too many people to keep it secure."

"Her cellphone safe?"

"Probably not, but Pink was careful. He disguised his voice and pretended to be some professor inviting her to a conference. He mentioned something that told her instantly who was calling. I pretended to be his secretary. We're good."

Indeed, the plan went off without a hitch. We met Dr. Knoe at an interstate truckstop where she left her car and rode back in the van.

She was striking as ever, her eyes penetrating mine with their puzzling intensity. We shook hands, which sent an electric thrill through my nervous system. Then she embraced Joan, or, rather, Joan embraced her. Anyway, they embraced, a tad longer than my comfort level accepted, and they spoke softly to each other and peered into each others eyes. The electric thrill drifted from my libido.

SACRIFICE

GETTING DOWN

Dr. Elizabeth Knoe accomplished two things as she launched her involvement with deciphering Elliot Burke. In the van on our way to the house she assured Joan and me she shared our suspicion of Wilde Laboratories and that she had taken precautions to avoid anyone from The Cottage or associated with Wilde tracking her electronically.

"It's an ultrasonic transmitter," she said, holding up her wrist to display a razor-thin digital watch held in place by an elegant gold braided band. She sat in the front next to Joan, who had taken over the driving in the event we needed some fancy maneuvering to elude a hot pursuit. "No one at Wilde knows I have this, not even Anthony," she added. "An old...um, friend who worked at the Pentagon gave it to me as a birthday present. Said the average person had no idea how much surveillance there is spying on us, it's everywhere. He said this might come in handy some day." She laughed, a light, innocent sound, before turning her head a couple of degrees further to include me. Sitting directly behind the driver's seat, I smiled at those electric eyes and felt myself begin to relax.

"Jams the signal?" I asked. A pure guess, from a vast ignorance of even such basic electronic gizmos as TV remotes.

"Not sure how it works, but my friend said it can actually change the signal of a tracking transmitter so it appears frozen, like it's not moving. You can turn it on and off with this little button so they think their hound dog – that's what they call the trackers – is working, and when it stops they think that's where you are.

"This was off when I left The Cottage, and I turned it on when I parked the company car and joined you guys."

"Too bad we didn't know this, Liz. I could've stayed awhile at the truck stop to see if anybody showed up," I said.

Joan laughed and caught my eye in the mirror. "Got it covered, Al. Mary Beth's boyfriend followed us up on Newgate's motorcycle. He's got the car staked out right now. You know, what really gripes me is that here's another example of how we keep getting short shrift. The Secret Service, I mean. Our budget's a fraction of what we need, our technology's obsolete...I didn't even know about this sonic transmitter Liz has, never knew it existed. Can you believe it? I'm protecting a former president and all I have is a goddam sidearm. Well, I keep a shotgun in the trunk, but that's from the Nixon presidency. We've been a goddam stepchild ever since Bush 43 put us under Homeland Security. We get shit the FBI wouldn't waste spit on. Sorry, rant's over."

I saw Dr. Knoe lean toward Joan and extend her arm. I saw it jiggle several times as she patted Joan. Then the arm returned and she straightened in her seat. I considered commenting on Joan's complaint about the underfunding her service received, but this was old news. She'd mentioned it several times in the White House. Ruth tried to intervene when she was president but ran into a bureaucratic minefield she quickly realized would have taken too much time and energy to navigate. Instead she diverted funds at her disposal for executive expenses to ensure that Joan and her protective team had the equipment they needed. I settled back in the seat and napped the rest of the way.

Back at the house, Dr. Knoe called a meeting of all the occupants, quickly establishing she was in charge. Even Doc Bot, whose house she was commandeering and whom I heard grumbling to Newgate, "Where in hell does she think she is," albeit appearing to do so reluctantly, fell under the charm of her professionally assuming manner and amazing blue eyes. She kept the meeting brief, introducing herself and exchanging a few pleasant words with each of the others she was meeting for the first time and then explaining to all why she was there. What was most surprising to me was her holding the meeting in the room with Elliot Burke, addressing him as respectfully and cordially as everyone else. When she'd finished and people started filing out she held me and Joan back.

SACRIFICE

"You two stay. We don't want Elliot to think we're playing good cop-bad cop with him, do we?" She smiled at Burke when she said this.

Burke's erection had returned, almost immediately upon Dr. Knoe's entering his room. It had the same effect as earlier of creating a small tent with part of his sheet. It was also obvious Burke had no intention of trying to hide it. Dr. Knoe chose to address this situation as soon as the three of us we were alone with him.

"Mr. Burke, ordinarily I should be flattered if not flustered by your show of affection here," she nodded at the little tent, "but for several reasons I am not." As Burke opened his mouth to speak, she continued, cutting him off at the raspy start of presumably a word. "First, the drug you've been given has this effect on all males, even mice. I understand your first erection here was in the presence of Dr. Pinkerton — not that I don't consider myself in excellent company, both professionally and personally, with Dr. Pinkerton, but you must agree that unless there is some gender confusion in your own mind, having the same libidinous effect in my presence as Dr. Pinkerton's takes a bit of the blush off the significance of your response." Burke was grinning sheepishly. Dr. Knoe continued, "In addition, I'm well aware that my unusual eyes have an almost hypnotic effect on most people. It's a phenomenon I've experienced ever since puberty and, while allowing me certain societal privileges it also has been somewhat a burden.

"Therefore, rest assured that although without a doubt under more advantageous circumstances you are a striking figure of a man, attractive and virile and perhaps even any woman's dream of an ideal mate, I was not, I am not flirting with you and I now respectfully ask that you allow your libido to do the decent thing so we may discuss important matters."

"Darlin' Dr. Knoe...Is that really your name?" Burke was smiling now. Dr. Knoe, poker faced, kept her gaze aimed directly at his eyes as she slowly nodded. "Yes, it is," she said, "And please don't try the 'Bond, James Bond' bullshit with me, Elliot. I've heard it a million times and I would hope you were cooler than the average dickhead I run across."

Still smiling, Burke said, "Oh, no, Dr. Knoe, I wouldn't dream of acting the dickhead with you. I just wasn't sure I'd heard you right. No, no, Dr. Knoe. I did wish to say, however, with your indulgence of course, that my erection is not directed at you personally. Damned thing just popped up by itself. In my condition, not knowing how long I might have to live and all, I just want to enjoy any little pleasure that comes my way. I hope you won't begrudge me that."

Dr. Knoe's face softened with amusement, and a mischievous sparkle danced in her laser eyes. She gave him a small smile. "That's OK, Elliot. I just didn't want you to get the wrong idea."

Almost immediately the little tent pole wavered, as if struggling against gale force winds, and slowly, incrementally withdrew its support until it brought the tent down with it.

SACRIFICE

CAN'T STOP NOW

Our first sign the knots in Burke's mind might loosen came with his response to the first question from Dr. Knoe, employing the interrogation equivalent of sailing a boomerang at a fleeing wallaby.

Her question: "Do you have any questions of us?" Burke's face crinkled in puzzlement. He squirmed under the sheet in his hospital bed and looked from Dr. Knoe to Joan, to me and back to Dr. Knoe.

"Yeah," he said. "What's that stuff you gave me, anyway? That drug?"

"What makes you think we gave you a drug?"

Burke rocked his head back into his pillows and rolled it from one side to the other. He grimaced when a kink in his neck cracked, then let his face relax. "Look," he said, his voice calm, patient, "I've had my share of morphine, OK? I know what morphine can do. What I feel now is not from morphine. I've done my share of acid, OK? I do feel a little like I've felt after an intense acid trip. But my head is clear. My head is clearer than it's ever been. Clear in a steady way, not with the herky jerky rushes I've had with amphetamines. Yeah, I've done speed. Probly every drug you could name...the sodiums, pentothal and amytal... oh yeah, done 'em.

"None of 'em have ever made me feel like I feel right now. So I know you've given me something and it's pretty cool. I'd like to know what it is."

"Not a problem," Dr. Knoe said and gave him a rundown, noting that she, Pink and I had also taken Vulcana.

"So now I'm supposed to have a conscience, that it?" he said,

"Join up with the angels?"

"I'm not really sure what to expect, Elliot. We don't know a lot about it yet, how it affects different people, different types. You're the first...um..."

"Bad guy?" He laughed, and I did, too. Couldn't help myself.

"Well, relatively speaking, I guess you could say that. You did try to kill Pink," Dr. Knoe said.

"Our orders were to take out Pink and anybody with him. No witnesses." He nodded at Joan and murmured, "Sorry, ma'am." I couldn't see Joan's face but I saw her shake her head.

She said, "Either your heart wasn't in it, Elliot, or you weren't on top of your game, thank goodness."

"Well, ma'am, you were pretty slick with that little Sig. Fact, I've never seen anybody shoot that fast. Guess I'm lucky to be alive." This time I saw her cheek bunch up a tad on my side in what I assumed was a smile.

Dr. Knoe jumped in to take back control of the interview: "So, yes, Elliot, you are without a doubt the first bad guy to be given Vulcana. This makes you our most..." Loud voices outside the room preceded a pounding on the door.

"Bot here. I'm coming in." The door swung open and Doc Bot stood in the entrance silhouetted by the hallway's brighter lights. "Jim called," he blurted. "Couple guys checking out the car at the truckstop. Wants to know what to do."

Joan jumped up and strode to the door. "You still have him?"

"Whattaya mean?"

"Is he still on the line? I need to talk to him!"

"Sorry, darlin', he hung up. Said it was two guys, came in the same kinda car he was watchin'. Crown Vic, he said. He got the license number. Here, I wrote it down." He handed Joan a slip of paper.

Joan turned to Burke, "You guys drive Crown Vics?"

SACRIFICE

"We always rent operational vehicles, ma'am. Usually try to get SUVs. We had an Escape for this mission."

"How ironic. Where'd you leave it?"

"Fire trail. About a mile away. We pounded in to the target site."

"GPS?"

"Oh, sure. They'll be looking for us by now."

"Great. Don't go anywhere," she said, backing out of the room. Burke lifted a hand and wiggled his fingers.

We gathered in Doc Bot's office, where Newgate was seated behind Doc's computer, his foot in a cast. Mary Beth wanted to come with us but her father vetoed the notion before we had the opportunity.

"Gonna need you here, Sweet Pea. Jim'll be OK. He'll pray the Devil away."

"Dad!" Bot's face cracked into a grin so alien to his normal mien it was hideous with its suggestion of mean sarcasm. Nonetheless it elicited a warm smile from Mary Beth, but only after she stuck her tongue out at him.

Joan, in full command mode, decided we would be less conspicuous in Mary Beth's Toyota Camry. "If they're from Wilde they would expect us to be in an SUV," she said. "If Chesapeake sent them, same thing. I'm surprised they're not driving one, except maybe they don't want to be conspicuous either."

"I'm surprised they don't have a massive search out for us by now," I said. "We've been missing nearly a month."

"Not if they're behind it," said Joan, "Or even if they aren't, if they think The Cottage is under attack. They'd be circling the wagons."

"You're losing me. Who would attack The Cottage?"

"That's a good question, but maybe somebody thinks Pink is still there, say, thinking we sent a decoy out to lead them away...but I agree that's pretty far-fetched."

"Oh yeah. All that for a better Viagra? I don't think so."

"Never underestimate greed, Al. If all Vulcana is is a better Viagra or that's what people think, we could have a war on our hands. If word got out what we think Vulcana can do besides that, we will have a war. Guaranteed."

Newgate tapped his keyboard decisively and rolled his chair around. "If I tell you who that license tag's registered to, can I try that stuff?"

"Vulcana?" I said, "Having menopausal issues Newgate?"

"Nah. I'm just looking for a heart. It's a rental."

"The car?"

"No, Geddes, my ticker."

Joan asked, "Agency?"

"Avis. No telling where from."

Joan to me: "Wilde uses National. Maybe it is Chesapeake."

"Only one way to find out," I said.

Joan got the car keys and Jim's cellphone number from Mary Beth, and we were off.

SACRIFICE

NOBODY DOESN'T LOVE A PARADE

Events broke fast when we reached the truckstop. The place was hopping. Twice as many or more cars than when we'd met Dr. Knoe there mid-morning. In the adjoining lot stood the same armada of big rigs or their identical twins, reefer trucks among them adding to the neighborhood din with engines idling to keep the coolers chilled. We were far enough below the interstate so the only sounds to reach us from its streaming traffic were an occasional miniaturized blast of a horn, the brum of a revving motorcycle or the descending pitch of engine strain in a downshifting truck.

Dr. Knoe's car was still parked where she'd left it but there was no sign of another Crown Vic or anybody near the car showing an interest in it. We parked next to the Indian, got out and walked closer to the antique bike as if admiring it. The muted thump of closing car doors drew my attention to a Buick Century station wagon that had disgorged a family with children two rows away. As I brought my eyes back across to the bike I saw someone who looked familiar.

"I know that guy, Joan," I said quietly, tilting my face slightly toward a man wearing baggy jeans and an untucked Hawaiian shirt. He was standing three cars away from the wagon. I quickly looked back at the bike and pointed at the speed gauge on the handlebars. Joan feigned interest in the gauge, as well, but stole a sly glance sideways at the man I'd indicated. She grabbed my wrist.

"It's Ashmore!" she said, rubbing her other hand next to her nose to help muffle her voice. Instantly it came together for me: Roger Ashmore, the renegade Secret Service agent nabbed while trying to abduct Ruth in the secret Rose Garden sting operation, working for the corrupt special prosecutor in a plot to discredit Ruth and destroy her presidency.

"What the hell? Is he still an agent?" I was trying to whisper but my voice started breaking through.

"Let's get inside, find Jim," Joan said, tugging my arm and keeping her face turned away from Ashmore. I did the same. As we approached the plate glass windows on either side of the entrance I could see by Ashmore's reflection he evidently hadn't noticed us. He seemed to be waiting for someone in the car he was standing beside, a Crown Vic.

Inside, the restaurant was abuzz with jovial voices amid the clink and clatter of tableware. Crisply uniformed waitresses bustled among the tables with trays of food trailing enticing aromas from the kitchen. Three other waitresses worked methodically between an open portal to the kitchen and a French-curved counter serving individual diners who perched on stools and planted their forearms on either side of their plates.

We entered to find half a dozen people just inside the entrance waiting to be seated. Joan spotted Jim at a table along one of the windows with a clear view of Dr. Knoe's Crown Vic. We joined him and ordered coffee.

"See that guy out there with the Hawaiian shirt?" Joan said.

Jim nodded. "He's one of them. Other one's still in the car."

"They done anything since we called?"

"Not really. Just keeping an eye on the car from where they are now. They ate a quick lunch in here before I saw them by the car. That's when I called you." Jim was a nice looking kid...I call him a kid, but he was, I'd say, mid-thirties, with a youthful face. He had all of his hair, brown and wavy, a little long, which added to his youthful appearance. He'd seemed friendly when we met him at the house. He was friendly now.

"So, Jim, should we be calling you Reverend?" He laughed, a pleasant easy laugh.

"That's just a joke, Mr. Geddes. I'm always talking philosophy and quoting poetry. Mary Beth's dad started calling me 'reverend' for the hell of it, I guess. It stuck."

SACRIFICE

This is when I heard an unusual strain of music. It didn't seem to fit the ambience of Ruckman's Oasis, and I looked around to try to see where it was coming from. Jim held up his cellphone and the strain became louder. Jim was smiling. "Mozart's Requiem," he said and peered at the lighted screen of his device. "It's Mary Beth." He put the piece to his ear. Soon his face grew concerned. He muttered something and handed the phone to me.

Mary Beth's voice was calm and deliberate, which did not reconcile with the information she conveyed. "Mr. Geddes?" I assured her I was he. "Well, Mr. Burke has escaped."

"What? Can you say that again, Mary Beth?" I tried to keep my voice as calm as hers.

"Yes, sir. Mr. Burke got hold of a gun, we think, and he's taken Dr. Knoe and Mr. Pink with him. They drove off in the van."

"Mary Beth, how long ago did this happen?"

"Just now. They just now drove off."

"Nobody got hurt, did they?"

"Not that I know of, Mr. Geddes. Mr. Burke pointed the gun at Dr. Knoe and told her to help him get to the van. He said he wouldn't hurt anybody if they did what he said."

"Did he say where he was going?"

"No, sir. They just got in the van and left."

"OK, thank you, Mary Beth. We can't talk any more right now, but please tell your father and Mr. Newgate that Joan and I and Jim will be back just as soon as we can. And we'll let you know if anything changes, OK?" I handed the phone to Jim but shook my head and motioned for him to turn it off. He spoke softly into the phone and then did something to it and returned it to a pocket in his pants. It rang again, but he ignored it.

After I explained to Joan what had happened she immediately took charge, handing out instructions as if she'd planned them well in advance.

"OK, here's what we are going to do," she said. "Jim, Al and I are going to confront those two men outside. I'm pretty sure...I'm positive they are going to run as soon as they see us approach. If they don't and something happens, a fight or even if you see guns and hear shots, keep your head down and wait until it's over. I don't want you getting hurt, OK?" Jim nodded. He started to speak, but Joan held up a hand and continued.

"Now, assuming they do run, I'm going to follow them in Dr. Knoe's car, and I want you to follow me on the motorcycle, OK? They will try to outrun me, and I will let them and at some point I will pull off the road. I will make it look as if I have lost control. I'll park the car and then you will take over following them. They won't be expecting a motorcycle tail, but still I want you to stay far enough behind them so they won't get suspicious. Stay just close enough to keep them in sight, OK?" Jim nodded several times throughout these instructions to indicate he understood them.

"And I'll be driving Mary Beth's car, I presume?" I said.

"Correct. I'll wait for you to come along behind the motorcycle. We'll take both cars to the nearest rest stop or gas station or someplace safe we can leave the Camry, then we'll take the Crown Vic."

"And?"

"I think I know where Burke's going." She arose from the table, adjourning the meeting. I put some money down and Joan and I headed for the parking lot. Joan motioned for Jim to stay at the table until we knew what Ashmore and his partner would do.

Joan, of course, had guessed correctly. We strode purposefully toward the car the two men had driven. Ashmore had gotten back in with his partner. Joan had her badge out and was holding it in front of her. I wasn't carrying mine, but I held up my wallet instead. I did have the revolver she'd given me, and I reached into my side pocket and gripped its handle just in case the two rogues decided to take us on. They didn't. We'd gotten to within about ten feet of their Crown Vic when the engine suddenly belched out a roar and the powerful car wheeled from its space, tires

SACRIFICE

screeching and smoking across the asphalt, and headed for the exit.

Joan ran to Dr. Knoe's car, clicking it open with the key holder remote as she reached it, and soon she was peeling across the parking lot in hot pursuit. I turned back to the truckstop to find Jim walking casually to the Indian, big grin on his face as if nothing unusual were happening. He hopped on the motorcycle, kicked it to life and rumbled on out to the interstate ramp. My walk to the Camry seemed anticlimactic and my exit wasn't nearly so dramatic, but soon I, too, was in this frantic parade, bringing up the rear.

MATHEW PAUST

CAVEAT EMPTOR

Driving the stealth car in this fake-chase/ghost-tail fandango was like being the ball carrier in a football delay play, waiting for the other players to do their thing to open the way for you to do yours. Gave me time to enjoy the odd mix of sensations – excitement that we were finally within striking range of proving who had hired the mercenaries, and relief that the burden of trying to save humanity from itself was no more. This last because Elliot Burke had just proven Vulcana wasn't the wonder drug we'd thought it was. Maybe it enhanced the better natures of people who already accepted and trusted the concept of a social contract, like me and Pink and probably Dr. Knoe, but now it seemed its effect on sociopaths simply enhanced their sociopathy in addition to giving them the power to will an erection up and down. If it turned Burke into an even more dangerously amoral monster than he'd been I could only imagine the havoc it would create if slipped into the martinis of "lords of the oligarchy," as Ruth liked to call the megamoney barons who ruled our government from behind their platinum curtains.

I waited until Jim had roared up the interstate ramp on Newgate's Indian and disappeared before I guided the Camry up the same ramp and accelerated until I was able to edge smoothly into the sporadic flow of mid-afternoon traffic. I squinted my eyes against the unapologetic sun in a vain search for the motorcycle, smiling when I spotted one and grunting when a closer look revealed it to be a Harley with a shapely female rider. I wasn't worried. My job was simply to drive until I saw Joan's Crown Vic parked somewhere beside the road and join her there, work out a plan with her for the next leg and then drive both cars to a place we could leave the Camry and proceed in the Ford to where Joan thought Burke and his hostages would be. Simple enough for someone like me, untrained in police procedures, to follow.

SACRIFICE

The notion of both Crown Vics and even the Indian leaving the interstate without my knowledge had just pushed into my thinking, making me wish we had some way to communicate, when I spotted a car the same dusty maroon as the bandits' Vic barreling toward me in the opposite lane passing every car in front of it. Sure enough, about six car-lengths behind it I caught glimpses of another car snaking through the slower traffic evidently in hot pursuit. I didn't see Jim, and hoped he'd also made the turnabout. The grass median was so narrow at this point that as the maroon Vic neared I could see a sunlit swath of the yellow and red Hawaiian shirt shouting through the windshield. I rolled down my window, reached my arm out and thrust my middle finger at the driver, catching the surprise on his face as we passed. For a moment's flicker I half-hoped he would lose control and wreck, instantly chastising myself for both thought and gesture. The whole point of our pursuit tactic was to track the bastards back to their nest. Other than the visceral satisfaction, watching them wreck would be pointless. I expelled a sigh of relief to see in my mirror the maroon Vic's driver evidently had weathered my withering insult and was managing to keep his car on the road.

After Joan passed I started looking for a crossover so I could get in the opposite lane, too. Just as I found one and turned off my lane, Jim roared past on the Indian, reassuring me our plan was holding together. Although Joan apparently had not seen the Camry, Jim recognized his girlfriend's car and held a hand up in salute. I got in behind him and let him drift ahead, extending the distance between us, but this time decided to keep him in sight in case our quarry tried another maneuver to lose Joan. We were coming up on a series of exits to U.S. 17, a likely detour for someone seeking more options for ditching a tail.

I assumed this is what happened when, only several minutes later, I saw the Indian peel off and head down an exit ramp about a quarter mile ahead. I followed and reached the bottom of the ramp in time to see the motorcycle disappear around a curve heading south on 17. I heard tires squealing as I entered the curve, and came out to find Joan's Crown Vic stopped crosswise in the median under a cloud of rising dust, hood aimed at my lane. I pulled off the road to the right to keep from being seen by the bandits if they were watching the spinout. I assumed Joan had done it where she knew they could see her, and I regretted having flipped off the bastards from a car they now surely would recognize. I parked on the shoulder and waited for her to climb out, look up the road after the others and give me a thumbs up when they were out of sight. I left the Camry on the shoulder and ran across to the median, admiring the arcing skid marks her Vic had left as she spun the car off the road.

I followed her as we drove north on 17. We left the Camry behind a Days Inn where I booked a room as cover and as a possible hideout should we need a place to gather our wits later before heading back to the house. Without taking the time to even check out our room we gassed up the Crown Vic and headed to the site where Burke's team had ambushed Joan and Pink.

"You think he took them there?" I asked.

"I think he lied to us about the GPS. Just a hunch, but I think he's after something in that SUV."

We were less than an hour away.

SACRIFICE

CATCH MY DRIFT

I drove the Crown Vic to the ambush site. Joan had tossed me the keys without a word after we rented the motel room. She climbed into the passenger side, her face drawn and haggard. She sagged for a moment against the door before struggling half-heartedly into her seatbelt.

"You think Pink's one of them?" I said, trying to inject energy into my voice to counter the sense of defeat Joan conveyed.

"I think Gladys is. I've never trusted her." Her voice was flat and she didn't bother to look at me. I waited for more, and when it became apparent she was finished speaking, I said, "Why?"

Now she turned her head and looked at me. She was frowning and one side of her mouth was stretched in a sneer. This told me she found my question irritatingly stupid, and, upon reflection, I had to agree. I added, "I mean, why always? I suspect her now, too, obviously because of her unusual disappearance and what's been happening since..."

Joan interrupted my rambling. Her face had relaxed some, and the sneer was gone. "I can't put my finger on it," she said. "There was just something about her. The way she sort of glommed onto Pink, wrapped him around her pinky haha. Too much personality, too manipulative for someone who's supposed to be a nerd."

"Woman's intuition?" I regretted it soon as I said it. It won me another sneer.

"How about just plain intuition? Or maybe a cop's sixth sense?" I kept my eyes on the road ahead. She let her words hang awhile, then added, "OK, maybe you're right. She definitely has a way with men that...I wouldn't call it jealousy, but I found it annoying how easily she handles men and how obvious she is about it. And maybe it doesn't have a damned thing to do with what we have now." She sighed and I could see one of her shoulders lift in a shrug.

"It might have made you more observant of her, you know, if you don't trust somebody, or even if you just don't like them you're apt to watch them a bit more closely."

"I suppose I did."

"So maybe you'll remember something you noticed but it didn't mean anything at the time and now it'll be like finding a piece to a puzzle, you know?"

"You read too many mysteries, Al. Or is it TV? You never used to watch TV."

"Never had time. Don't watch it much now."

"I caught you reading a mystery once in your office, before I 'died'."

"I remember that, Joan. You needled me about it, too."

"I did. Said I'd tell Ruth you needed more to do. I think I can even remember the name of the book. Something with a song title...wait, don't tell me...Bad Moon Rising! Ha! Am I right? I am! That's what you were reading!"

"Wow, talk about a cop's memory! That was a while back, too. You got it. Bad Moon Rising. One of Ed Gorman's Sam McCain series. Set in Iowa. I've read 'em all."

"I had a crush on John Fogerty. Still do, truth be told. Creedence." She reached to the dash and ran her fingers over the buttons. Finally looked up at me, smiling. "Know how to turn this radio on?"

"I haven't a clue, Joan. There should be a power button there somewhere."

She fussed some more and finally gave up. "We need a child here to show us how. Kids know all that tech stuff."

She'd gotten fidgety, squirmed in her seat, looked out the windows as if trying to be casual, but her movements were

SACRIFICE

abrupt. Were she a smoker I'd've figured that was the problem, that she needed a cigarette.

"You don't smoke, do you, Joan?"

She turned her head, frowning. "You ever see me with a cigarette, Al?"

"No, but that could mean you're just careful. It was just a question. You seem antsy."

She barked a laugh. No mirth. "I'm worried. Are you surprised?"

"That sounds a little defensive, Joan. I guess I am surprised in a sense. You're usually the cool professional."

"I'm usually driving."

"Hey, you want the wheel, it's yours. You tossed the keys, remember?"

"I was fucking tired, OK? I'm still tired. And worried, but I'm OK. Don't be worried about me, Al." After a long pause she said, her voice still strained but not as cutting, "Al, what the fuck's going on?

"It's Liz, isn't it."

"Did you say 'Liz'?"

"I did."

"So what are you trying to say, Al? Why don't you just come out with it?"

"An odd choice of words."

"Oh, shit. Al. What the fuck?"

"What, you don't trust me?"

"Al, Jesus Christ. Gimme a break, huh?"

"Why don't you come out with it, Joan? It's just you and me."

"Goddammit, Al...LOOK OUT!!" We'd come up too fast behind a farm truck loaded with implements. The truck was pooping along.

MATHEW PAUST

Before I realized the difference in our speeds it was too late to do anything but whip the steering wheel and get around it, hoping the damned truck driver wouldn't try to swerve into the lane to let me by, thereby guaranteeing I'd hit the sonofabitch as we both swerved, and likely kill us both.

We were lucky the road was dry. It shouldn't have been. It was late April and what looked to be another nasty storm front had been inching up from the west all afternoon. Whipping the Crown Vic in a sharp maneuver on wet asphalt would have sent us spinning into an existential future Mother LaMarr, Palmist & Crystal Ball Gazer Supreme, could have forecast in naught but a mushroom dream. As it was, horns blasted, tires scritched and oaths gasped, and in an instant we were around the clog and I could see a middle finger extended out the truck driver's window in my mirror. My nervous laugh was not shared.

"Jesus Christ, Al, maybe I should drive."

"Asshole was going too slow. I'da been alone I'da rammed his ass."

"Oh, big bad Al, huh? So what was it you were asking me before you lost control of the car?"

"I didn't lose control."

"You sure as hell did. You recovered quickly and you – we – were lucky, but if you'd been paying attention you'd have seen that asshole in time to avoid scaring the piss out of me."

"Really?"

"Really what?"

"Secret Service Agent Joan Stonebraker pees pants in harrowing highway...something or other. I tried journalism before I got into law. Couldn't get the hang of headlines."

"Don't change the subject. You know I know all that. It was me had to vet your skinny ass when you came on board. I know more about you than your shrink does. So you want me to come out to you, huh? Right here, right now?"

SACRIFICE

"Why not?"

"Because my sexuality is none of your god damned business, that's why."

"Who's talking business? I was just..."

"What, you hitting on me?"

"Not if..."

"Oh, shit! 'Not if!' What a chickenshit thing to say. You hitting on me or not? Out with it!" She was grinning now.

"Well, Joan, that grin does tell me quite a lot. Well...it's telling my libido quite a lot, if you catch..."

"I catch. Keep it down for now, cowboy, OK? Let's finish the mission. We can explore this new development later...if...um, the development is still developed, if you catch my drift, and if there is a later." She patted my thigh. High enough. I was grinning now, too.

HARM'S WAY

The amphetamine effect of confirmed mutual physical attraction helped me focus on the upcoming challenge. Joan seemed revived, as well. Amazing, I thought, how something so basic and simple can be so transforming. And this extended to my perception of her as a woman. Until then I'd repressed sexual feelings toward her as if we were siblings. Even trying to look at her sexually, appreciating the way she held herself, the arch of her back, an athletic grace, how the tandem spheres of her ass moved under the faded denim of her jeans, looking at these aspects with admiration, the de-eroticizing filter of, I assumed, professional propriety along with uncertainty about her sexual affinities, kept my libido pretty much out of the assessment process.

We were two different people now, at least in my mind, stalking lethal danger along the edge of an unfamiliar woods. The sexual tension I felt between us after we alighted from the Crown Vic had shifted subtly from restraint to restrained anticipation. We were imminent lovers, my libido told me, just one deadly job away from consummation. I accepted the remote possibility it might have been delusion on my part. Remote, I say, because I knew her well enough to interpret with confidence a grin and a pat near my groin, and friendly recognition of my instant natural response, and then her perking up almost as soon.

I was aware her perking up could have been simply professional reflex as we approached our target. I allowed for that, and yet a door had opened for me, for my imagination, stimulating me to potentially greater reliability as a fellow warrior in the test ahead. Had she opened that door merely for the tactical advantage of increasing our odds of survival with a bonus shot of testosterone, I was good with that. The cynicism would disappoint were it realized, which I well knew, but, as I say, that prospect was remote at the moment and thus not as bothersome as it could

SACRIFICE

have been and yet could be. What the hell, at my age I was, and am, quite happy accepting practically any pleasantry, no matter how illusory or ephemeral.

On the road Joan sensed our proximity to the ambush site before I did.

"You wanna start slowing down, Al, we're getting close. Not too slow, but I wanna be able to see the car if it's parked in there. Whether we see anything or not, just keep going. We'll park up the road a ways and then hike back."

"Yes, boss." I flashed her a smile, but it bounced off without noticeable effect. She was scanning the treeline streaming by outside her window. Traffic was light, but an SUV had come up behind us, riding the bumper, and its driver seemed reluctant to pass. I was holding the speed to the 55 limit, but because my tailgater stayed so close I assumed he found this too slow. We were on a stretch of road with several curves, which, with the occasional oncoming vehicle, justified the SUV playing it safe. Yet, following us so closely was also dangerous. Finally I rolled down my window, stuck out my arm and motioned that he should pass. I even slowed a tad more to encourage him. Suddenly he pulled out and started accelerating around. When the SUV was even with us I could see its driver appeared to be female. I raised a hand in cordial salute but she roared on around us without appearing to notice. I sighed involuntarily, recognizing I had harbored a small worry the SUV might have been the enemy.

Joan, her eyes fixed on the roadside, seemed to have missed my little drama. I decided to let it pass without mention. "It's in there," she said, her voice so calm I almost missed the import of its message.

"Doc Bot's van?"

"Yeah. It's right where Burke said his SUV would be. Looks like a logging trail. I just caught a glimpse of the van. It was back in there."

"People?"

MATHEW PAUST

"I didn't see anybody. Or the SUV."

"You figure they switched rides ?"

"Might have. Let's leave the car at the first turn-off you find. See if we can get back there on foot. Scout around a little."

"It's gonna rain, Joan."

"Yeah, well."

"OK." Within half a mile we came to a 7-Eleven. I pulled in and parked out of the way, next to a dumpster. We got out and stretched, went into the store and bought coffee and a couple more disposable cellphones. Joan used the restroom. Before we started out she opened the Crown Vic's trunk to reveal what looked like a trombone case. Inside that was a stubby pump shotgun, which she withdrew and loaded with shells from a box nestled in the case. I stood behind her to shield her from any nosy types who might happen by. She fed the brass-based red shells into the tubular magazine one at a time, clacked the action shut and handed the weapon to me.

"Remington 870. Ever use one?"

"Nothing this short. I had an old Winchester pump for pheasants back in the day."

"Same thing. Smoother action. You have seven 12-gauge double-aught buck in there. An eighth round's in the chamber. Safety's on. See the button?" She pointed to an aspirin-size steel button at the rear of the trigger guard. "To disengage the safety when you're ready to fire, push it from the right side so the red band on the left side is showing." She demonstrated, clicking the button to the left, then, after making sure I saw the red band, she clicked it back on safe.

"Wouldn't you be better off with this?" I asked when it became apparent the Crown Vic's trunk held only one shotgun.

"I would. We would," she said. "But you look more like a shotgun guy. We're going in with psy-ops on this one." She was smiling. She added, pointing at the pistol on her hip, "Besides, I'm not too

SACRIFICE

bad with this, you know."

"Indeed. And Burke sure as hell would agree."

She slammed the trunk lid shut and we walked to the shoulder and headed north. I'd almost forgotten in the adrenalin rush of launching our patrol what awaited me to reward a successful mission, but then my eyes drifted to those tandem spheres working gracefully under the denim directly ahead and another rush, this of urgent enthusiasm, filled my heart. I squelched an urge to bellow, Get 'em up, move 'em out.

MATHEW PAUST

AMBUSH

First, good news that it didn't rain. Sure as hell looked, felt and smelt as if it would, heavy, dark, menacing clouds bearing down with intermittent lightning, occasional breezy gusts stirring the humidity, thick with pungent ozone. All this, but no rain. Our karmic reward, I wondered, for the earnest gratitude we'd both expressed for not getting pneumonia from our last bout of maelstrom.

Second, more good news that we didn't have a shootout. That's because there wasn't anybody to shoot at or shooting at us. There was nobody where we found Doc Bot's van. Joan, whose eyes, unlike mine were working professionally, spotted it first. She held her hand to the side and patted it downward, telling me, I assumed, to stop, which I did.

"We're getting close," she whispered. "I saw the van through that opening." She pointed into the trees. I saw no opening, no van, although I nodded as if I had. No sense questioning her at this point. She crouched and crept forward, stepping oddly so that her feet touched the ground heel first and then rolled up to the toe, doing it carefully and smoothly I assumed to minimize the chances of stepping on something noisy, a stick that could break or a pile of leaves. She looked like a cat creeping up on some oblivious small critter the cat considered prey. I tried to imitate her walk, but after producing several loud crunching sounds, drawing stern looks from my leader, I moved onto the shoulder of the road where such blunders were less likely on the fine gravel. Eventually I saw the van peeking through the trees, too.

"There it is," I whispered loudly. She wheeled around, holding an index finger to her lips in the universal librarian's signal to shush. I nodded, chastened and a tad embarrassed, but, as I was falling in lust with the woman, I let that slide right off into the underbrush.

SACRIFICE

I moved up behind her and, obeying her hand signal, to one side. We proceeded, crouching, to the tree line and took cover behind the trunks of adjacent loblolly pines. I let her peek around first, which she did, holding her sidearm with its barrel pointed down and pressed against the tree.

I gripped the shotgun with both hands after finding the safety button and snapping it to the left to reveal the red band. Knowing the trigger was now a slight tug away from releasing the firing pin converted the weapon's personality from having interesting potential to one of imminent lethality. It seemed to throb with unstable intent. Without any signal to me, Joan pushed away from her tree and stepped quickly around and into the clearing.

"Freeze!" she ordered, her voice low and firm. "Secret Service! Drop your weapons, keep your hands away from your body and step away from the vehicle! Do it! NOW!"

I waited until she glanced back at me and signaled quickly with her head before I, too, stepped into the clearing. I moved less deliberately, keeping my eyes on Joan and hoping my peripheral vision would pick up any movement elsewhere. I held the Remington in front of me, barrel pointed toward the van as I sighted down its eighteen inch plane, keeping my focus on the gold bead at its end. Joan, holding her pistol with a two-handed grip and pointing it at the van, repeated her orders, using the same steady voice with a tad more volume than before.

We then waited for what seemed like an hour or longer but which was more likely less than a minute during which we saw nothing human move, either outside the van or visible through its windows, and heard no nearby human-made sound, Joan signaled me again and we crept slowly forward, keeping the barrels of our weapons pointed at the van. We approached to within three feet of the doors on either side when she loudly ordered me to stop.

"Al, this van may be boobytrapped. Burke was special ops. They never left anything behind worth stealing that wasn't rigged with grenades or plastic. Look, the key's in the ignition. The bastard doesn't care if some innocent kid or civilian decides to see if it'll start."

"They wouldn't be innocent anymore if they tried to steal it," I said.

"True enough. But last I heard grand theft auto wasn't a capital crime."

"So what do we do?"

She was looking through the window into the van. "I see what looks like a piece of paper on your side, on the seat," she said. "Maybe it's a note. Check it out, but don't touch it. OK?"

I moved up to window on my side and saw the paper. It looked as if something was written on it in large block letters. I had to squint in the feeble ambient light to make out what it said. I looked up at Joan through the two windows. "Cottage," I yelled.

"What?"

I backed away from the van to give my voice more room. "It says 'cottage.' That's all. Looks like somebody wrote it in a real hurry."

"Shit," Joan muttered. "Looks like you were right, Al. Inside job. They're back at the Cottage."

"Maybe that's just what Burke wants us to think," I said, drawing from my career of working with devious politicians to keep our options open.

Joan walked around the front of the van and approached close enough for me to smell her sweat through the trace scents of soap and shampoo. She holstered her pistol and with both hands free grabbed my shoulders and pulled me down for a kiss. Yes, indeed, she gave me a kiss, one helluva hot, wet kiss right smack on the lips. I about tore my briefs before she released me (I was still holding the shotgun, terrified the damned thing would go off if I tried to set it down.).

"Let's get back to the room, cowboy, and, um, talk this over. I think you're right. Burke's too smart to let them leave a note out in the clear. They may well be at The Cottage, but before we do anything we need to check and see if Jim, the guy on the motorcycle, has anything, you know? For all we know they're all

SACRIFICE

working together."

"Wh...what about the van? Shouldn't we secure it somehow. You know, if it's, um, boobytrapped?"

Joan laughed, a healthy sound from her belly, and reached up and patted my face. "You shoulda been with the Service, Al. You sure you weren't a cop back when?"

"Just read a lot of crime novels. You know, those..."

"Oh, yeah, Bad Moon, um, Rising. We'll get the locals to check this out. It's probly safe, but they've got bomb guys, too. Nobody's gonna mess with it tonight anyway. It's gonna rain."

It did, but it waited until we'd giggled our way back to the Crown Vic and were on the road to the Day's Inn.

MATHEW PAUST

GETTING TO KNOW YOU

Did I mention it rained during our drive back to the Days Inn? I was wrong. It dumped. It deluged across the highway in sheets so thick and furious at one point I lost sight of the roadway but was afraid to pull the Crown Vic onto the shoulder because I couldn't see it either and couldn't remember how deep the ditches were along that stretch. We slowed to a crawl, not worried some maniac might ram us because anyone stupid enough to drive over 5 m.p.h. in that stuff would soon have been boogying off road to nowhere fun. Nonetheless at the first flash glimpse through the wall of rain I eased the Vic off the roadway and put it in park. I kept the engine running so I could leave the flashers on just in case our theoretical maniac managed to make it that far in one piece.

With the rain doing a Gene Krupa solo on the car and sealing us from view or viewing, our closeted intimacy spoke urgently to my already anxious libido in a voice I hadn't heard since my salad days. I turned toward Joan with what I'm sure she saw as a wolfish grin on my face. Her expression was ambiguous, offering just enough warmth that I started to lean in with obvious intent.

"Al," she said in a voice that sounded more professional than I was expecting, "Liz and Pink may well be dead."

As I scrambled to come up with something to say that wouldn't sound stupid, she continued, "That would have been the place to do it. He could have buried them and booked before we got there."

"Should we go back?" I knew this was stupid the instant I said it. Oh, well, I figured, it could be the first test of our nascent mutual affection.

"No point now, Al." She gave me a gentle smile, letting me know

SACRIFICE

she was withholding the deserved duh, but carrying a sadness as well. There was personal loss for her in this grim prospect. I had found Dr. Knoe attractive, but, then, fresh out of prison as I was I'd been finding myself taken with almost every nubile female who caught my eye. I half-expected these musings to dash a bit of cool water on my enthusiasm of the moment. Oddly this didn't happen. It seemed our shared concern over the fate of these two associates, albeit in the privacy of our individual thoughts, made us all the hornier.

Joan leaned toward me, too, as our eyes locked on each others. Hers captured the little light available in the car and set it to dancing as if tiny Tinkerbells had emerged from her pupils flicking fairy dust from under her lashes. Despite the magical hold of her gaze I couldn't help but catch a glimpse of her small but distinctly female breasts as she gave her T-shirt a furtive tug, freeing the sweat-damp cloth from pulsing nipples that peeked out like sandy brown buttons. We lurched forward at the same time, closing the extra inch or so that brought our lips and noses together to play their own game of getting to know you, brushing and stroking, lips nipping then grabbing lips, and tongues teasing and tasting.

A new aroma soon engulfed us with its entwined hormonal musk, and our hands got involved, fingers probing and stroking, sliding and then my left hand was under the T-shirt loving those small distinct dear breasts and poking and pinching their naughty nipples. Her moaning stopped for a moment as she gasped, trying to speak. She pulled an arm free and gestured toward the back seat, nodding up and down and smiling dreamily, then shifted in her seat and lifted a leg. I repositioned myself and helped her climb over the soft upholstered seat back onto the wide, unobstructed back seat. I couldn't see out the steamed-up window, but, from the thundering of water on the car roof knew I could be washed away if I tried to join my lover by jumping out my door and entering by the back. Not as limber as she, I nonetheless kicked off my shoes, tore off my jeans and climbed over the back seat as she had. She was already completely out of her clothes by then. I'd heard her pistol clunk as her jeans dropped to the floor. We were both cooing and moaning and sharing little chuckles as I lowered my stinking sweaty self onto her amazingly beautiful musky, sweet, slick, squirmy body.

Wrapped tightly in each others arms afterward, we slept long enough that the rain had dropped off to a steady sprinkle when we awoke. I was almost afraid to poke my head up, for fear we'd be sitting half out in the roadway or so near a steep dropoff our rocking could have tipped us down an incline into a stump-filled hollow or stony creek bed. But somebody had to check out the terrain, so poke it up I did. We were fine. A couple of feet off the asphalt on a gravel shoulder that feathered into a shallow ditch we might not even have noticed had we parked half in it. I'd already kissed Joan awake and now I helped her with her clothes. She broke into a wide smile every time our faces met, reached up once with a hand and patted my cheek, then pulled herself into a sitting position and kissed me full on the lips. I was erect again and mumbled something silly about the danger of trying to climb back into the front seat. Quick as a pit viper her hand shot out and she snapped the end of my penis with her middle finger. It took three sharp snaps before it was "safe" for me to make the climb.

"That wasn't very loving, Joan," I said, trying to sound hurt. Well, it did hurt.

"I was an LPN before I joined the Service. That's how they taught us to tame randy patients. Sorry, Al, darling, I was only looking out for our interests."

The banter continued in this fashion during the remainder of the drive to the Days Inn. Joan tried several times to contact Newgate for an update...on anything, but we were especially interested in what Jim might have learned following Roger Ashmore and his partner. But Newgate wasn't answering his phone, and it didn't have Voicemail.

So, exhausted and hungry, we picked up some burgers at a drive-thru Wendy's, took them back to the room, ate, showered, made love and slept undisturbed until we were startled awake by Joan's cellphone playing *Hail to the Chief*.

SACRIFICE

THE PLOT CONGEALS A TAD

"It's Ruth," she stage-whispered to me, shielding the cellphone with her hand. The conversation didn't last long, with Joan's contributions mostly single words: "Six. No. Six." She spoke no names, finished the conversation with a crisp, "K. Gotcha. On our way." Her face was dark with concern when she flipped the device shut.

"What's the matter? Six isn't enough?" I said, reaching an arm over. She slipped out from under it before it could land with its twofold intent, to comfort and/or to test the waters. She was already tugging into her jeans before my own feet reached the floor. Her explanation came out in strained spurts as she continued dressing.

"You men...Jeezuz Christ, Al! Is it any wonder...some of us...unh...are..."

"Sorry, Joan. It takes me awhile to get up to speed...or down. I withdraw the question."

"Thanks for leaving out the um. Maybe there's hope for you. Ruth said Edna's worried. Says Warren won't return her calls."

"That's all? Sounds like a management problem. I'm surprised it took Edna this long to catch on to Hendrian."

"She wants us to meet her there."

"The Cottage?"

"Yes. Coincidence, isn't it."

"So where is she?"

"Didn't say. Didn't say much of anything. He phone's supposed to be secure, but she sounded unusually cautious."

"Edna be there, too?"

"Didn't say. Probly not. Edna delegates, you know. Hates to leave her Baltimore penthouse."

"Delegates to the president? That's arrogant."

"They're old friends, Al. Sorority sisters. Edna always treated Ruth with proper respect when Ruth was in office."

"I met her once. At one of the early fundraisers. Attractive woman. A little distant, but..."

"But?"

"I heard her laugh. It wasn't one of those fake society laughs. A real gut-busting laugh. I liked her then."

"You're a cheap date."

"One of my charms."

"I see. That why you don't get laid much?"

I decided to let Joan have the last word, and so merely gave her a wearied deadpan look, which prompted an "uh huh" from her, which I ignored as I finished dressing.

I left a ten-dollar bill on the pillow for the maids, settled up at the office and we were back in the Vic on our way north, this time with Joan driving. We were on the road less than half an hour when Joan got another call. Ruth again.

"Change of plans," Joan said after flipping her phone shut. Her end of the conversation again had consisted of single words, most of them "yes" and "no." No numbers this time. "Ruth and Bob are meeting us at Merle's."

This meant nothing to me, but I soon learned there was a small marina a couple of miles south of The Cottage where we could hire someone to deliver us by boat to a landing within walking distance of our destination on the Bay side of the property. Ruth would be accompanied by Bob Rose, who had succeeded Joan as acting chief of the Secret Service White House security detail after her supposed death, to fool me, and was now assigned with Joan

SACRIFICE

to guard the former president.

"Small" was definitely the right adjective for Merle's Marina. We reached it at the end of a narrow gravel road that wound down through scrub pines and cedars nearly a mile from the highway. Surrounded by a gravel parking area sat a squat cinderblock building facing three finger piers that reached into the Bay each with slips for no more than a dozen boats, six on either side. At least half the slips were empty. The glow of a red neon sign in the picture window next to the entrance affirmed that the office was open. I was surprised there was no sign indicating this was Merle's Marina, and then realized it wasn't necessary as the boat-shaped sign at the highway end of the road proclaimed the name and there was no other business to confuse anyone who traversed the road's length to its end. It was shortly before noon. There were three vehicles parked in front of the office – a pickup and two SUVs, neither of them Ruth's. Joan parked the Vic on the side opposite the road and we crunched across the gravel and entered the building.

The place looked bigger inside. It had a store for boating supplies on one side and a cafe area with half a dozen tables on the other. A grizzled fellow of indeterminate age, wearing a weathered Orioles cap, faded jeans and a T-shirt bearing the nearly bleached-out words in blue cursive, Merle's Marina, was behind the counter waiting on a yuppie-looking couple in Tees and chinos. We walked into the cafe area and sat at table near the window. Most of the storm clouds had passed but the sun was high enough that all we saw of it was its reflection rippling on the Bay. A fellow looking to be in his early sixties sat at a table in the back of the room and a couple about a decade younger were two tables from ours. As we settled ourselves in the wooden chairs a small woman wearing a yellow apron around her waist, with short, curly gray hair appeared and put nautical-themed placemats and silver rolled in a paper napkin in front of us.

"Coffee?" she said for perhaps the three-hundred and fifty-thousandth time in her career, while still managing to make it sound inviting. Her smile was tight but durable and she held it while switching her pale blue eyes from Joan to me and back to

Joan. We accepted her offer and she returned moments later with two heavy cups and a steaming glass pot. Small bowls holding packets of sugar and plastic containers of creamer sat next to an aluminum container of paper napkins in the center of the table, which was also of a solid wood that matched the chairs.

"Our specials today are crab cakes or broiled flounder," she said as she poured the coffee.

"That sounds good," said Joan. "We're expecting another couple to join us. We'll wait until they get here, if that's OK."

"You just take your time, honey," she said and headed back to the swinging door, where I caught a glimpse of someone bustling around in white chef's clothing when she pushed it open.

We'd nearly finished our first cup of coffee, growing more concerned with each sip, when Joan plucked her cellphone from it's holster on her belt. She'd put it on vibrate so as not to draw attention with it's Hail to the Chief ringtone. Another brief conversation, with only one contribution from Joan this time, several Oks.

"It's Anthony. Something's wrong. He's coming here."

"Ruth?"

"He can't reach her."

"Did he say..."

"That's all. He couldn't talk. He was practically whispering. He's bringing one of the security boats."

We stared at each other and finished our coffee.

SACRIFICE

WTF?

The security boat, a 24-foot Boston Whaler festooned with broad red and blue stripes to vaguely resemble a Coast Guard motor launch, eased into the marina and docked as we were finishing our lunches. The man with the Orioles cap, whom I took to be Merle, trotted down the pier to help the man who'd climbed out of the boat secure it in the slip and drape canvas covers on each side along the prow, presumably to cover the Coast Guardish stripes. The two men then headed up the pier toward us, conversing with an animation that suggested they knew each other.

Had I known Cromwell better I'd have had a better chance of recognizing his physical appearance and movements as he walked up the pier. At that distance and wearing jeans and a T-shirt, he looked like any slim athletic young man. He seemed taller than I expected, but that could have been an illusion from his proximity to the shorter "Merle." The man I assumed was Cromwell had a confident stride. He wore a brimmed white cloth cap that shielded enough of his face, with his eyes covered by aviator's sunglasses, that I couldn't be certain it was him until he removed his sunglasses and was standing across from us.

"Ms. Stonebraker. Sir," he said gravely nodding first at Joan, then me.

"Anthony, for Christ's sake, drop the goddam 'sir', OK?" I smiled when I said it, but Cromwell's face remained impassive. Joan, smiling too, added "And the 'miz', too, Anthony. You had me almost looking around to see if my mom had just walked in. Have a seat. Join us. Please."

He pulled a chair out, lifting it slightly to keep from scraping the floor, while apologizing. "Too long in the Corps, I guess. Hard habit to break," he said quietly as he settled onto the wooden chair. Cromwell had been decorated for valor by the Marines, but was uncomfortable talking about it. I'd pegged him for a lifelong Boy Scout the instant I met him, in the Rose Garden when he led the team of animal control officers that prevented the president's abduction and possible assassination.

"People are animals too, sir," he'd said to my angry challenge when he identified himself after I confronted him among the FBI and Secret Service agents staked out around the Rose Garden awaiting the arrival of a group of conspirators Ruth had knowingly invited to a sting operation disguised as a ceremony to honor a movie starlet who happened to be one of the conspirators. Cromwell and his team were assigned to the sting unbeknownst to me by another White House staffer in what might well have ended tragically – and almost did – as a consequence of nearly unimaginable miscommunication. As it turned out it was Cromwell and his team who saved the day.

"We're all in danger," he said now, leaning forward across the table, his voice approximating a Clint Eastwood whisper. We stared at him. I felt my eyebrows shoot up inquisitively, glanced quickly at Joan and saw that her forehead was reacting conversely, scrunched into a severe puzzlement. Cromwell waited politely for a vocal reaction. Receiving none, he continued, "It's Hendrian. We think he got into one of Pink's chemicals. Roger saw him coming up from the lab. He's been acting very strange ever since."

"Roger?" Joan asked. "Who's Roger?"

"Ashmore. He's been working for me since leaving the Service. I thought you knew that."

Joan and I turned and melded our mind-blown glances. Joan turned back to Cromwell. "What the fuck, Tony? Ashmore's a felon. He ran from us yesterday, like a scared rabbit."

The waitress appeared and we suspended the conversation while Cromwell ordered coffee and the flounder special. He continued after the waitress had returned to the kitchen. "That was our little secret, Joan. Roger was under quadruple cover then,

SACRIFICE

working for Animal Control as well as the Service while pretending to work for the special prosecutor and the conspirators. It did get confusing...

"Wait a minute. Waaaaait just a goddam minute, Cromwell!" I blurted, beginning to wonder if someone had slipped something into my coffee. "Ashmore was working undercover for you? What the fuck, if I may be so blunt?"

Cromwell squirmed a tad, and I noticed he was drumming the fingers of his right hand rhythmically on his napkin.

"Ashmore informed us Mr. Cohen was mistreating the family dog. As Ashmore was already in Mr. Cohen's confidence vis a vis the sting operation I rigged him with a miniature camcorder to gather evidence. It was actually the animal abuse case that forced him to resign as special prosecutor. He accepted that charge in a plea agreement, but then realized the negative publicity would hound him from office eventually. Pardon the pun, please. It was my first one." He quickly ceased drumming his fingers and moved them to cover his mouth, but a self-conscious giggle escaped between them anyway.

"Anthony!" Joan, ignoring the moment of levity, raised her voice to its highest decibel level yet. "Why wasn't I informed of this?"

"Ma'am..."

"Cut the shit, Anthony! This is inexcusable!"

"Ma'am!" Cromwell raised his voice to match her volume. He continued in a more conversational tone, "With all due respect, Joan, I did not know you didn't know..."

"Bullshit, Anthony. You said 'our little secret,' remember?" Her words were harsh, but her tone matched his. We were not creating a scene.

"It was need to know, Joan. I assumed you knew, and you caught me by surprise when you indicated you didn't. I'm sorry. I apologize."

Joan had pulled herself up to full height in her chair, her back straight as a board and I imagine quite as rigid. "Anthony, I am having trouble getting past this. I'm assigned by the United States Secret Service to protect a former president of the United States. How could you or anyone else explain why I or anyone else assigned to protect a former president of the United States – the...United...States – should not need to know something of this vital nature? Someone could have been killed yesterday because I was not informed that Roger Ashmore was working for you! Thank God Ruth wasn't with me!"

Cromwell stared at the placemat in front of him.

"I'm sorry," he mumbled.

I reached over and patted his nearest forearm. "It's OK, bubba. We all make mistakes. This is your first one, I believe." I looked up, forcing a bright smile, and said in my cheeriest voice, "Two firsts in one day, a pun and a mistake – how about that!" No one laughed, but Joan flashed me a tense grin and settled back in her chair. Cromwell cleared his throat and looked up at us, his face returned to unreadable implacability.

"Well, anyway, we have a new problem. A much worse one, I'm afraid. Hendrian is staging a coup. He's brought in some security people and ordered our arrests, me and my staff. I believe we've all gotten out, but our communications are no longer secure. I called you on a disposable. I'm sure they'll be looking for me."

Joan said, "Have you heard from Ruth?"

"One call, this morning. It broke off before we could say much."

"She say where she was?"

"No. Joan, Al, we've got to get back in there. Hendrian has Pink and Dr. Knoe locked in one of the lab rooms. I heard some screaming from down there this morning. I think they're being tortured."

"Cromwell," I said, trying to sound confident, "You got out, so you must know how to get back in." I knew this wasn't representative of my best thinking, but he didn't seem to notice. Nor did Joan.

SACRIFICE

"The tunnel," he said, back to his Eastwood whisper.

MATHEW PAUST

MISSION INSCRUTABLE

Anthony Cromwell was about finished with his flounder special when we saw the Crown Vic we'd chased the day before drive past the front of the place, and soon thereafter we heard car doors slamming. Soon thereafter that, in walked Roger Ashmore and someone I didn't recognize, a stocky man with a stubble of graying hair who appeared slightly older than Ashmore. Both men wore rumpled chinos under baggy Hawaiian shirts.

"Pull up chairs, fellas," said Cromwell. "Have some coffee and something to eat. We're getting ready to go back in. You know these folks." He nodded in our direction.

"Mr. Geddes, Ms. Stonebraker. Good to see you," said Ashmore, as he removed his sunglasses. He indicated the other man. "This is Cranston Case. He goes by 'Crank'. We go back a ways. Special Ops." Neither man smiled, but they did as their boss suggested and joined us. Ashmore seemed uncomfortable, especially with Joan. He shot her a couple of quick glances after sitting and then feigned fascination with the menu. I decided to chip at the ice.

"So, Roger, how come you guys ran from us at the truckstop? We're not that scary, are we?" I said this smiling, and won a weak one-corner mouth tug and another quick look at Joan, who stared at him as if he were across a steel table from her in an interrogation room.

Cromwell answered: "I had just called them, Al. Told them we were under attack and to head for cover. No time to explain. They must have thought you were hostiles. Right, guys?"

"I recognized you both, Mr. Geddes, but like Tony...Mr. Cromwell said, we were following his instructions," Ashmore explained. Case merely stared at me with no expression and no visible acknowledgment of anything. He'd not removed his sunglasses. I

SACRIFICE

couldn't resist jabbing the needle.

"Mr. Case. Crank, is it? What say you to all this?"

"Larry summed it up pretty well," he said, his voice oddly soft from such a hardened impassive demeanor. His sunglasses never left what I presumed were my eyes.

"I see. So you recognized me and Special Agent Stonebraker here, too? Is that right?" I waited a beat, then continued, "Where, might I ask, had you seen either of us before?"

Case remained stone still, continuing to stare at me as if I were an insect he loathed but would wait until it approached within range before crushing. He shrugged. "I've never seen either of you before," he said, his voice sounding almost kindly. Then he reached up and slowly removed his sunglasses, revealing the most startling, intimidating eyes I had ever seen – large coal-black irises that filled the sockets and reflected and focused the room's ambient light in a way that seemed to be directing white laser beams straight into me. He held me with these paralyzing eyes while he used a paper napkin to calmly, slowly clean his sunglasses. When this was finished he casually put the glasses back on, shielding anyone he looked at from the full effect of those humongous glistering merciless irises. He picked up the menu and studied it, worrying me that even with the sunglasses it just might burst into flames before he decided his order.

I had the sense Joan never took her eyes off Ashmore from the moment he entered, other than to toss a nod at Case when he was introduced. Without either of us saying a word, Ashmore seemed to read the question on our minds, but he addressed his answer to Joan.

"The guy on the bike? We made him right away, Agent Stonebraker. Led him around until he ran out of gas. Haven't seen him since. He yours?"

Joan ignored Ashmore's question. She sighed, shook her head wearily and turned her attention to her coffee.

To me Ashmore said, after cracking a small grin, "Mr. Geddes, that wasn't very professional of you with the finger. Crank here could have gotten angry and lost control...of the car." Case ignored the comment, continuing apparently to study the menu.

"Roger, let's cut the shit with the formalities, OK? Seems we went through this once before, as I recall. You Roger, me Al, your buddy here, Crank. Keep things simple. To respond to your comment, though, no, my flipping you off wasn't professional. I'm not a cop. Never been one. I don't know shit for tactics, but I am creative and I'm senior. Joan will lead this operation, with Cromwell her XO. Crank, are you gonna stare at that menu all afternoon or will you be ordering something? I suggest a sandwich and a drink to go. Time's a'wastin'"

Case ignored me, but caught the waitress's eye and ordered a burger and fries and a coffee to go.

Joan decided to leave both cars at the marina, parked in back out of sight. We would take the boat to within hiking distance of The Cottage. Merle agreed to skipper the boat and bring it back to the marina after dropping us off. Joan and Ashmore procured the weapons from the car trunks – her shotgun (mine now) from ours and a carbine and a shotgun from the other. Merle brought out a sawed-off double barrel from under the counter in his store and handed it to Cromwell along with a box of shells.

"Slugs. Twelve gauge," he said.

We climbed aboard the boat, crammed so tightly into the passenger compartment the scent of Joan's shower soap gave me the start of an erection, which I quickly willed to return from whence it came. Merle backed the boat out of the slip and eased it along the shoreline toward The Cottage.

Some twenty minutes later he steered it in and tied up to a small private pier that jutted out from the woods. I could see a cottage on stilts up an incline through the pines. We climbed off the boat onto the pier and marched up its creaky planks to the narrow beach, and by the time we'd stepped onto the gray wet sand and turned back to the Bay, our boat was chugging quietly away.

SACRIFICE

PENETRATION

We made our way to The Cottage infantry-patrol style, in single file along a narrow path worn through the undergrowth to the hard-packed soil presumably by a habitual procession of feet - human and wildlife. A scraggly row of coniferous trees and wax myrtle shrubs partially shielded us from the Bay. The scrub pine and cedars also intervened with the afternoon sun's pitiless assault on my still soft, prison-pallored complexion, and a merciful breeze wafted off the Bay to help mitigate the discomfort of our mile-long-or-so trek. Cromwell walked point, with Joan close behind. I followed her and could hear Ashmore and Case tromping along behind me.

Joan, crouching, signaled me with a downward wave of her hand when we reached the end of our march. I turned and did likewise for Case. Cromwell moved back along the line and grouped us together. He produced a drawing of the rear of the antebellum house we would enter and in a whisper pointed out several key features. Most importantly, he hissed, was the entrance to the tunnel, which would lead us from near the beach end of the pier under the slope up to the building's foundation and into the subterranean levels where the laboratory was located.

Cromwell held up his remote security module, pointed it into the trees and pressed a button. A small bulb on the unit flashed red for less than a second and the module emitted a single high-pitched beep.

"I've deactivated the gulls," he whispered. "I'll go first and open the tunnel, then the rest of you join me. Don't come all at once. First one, then the next until we're all together. OK?" He slipped away through the underbrush and down the several feet to the beach, crouching low as he made his way to a protuberance at the base of the grassy slope that led up to the house. After fussing with something he raised hand and motioned for the next person. Joan then followed the same course he had taken, motioned likewise and suddenly I was crashing through the brush and crabbing down to the sand next to the water.

I felt the old mansion's presence before I turned my head to look up at it. It gave me the same chilling sense I knew from childhood feeling a parent or teacher silently observing me doing something I knew I shouldn't. Yet actually looking at the house dispelled this feeling. I hadn't seen it previously from the back, but it appeared fairly ordinary, what I could see of it. Crouched as I was, the slope hid most of the lower third of the house. I could see the outer rail of the deck where I enjoyed my breakfasts, and the top half of the kitchen door that led to it, but the deck itself and its tables and chairs were below my sight line. Thinking it likely a general alert for us would be in effect, I was surprised and relieved to see no sign of anybody who might notice our invasion.

When all five of us were gathered at the tunnel entrance, Cromwell removed a small container of what appeared to be some type of lubricant and applied its contents to the hinges of an iron gate that blocked access to the passageway. An opened, badly tarnished padlock hung from matching iron rings on the gate and its frame. Cromwell tugged carefully on the gate. Its hinges immediately squeaked in protest, so he squirted some more lubricant on them and worked it in by moving the gate back and forth slightly until the squeaking stopped. Pulling it all the way open, he whispered some more instructions:

"I'll go first. There's no light in here. I have a flashlight with a blue light that won't hurt our night vision. This tunnel was built during the Civil War as an escape route for the occupants if Union troops approached from the front. I don't think it's been used since then except by rats and god knows what else – and me when I came out a couple hours ago. Smells bad and there's no ventilation. The floor is dirt but the walls and ceiling are sturdy, made of stones.

"The door at the other end opens into a room Pink uses for storage. It's not easy to recognize from the inside and I doubt

SACRIFICE

Pink ever noticed it. Once we're inside we'll take the main corridor to a series of small rooms at the other end of the house from the lab. They were slave quarters. That's where Pink and Liz are being held. Our plan is to get them out and retrace our steps to the tunnel and back to the path. I'll signal Merle and we'll be safely away before anybody else is the wiser."

"How many security people has Warren brought in?" I asked.

"I don't know, Al. I saw at least half a dozen before I evacuated. They came in black SUVs that dropped them off and left. They're zombies, Chesapeake's field zombies. So much body armor they look like robots. Soon as I saw them I knew what was up, the way Hendrian was acting. It will take them awhile to get the lay of the land here, but they have Hendrian helping them and the guy that brought in Pink and Liz. They got here yesterday."

"The guy who brought in Pink and Dr. Knoe is Elliot Burke. He's with Chesapeake. He was shot in the leg when Joan and Pink ran into the ambush last week. Is he limping?"

"A little. Not much."

"He's one tough bird. He'll be running the zombies."

Cromwell nodded. "OK, we ready? Let's go in."

This time I followed Cromwell, with Joan next and the other two behind her. The tunnel was too small to stand up in, so we crept along on hands and knees. Cromwell was right about the smell. Considering you might be eating while you read this, I'll skip trying to describe just how awful it was. The dirt floor was hard but damp, as were the stone walls, through which various organic roots protruded and seemed to be grabbing at us as we brushed past. Something scuttled over my right hand, pricking the skin with claws as it launched itself from the unfamiliar surface and scurried on up the tunnel. I couldn't see if the claws had broken the skin, but a quick brush of the back of my hand against a cheek indicated there was no blood. I made a mental note to dab hydrogen peroxide on it anyway, first chance I had.

Climbing upward through the rank, musty darkness seemed to

take longer and require more stamina than our march along the Bay rim. With the humidity and lack of ventilation I sweated profusely and was soaked by the time Cromwell flashed the blue light back at us signaling we'd reached our destination. I heard him work some kind of latch and felt a rush of cool, fresher smelling air wash down over us.

SACRIFICE

GUN*PLAY?*

We caught our breath and cooled off in the darkened storage room. Cromwell had cleared a space, moving lab furniture and cardboard boxes from the wall to locate the door. He'd found it on old blueprints of the building after Edna Usher hired him at Ruth's recommendation as head of Cottage security.

"If you didn't know what it was you would have thought it was just an odd piece of paneling," he told us. "The latchwork is inset near the floor and barely noticeable. An ingenious design. I found the hinges right away. Leather strips at the top. Still in good shape for nearly two centuries." The thin wooden door was was rigged to swing in and up like the smaller version of what some people install for their cats except this one swung only one way.

With only the blue glow from his pocket flashlight, we studied diagram's Cromwell had passed out of the floor we were on. The storage room was marked as was the rest of Pink's lab complex, the corridor, elevator and the rooms that were being used to hold the prisoners.

Cromwell exhibited what I thought was sound tactical sense when he laid out the plan of attack. He, Joan and I would turn right when we reached the corridor and head down to the locked rooms. Cromwell had the keys. We would release Pink and Dr. Knoe and bring them to the storage room. Ashmore would stand guard at the corridor just inside the entrance to the lab complex and Case would be further down the corridor to the left at the elevator.

Our execution began with the precision one would expect of seasoned warriors. Cromwell unlocked the door to the first room and threw the door open as Joan and I covered the entrance with our weapons – she with her pistol and me with the 12-gauge. The room was without light of any kind. The dim blue from

Cromwell's flashlight revealed what appeared to be a human form lying on a cot against the rear wall. The figure struggled to a sitting position, bare feet thumping as the hit the floor. It was Pink.

"Pink," said Joan. "We've come to get you out of here." A sound that resembled a foghorn several miles distant was followed by an attack of coughing. When he stopped coughing, Joan asked him if he was all right.

"Uh...uhhhh...who there?"

"Mr. Pinkerton, it's Anthony Cromwell. You're safe now. You can come out now." But Pink remained seated on the cot. He rubbed his eyes and had another coughing attack. This time when the coughing ended, Joan asked him if he knew where Dr. Knoe was.

"No?" came the ragged voice from the darkness.

"Liz, Pink. Is Liz OK?"

"Lizzzz..."

"Oh, Pink, what have they done to you?"

It was right about then that a blood-chilling shriek pierced the subterranean stillness and tore our attention from Pink to the direction from which the scream had come. Before we could react beyond simply pivoting toward the sound, another even ghastlier cry resounded down the corridor from the same direction. These horrifying emanations of unconscionable human suffering were coming not from the room next to the one in which we'd found Pink, but further away, at the very end of the corridor, it seemed.

Joan beat us in her dash to the door behind which we now heard the tortured soul's sobbing. Cromwell and I were only two or three steps back. Within seconds he'd pulled this door open, and we knew immediately his blue light wasn't needed.

Two people sat at a small table apparently playing cards. A floor lamp and a smaller lamp on a table next to a cot provided ample lighting. Elliot Burke was one of the card players. The other was a

SACRIFICE

woman I had seen before, but it wasn't Dr. Knoe.

"Gladys?" The name erupted simultaneously from Joan and Cromwell. Of course. Pink's lab partner and lover, whom we had set out to "rescue" before finding we too were being sought, but not in a good way. Gladys Alabi, as gorgeous now as she was when I met her. The only difference was the expression on her exotic face. The adoring glow she'd exhibited when in Pink's presence was replaced now by wide-eyed gaping fright. I raised the barrel of my shotgun to cover Burke, whose face registered mild surprise. Fortunately for both of them neither Gladys nor Burke made any attempt to move. Then Burke slowly raised his hands from the table, fingers splayed, weaponless.

"I can explain," he said calmly.

"Freeze," Joan ordered. "Don't either of you move. Don't even develop a nervous tick. Yes, Burke, you will explain, and so will you Ms. Alabi. But right now this is the perfect place for you both..."

Before Joan could finish another series of hideous screams pierced the air.

"Recording," Burke said. He jabbed his thumb back down the corridor. "Empty room..."

A shout of dire alarm assaulted our ears from further away, overriding his explanation. Cromwell and I wheeled from the door to see three figures at the corridor's other end. All were in a crouch, facing off. Artificial light silhouetted the three, but one appeared to be Case. The other two were, considerably larger, were sidling apart from each other, both continuing to face Case. A ragged tongue of fire flashed in front of Case followed instantly by a blast that jolted the building. The blast's concussion pummeled my ears.

I saw one of the taller figures stumble backward and fall to the floor as Case swung his shotgun toward the other. Cromwell and I had started down the corridor toward the scene, but stopped when another flash, a brilliant green, blinded me temporarily. When my vision returned I was aware of two things. First, there was no blast. Second, someone had begun an unearthly interminable screaming. Case. The screaming finally ended when it looked as if his midsection exploded in a bloody cloud. The explosion seemed to have severed his torso, yet, with one hand gripping his pants to hold himself together he began screaming again, a choked, gurgling sound, and shuffled toward the standing black figure, which had started backing away from him.

Case crashed to the floor before he reached his killer, who now turned toward us, blinding me again with light, only this time instead of the green from whatever weapon had been used on Case, a brilliant white spotlight. I directed my shotgun barrel down the corridor and saw Cromwell raise the sawed-off double-barrel he'd gotten from Merle at the marina. A commotion behind us broke our concentration. I heard a heavy thump and some shoes scuffing on the concrete floor. Joan cursed, sharply. Burke crashed between us, limping badly as he ran toward the figure that was stalking down the corridor toward us.

"NO!!" Burke shouted. He'd lifted his arms and was holding his hands over his head, fingers still splayed. "NO!! GO BACK!!!" He continued his jerky sprint toward the figure, which showed no sign of slowing its pace toward us. As the two neared each other Burke shouted, "I ORDER YOU TO STAND DOWN! TURN AROUND AND GO BACK TO YOUR STATION!!"

This time the green flash was partially blocked by Burke's body, but the explosion of his midsection was more visible than the one with Case. It appeared steam was part of the grisly eruption spewing a sickening pink, hissing mist that filled the corridor's entire width and height where Burke stood. Burke took no steps as had Case, but collapsed to the floor, his head meeting the concrete with a terrible crunch.

I immediately opened fire at the approaching figure, as did Cromwell and now Joan, who had moved up to join us. The figure fell backwards to the floor but struggled to its feet and scrabbled down the corridor toward the elevator. The other figure had gotten to its feet by now and was holding its abdomen as if in pain. Ashmore stepped out of the lab entrance and started

SACRIFICE

shooting at this figure. All four of us had emptied our weapons by the time our two attackers dragged themselves onto the elevator and disappeared, presumably headed to a command center on one of the building's upper levels.

BAD MAN'S LEGACY

The biggest problem we faced initially, after the last shots were fired and the two "zombies" had escaped in the elevator, was trying to communicate with each other without speaking. The concussions of the shots fired in the corridor's acoustic confines had deafened us temporarily. I saw Joan 's mouth moving but I heard nothing. I tried to speak to her, but couldn't hear my own voice. I knew my vocal cords were vibrating only because I felt them. I threw my hands out to the sides and shrugged, smiling helplessly, about the same time she did the same. I saw her shoulders shake a few times as if she were laughing, but if she was I heard nothing.

Much of what happened in the next few minutes I've pieced together from talking with the others after we regained our hearing. At the moment, when Joan left me to find Pink, my attention shifted to Elliot Burke, who lay on the concrete floor in a widening dark red pool about ten yards away. I assumed he was dead, thinking no human could survive more than a second or two with an exploded midsection and a shattered skull. I expected to find brain matter in the spreading blood. When I looked down the corridor at him now I saw something move. A hand. Its fingers were flexing. I laid my shotgun on the floor and ran to him.

The stench as I drew near was a putrid mix of raw viscera and feces with another, incongruent odor I later decided was what boiled chitterlings must smell like. We eventually learned that the blinding green beam used on Burke and Case was composed of an extraordinarily powerful laser mated with a concentrated microwave beam that literally seared into and boiled the innards of both men in less than a second after contact. Abdominal fluids turned to steam and burst out of their bodies with the intensity of an exploding dynamite stick. These weapons, being designed for military and police use, were still in a prototypical stage.

SACRIFICE

Chesapeake Security's aerial drones and "field zombies" were the first to deploy them outside laboratory conditions.

Hunkered next to Burke's head I could see it was his nose apparently that took the brunt of the force when his head hit the floor. The impact broke it sideways and it lay flat against a cheek. I knew this was fortunate, as a straight-on blow could have driven the two nasal bones into his brain, killing him instantly. His head was on its side and his eyes were open, staring intensely into mine. I saw his lips separate and his jaw start moving. He was trying to speak. He had at most only seconds left to live, and likely would be dead before I could hear what he said.

Cromwell at this moment was escorting a stunned and feeble-looking Dr. Knoe from the room next to the one Pink had been held in. I tried to holler at him, to no avail. I waved my arms. This got his attention, and when I started pointing excitedly at Burke's face and then at Dr. Knoe and motioned for him to bring her to me, he seemed to understand. As they approached, I pointed at Burke again and then at my ears, then shook my head and pointed and nodded at Dr. Knoe, whose hearing I assumed the blast concussions hadn't affected as they had ours. It worked. Depleted and confused as she was by her captivity and the sudden chaotic rescue, she understood what had happened and what was expected of her.

She sat in the blood that still pumped from Burke's dying body and leaned close so that her ear was within a couple of inches of his mouth. She remained this way for what seemed like an hour or more but was probably no longer than ten or fifteen minutes. She sat up and shook her head when he lost consciousness. I helped her up and escorted her to the storage room.

While this was happening Joan took Pink to the storage room where she then began searching for the supply of ammunition Cromwell said he'd stashed there. The first thing Cromwell did after the shooting stopped was to run back to the room where we'd found Burke and Gladys, who was standing in the doorway looking on in disbelief. Cromwell shoved her back inside and locked the door. Then he moved to the room where Dr. Knoe was being held.

After rescuing Dr. Knoe and leaving her with me and Burke, Cromwell ran down the corridor to his two employees. He found Ashmore with a distant look on his face, kneeling beside Case and holding his dead hand.

"Bravest man I ever knew," Ashmore told us later. "We were on a mission in [location deleted] when our Black Hawk went down and I was trapped and bandits were moving in. Cranky had gotten out and was covering me. All he had was two SIG .357s but he charged at those bastards. He came out from cover and ran at the bastards screaming like a Comanche and firing those goddam SIGs. He killed three of them and then chased after the last two when they tried to get away, and killed them, too.

"I didn't know until he came back to check on me that he'd been shot. Twice. 'Fuck it,' he said, 'They're mere flesh wounds.' then he laughed like a madman. Only time I ever heard him laugh. He stayed with me until the rescue chopper came. I loved that man."

Responding triagely, knowing our having kicked the hornets' nest compromised the likelihood of our escape undetected via the tunnel, we abandoned the corpses where they lay and reassembled in the storage room. By the time we'd accomplished this my hearing was pretty much restored, as it seemed as well with the others. We'd agreed to keep Gladys on ice in the room where we'd found her and to keep this information from Pink for the time being. Although what she knew was undoubtedly valuable, we could not be certain if she was trustworthy, especially considering the dynamic between her and Pink.

"Dr. Knoe, was Burke able to give us anything useful?" I asked.

She shook her head and heaved a weary sigh. "Hard to tell. Hard to make sense of what he was saying. He'd been acting strange all the while we were with him, different moods, even different voices. It was as if there were two or three or more separate people inside him struggling for control."

"Vulcana," I said and saw Pink nodding affirmation. Pink hadn't said anything beyond some incoherent mumbling since we found

SACRIFICE

him. I wondered if he'd been drugged.

"I think so," Dr. Knoe said. "I think he was in charge of those creatures he called zombies. They were here when we arrived, and I think they were the reason he brought us here. He seemed to communicate with them through a small microphone clipped to his collar."

"But he was shouting at them just now when they shot him," said Joan. "What do you suppose happened? Hadn't they seen him in person?"

"I don't know. Maybe the mic wasn't working or maybe they didn't recognize his voice, depending on which one of him was speaking. Maybe someone else had taken control...

"There was one thing he kept trying to say, I think. Kept repeating it. Sounded like the word 'arm'. He said it several times, and once it sounded like he said 'pit.'"

"Armpit?" Joan said.

"Maybe so. Could be."

"His armpit? No, that doesn't make any sense. Hmmmmm. Maybe he wanted us to know that's where these zombies are vulnerable," Joan said.

MATHEW PAUST

MASKS COME OFF

Continuing in triage mode, we agreed finding a way to disable the "zombies" was our first priority. We almost agreed, that is. The lone dissenter, Pink, interrupted our discussion.

"Where's Gladys?" he blurted.

"Gladys?" Joan and I responded simultaneously, trying to sound puzzled.

"I heard her screams. They were torturing her," he said, his voice steadier, edging toward the accusatory.

I turned toward Joan and saw she had turned toward me. She shrugged. We both turned to Pink.

"She's in a room down the hall, Pink," Joan said.

"What? Bring her here!" Pink demanded, now seemingly in full control of his capacities.

"She was not being tortured," I said quietly.

"I HEARD HER SCREAMS!!" he shouted.

"SHHHHHHHHHHHHHH!" everyone hissed, except Pink. I said, "That was a recording, Pink."

"IT WAS HER VOICE! I KNOW HER VOICE! IT WAS HER!!"

"We think they were using her to get to you."

"But...but why? All they wanted from me was the formula. Gladys already knows the formula. She helped me develop it!"

"Evidently not, Pink," said Dr. Knoe. "Evidently she was playing you. I'm sorry."

"But Gladys loves me! And I love her! That's real!"

SACRIFICE

Dr. Knoe said, "Maybe it is for you, Pink, but not for Gladys. Maybe never for Gladys. She was never in any danger. I saw her kissing Burke right after they brought us here. They didn't know I could see them..."

"Stop! Stop it, Liz! I don't believe you! You're mistaken! I wanna talk to her!" Pink had gotten up from the wooden crate he'd been sitting on. He was waving his arms.

Joan said, "OK. We'll bring her here, but she's going to be in restraints. Maybe you trust her, Pink, but we can't afford to take any chances. I'm sorry, Pink. I really am. I'm so sorry."

As Joan and Cromwell started toward the corridor to bring Gladys back, Pink insisted on accompanying them. We tried to discourage him but failed, so I went along to keep an eye on him. When Cromwell opened the door we saw Gladys at the card table playing solitaire. Her beauty radiated when she looked up. Her face registered surprise, which quickly segued into a welcoming smile.

"Glad! Glad!" Pink shouted and started for the door. I grabbed one of his arms and pulled him back. I noticed that Gladys seemed to cringe when she saw Pink, but I doubt if this registered with him. Joan and Cromwell, moving swiftly, subdued her without visible resistance. They bound her wrists behind her back with nylon cuffs and led her to the door. Pink called her name several more times, but she looked past him as if he weren't in front of her. By now I had him in a bear hug, pinning both of his arms to his sides. He struggled fiercely at first but I felt the fight dying in him as it became clear Gladys was deliberately ignoring him.

"Where's Elliot?" she said in a timid voice. As soon as she said this she saw his body on the floor. Her eyes widened. "Elliot!!!" she screamed and in a furious burst of speed tore loose from her captors, rushed down the corridor and threw herself on the bloody corpse, sobbing hysterically. Pink's sobbing soon joined hers, and I released my grip on him. Pink walked slowly, as if dazed, toward the two bodies on the floor. He reached down and tenderly put his hand on the shoulder of the one writhing in grief.

"Why, Glad?" he asked, his voice breaking with emotion. "I love you. How could you do this?"

Without looking at him, choking back sobs, she said, "I'm sorry, Pink. I didn't want to have to do this to you."

"But why, Glad? Why, darling?"

"It was a job," she said, her tone gone flat with scorn. "That's all. Just a job. I was never who you thought I was."

Pink sat down now, too, in the thickening blood pool. He stroked Gladys's shoulder with one hand and reached his other to her face. She finally turned her head to meet his eyes. "Can you get them to undo my hands, Pink? It's hurting my wrists."

"Can't do that, Gladys," said Joan. She, Cromwell and I were standing next to them. "At least not until you give us some information, such as who you are working for?"

"Oh, shit, I suppose there's no point in pretending any longer, is there?" Gladys said with no emotion. "That was a rhetorical question. My credentials are in my jeans, right back pocket. I am Major Gladys Alabi, Nigerian Intelligence Service, and I have diplomatic immunity. I demand to speak with a representative of my consulate immediately!"

Joan knelt next to the bloody pile and pulled a dark green leather folder from Gladys's jeans. She opened it scanned it briefly and tossed it into the pool of blood. "Looks bogus to me," she said. "Besides, if you had been shot to death right now instead of captured, without us knowing what you claim to be, that would be tough shit, wouldn't it? That was rhetorical, too." She stood up, walked to the green folder and pushed it into the blood with her toe. She stirred it around until it was completely covered with reddish brown gore.

"There. Now, would you like to tell us about Mr. Burke here? Who was he working for?"

"He was working for Chesapeake Security, too. We fell in love, which complicated things a little."

SACRIFICE

"Too?" Joan said. "You just told us you were with Nigerian Intelligence. What have you been smoking, girl?"

"I am...or was." She shrugged. She was sitting up now. "I was assigned to Chesapeake Security, as a consultant. We knew they were working on something important."

"Vulcana?"

"Bingo. Score one for the dyke."

Joan was on Gladys before any of us saw it coming. She shoved Pink out of the way, grabbed the Nigerian woman's hair in one hand and pulled her off Burke's corpse head first onto the floor, holding her face in the gore as Gladys gasped for air between shrieks of rage. Joan finally let go of the other woman's hair and shoved her onto her back, then stood up.

"You can take the cuffs off, now, Anthony," she told Cromwell.

MATHEW PAUST

GLADYS SPILLS

By the time we got Gladys to the storage room she'd already begun, on her own, to cooperate with us.

"If I'm nothing else, I'm pragmatic," she told us with a wink in the adjacent lab where we'd gone to clean off Burke's gore. This meant changing clothes, as well. Fortunately Pink and Gladys kept spare clothes in the room behind the lab they'd shared in happier times. Gladys and Joan changed into clean jeans and T-shirts. My Carhartt work shirt had escaped most of the splatter but my chinos were ruined. Pink had a couple pair of jeans. With the cuffs rolled up an inch his extra pair fit me fine. The four of us scrubbed our sneakers in one of the deep basins. Ashmore and Cromwell had reloaded their shotuns and stood guard at the entrance to the corridor.

Back in the storage room we began bombarding Gladys with questions, randomly, spontaneously, and she answered every one. This convinced me she was genuine. A professional might be able to anticipate the progression of a contrived sequence of questions but not a flurry such as ours. My questions dealt more with strategy while Joan and Cromwell wanted details on the "zombies" and how possibly to defeat them.

"That can't be Kevlar they're wearing," said Joan. "That stuff's too heavy. Once the first guy went down he'd've stayed down. And I know I got the guy who killed Burke with at least one neck shot and you guys hit him with slugs and buckshot. He just kept coming."

"Elliot said it was some new alloy," Gladys said. "Light as titanium and twice as hard as chromium without being brittle. He said you'd need diamond-tipped bullets and even then most of them would bounce off.

SACRIFICE

"We saw them when they got off the bus. Just boys. Teenagers. Skinny, goofy looking. Video game nerds, Elliot said. Carried their zombie suits in duffle bags. Handled them easily.

"Teenagers?" This was Joan.

"Well, all but one. The older guy seemed to be in charge. He carried a duffle bag, too."

"He was the one who shot Burke." Joan made this a statement of fact. "You said Burke was supposed to be giving them orders? If so, this older guy decided it was time to take over. That's what happened down here. Somehow the older guy knew Burke had turned."

Gladys shrugged. "Don't look at me. I thought he was running the whole show...except for Hendrian. He's the guy you need to talk to."

"What's his game?" I asked.

"Haven't a clue. He's who Elliot reported to. That's all I know."

"So Nigeria wants the formula for Vulcana?" Me again. "What's with that? I thought all you do there is solicit American men for prostitutes?"

She glared at me, then laughed heartily. "Yeah, we do that," she said after catching her breath. "American men are so gullible...sorry, Pink." Pink's face was blank. He seemed to have returned to the daze he'd been in when we found him. Gladys continued, "Nigeria wants to enter the world market with something everybody else wants - besides whores and oil, that is. If we have Mr. Pinkerton here to show us how to make the stuff, we'll have a monopoly. I thought he could teach me the secret, but he's mister sly guy. Kept a little something up his sleeve." She shot him a knowing grin. Pink lifted a corner of his mouth enough to register acknowledgment.

"I thought you loved me, Pink," she said softly.

Pink looked away, sighed, then turned back her. "How did you know?"

"I made a little batch myself. You didn't even notice. I followed the formula right down the line. Gave some to Ratso and put him in the cage with the Seven Sisters. He screwed them all to death and never shed a tear. That's when I knew you didn't trust me."

"You said they got sick. You didn't tell me..."

"Pink, once I knew you lied to me I decided all bets were off. You lie, I lie. That's not love."

"Gladys! I was under strict orders!"

"From who, Pink? Who told you to lie to me?"

"Mr. Hendrian said it was a matter of national security. And now I know what he meant. You were lying to me all along. And you're still trying to play me!"

Gladys threw back her head and laughed. "Pink, you're the cat's pajamas. You know that? I really do like you. It's too bad we had to meet like this."

Much as I was enjoying this little melodrama, I had to break in. Time was a'wastin'. "What I don't understand, Gladys, is why your government would want a drug for which there would be no demand, no market. A super aphrodisiac, sure. Build a better blue pill and the world will beat a..." I broke out laughing. Gladys and Joan joined in. "Sorry...that just slipped out. I mean, Gladys, you already know the formula for that. Isn't that all your government really needs?" She stared at me, an odd expression on her face. I continued:

"I mean, the enhanced formula, which we now know works because we just saw Elliot sacrifice himself for a principle, will not only not have a market but will be outlawed, just like hallucinogens, as soon as the corporate overlords find out what it does..."

Gladys interrupted me: "Principle? What principle did Elliot die for?"

Now it was Pink's turn. He stood up, stretched and walked over to where we were clustered. "It's not really a principle, Glad. It's

SACRIFICE

more of a spiritual thing. What the enhanced formula does is to stir up enzymes in our brains that make new connections to override our primitive instincts with the part of us that knows better, that knows the only way we can survive as a species is to look out for each other instead of simply looking out for ourselves.

"It's what we used to talk about when we got stoned together. Remember? How we felt? How we loved that feeling and knew it was right, that we weren't just high but were somehow better people when we felt that way? Remember, Glad? When I first told you I loved you and you said you loved me, too? Wasn't that real?" He reached a hand out to her but she drew back.

"I'm sorry, Pink," she said, her voice barely audible.

I broke in again. "So if I'm understanding this, what your government wants to do is blackmail the rest of the world. You'll keep Vulcana out of the soft drinks and the public water supplies and whatever other delivery systems you can use to make the world a better place, to maybe give the human species a chance to survive, for what? Money? Is that really what it's all about?"

"I know," Gladys said, staring at the floor. "Stupid, isn't it." She looked up, straight into my eyes, her face radiating a different kind of beauty, a remote sense of sadness, remorse mixed with a tinge of hope. "It's why I'm not going back. I was hoping maybe you could help arrange asylum for me here."

MATHEW PAUST

PINK'S DA MAN

After reassembling in one of the lab rooms, where we had light, we started planning our next move. We decided our best chance of getting Pink to safety was to attack. Too risky, we figured, creeping down the tunnel back to the Bay, as by now somebody was sure to be stationed behind The Cottage and be able to block the gate at that end, trapping us inside. This part of the discussion came after a quick scan of why, now that there seemed to be no danger of Gladys spiriting Pink off to Nigeria, there was any reason to believe Pink was in any danger at all.

"They hired us," Gladys offered.

"They?" Several of us asked this at the same time.

"Wilde. Hendrian. He's the one who hired me."

"Did he know you were with Chesapeake?" Joan asked.

"That's where he went. He wanted someone to keep an eye on Pink. Chesapeake recruited me from the consulate. I was their science attaché."

"But Pink said he met you through the Internet?"

"That was part of the plan. We exchanged photos. It was cute."

Pink turned away, head hanging.

"Why would a security company go to the Nigerian consulate looking for a scientist? Something doesn't add up here, Gladys."

"Elliott. I'd been seeing Elliott since my speech to the U.N. on the need for international cooperation in scientific research. He worked security there."

"OK, so why do you think Hendrian didn't trust Pink?"

"Good question. All I can say is I don't trust the fat little

SACRIFICE

bastard...not you, Pink. You're lean and mean." She winked at Pink as Joan and I laughed. Cromwell turned his head, as I saw his lips stretch into the semblance of a grin. Dr. Knoe smiled agreeably and Pink showed nothing.

My theory? Hendrian wanted the formula for himself. One of the simplest, most basic motives of all: greed. I didn't share this with the others, as they'd already indicated they were satisfied Hendrian was not to be trusted, and we moved to the next step, which was planning our siege of his office.

First, how to get out of this level. Obviously they'd be watching the elevator. Gladys said so far as she knew there were six zombies. We figured the one Case had knocked down would be out of commission awhile. At least two of them would have to be guarding Hendrian's office, and at least one would be stationed on the beach. Of the remaining two, one would guard the elevator, with the other as backup.

"Where are the stairs?" I asked.

Cromwell walked over to one of the lab tables, climbed onto it, reached up to the ceiling and pulled on a small loop of rope, opening a trap door that swung down to within an inch of the table and revealed an attached set of stairs. There was no light in this drop-down stairwell, which ascended into an undecipherable blackness.

"What, ah...where does this go?" somebody asked. One of the women, I recall.

"My office," Cromwell said. "It opens in the closet where I keep some...equipment. I'll go first."

"But..." I was curious. "Why go to so much trouble to put in hidden stairs? Why not just put in a regular stairway?

"Found this when I moved in. It was probly installed when the house was built. Goes with the tunnel, I imagine. Escape down the stairs and then down the tunnel. The everyday stairs were probly where the elevator is now. If they were blocked off, say, by soldiers or for some other reason, this would've been a fallback."

"Fallforwardforusteeheehee."

"Pink! You're back!" said Gladys, the joy in her voice sounding sincere. Pink gave her a timid smile.

Our discussion then moved to tactics. Assuming we could reach Cromwell's office undetected, how could we get past the "zombies" that would find us almost as soon as we stepped into the hallway, or at least at some point before we reached Hendrian's office.

"I'm sure they have some sort of electronic detection system in those suits," Cromwell said.

"Any way to jam it?" Joan held up her remote, the one we used to control the surveillance gulls.

"We can' t be sure," said Cromwell. "Probly not. We'll need to be able to strike fast from as far away as possible. I don't think our firearms would be very effective." His voice tapered off and his attention drifted inward. After a long pause in which he seemed lost in thought, he turned to Pink. "How much Vulcana do you have right now?"

"Three or four ounces. It's not dosed out yet," Pink said. He spoke rapidly, but did not seem as manic as before. Fortunately he was dropping the teeheehees.

"Powder?"

"Oh, yeah. Why?"

"Can you mix it with something? Make a liquid version?"

"Sure. It stays stable in ethyl alcohol. What..."

"How long would it take?"

"Wouldn't take any time at all. What..."

"Mix some up for me, Pink. I think I know how to handle these guys."

Now it was Cromwell speaking rapidly, the most excited I'd seen him. While he explained his plan, Pink moved quickly to another

SACRIFICE

part of the lab and began fussing with glass containers.

"We can't stop these guys with our guns, but we can stun them. Disorient them. They recover quickly, though, and you saw what they can do then. We can't let them recover enough to use those lasers on us. So before they can, we will shoot them with Vulcana. I have my animal control air gun in my office upstairs."

"Anthony," I said, his excitement rippling over to me, "this is brilliant! I'm assuming you've figured out a way to penetrate those bulletproof suits with your darts?" I know it looks in print as if I were being sarcastic, and maybe it did sound that way at the time. But I wasn't feeling sarcastic. It was hope driving my questions now, because without a chance his plan could work, we'd soon be exploding in clouds of steam and gore.

"The armpits," he said. "That was the word Burke kept saying to Joan before he died. Armpit. We have to assume he knew the one place in those suits that was vulnerable. Makes sense, too. They need mobility with their arms. Everything else can be covered with armor except under their arms at the shoulder. It wouldn't have to be much room, but just a crack is all I need. Those air guns are surprisingly accurate."

"How will you get them to raise their arms, Tony?" This was Joan. The ripple had reached her, too.

"We'll need a diversion. Remember, these zombies are kids. Their only experience in combat is with video games. They have great reflexes but they're programmed to expect certain sequences. They have no experience with the unexpected. We have to give them something that confuses them."

"What about their leader?" Joan again.

"Good point. He's most likely a seasoned warrior. He's the one we need to take out first. Once he's down the kids will panic."

Ashmore, who was guarding the door to the corridor, turned around and added his suggestion: "We blast the living shit out of him with everything we got. Knock him on his ass, then Tony can stick him with one o' them darts."

"Meanwhile the kids boil Tony's intestines and blow him in half," Cromwell said dourly.

"Sorry, boss. Just a thought."

"Forget it, Roger. Keep your eyes on the corridor. Don't worry. We'll think of something."

Pink walked over, holding a flask of cloudy liquid. He held it up to Cromwell, who took it, examined it and set it on the lab table far enough so none of us would accidentally knock it over.

"Perfect, Pink. This should work. Can you measure it out in individual doses? We don't want any zombies to OD." Sporadic chuckles. Pink nodded and said he would put the doses in separate tubes. Instead of returning to his work area, though, he held up a hand, like a student in a classroom.

"I have an idea," he said. All heads turned to him. "I'm the only one they can't kill, right? I mean, I'm the reason all this is happening. They want me. Want me alive. I could walk up to them and hold one of their arms up so you could shoot a dart into their armpit."

Several jaws dropped, including mine. Pink continued, "I'm stronger than I look, and they can't fight very well with all that shit they're wearing. Maybe it's light, but it restricts their movements. They're like knights in titanium armor or something, right?"

Heads nodded, jaws still hung.

"I'll just walk up to their leader, grinning and going teeheehee. Blow his fucking mind. Huh?"

"What if they can put those lasers on stun, Pink?" I said. "Not kill you but knock you out of the game?"

Pink shrugged. "Then I guess you guys are fucked teeheehee."

SACRIFICE

THE GAME IS AFOOT

It's a good thing I had to pee before we started up the hidden stairs to head into battle, because by the time I got back to the group waiting at the base of the stairs our plan was changing. And a good thing it was. Evidently Gladys was the one who brought up the likelihood Pink's life no longer was necessarily valuable to anyone but himself.

"Look at it this way," she argued. "Nigeria wants him alive because he's the only one who knows how to make the enhanced Vulcana, which they want so they can blackmail the developed countries, the oligarchies. That was my job, to get him safely to Nigeria. You can bet Wilde Labs has no interest in the enhanced formula. Their only interest is profits. They think I can make the basic stuff, which is where the money is. They don't need Pink, long as they've got me."

"What if they think you're dead?" This was Joan.

"A lot depends on how much Hendrian knows," said Gladys. "He hired Chesapeake, but he might not know Elliot's dead. There's got to be some confusion in the ranks. The zombies are just kids. They don't know shit, except for the head zombie, who's probly Kelleher, their chief operations officer. This is their first field op. I can see Kelleher leading the team. I can see him taking Elliot down, too. Those two never got along."

"What we need to know is whether Kelleher - if that's who it is - is more than a tactical commander," said Joan. "If Elliot was the contact point with Hendrian, Kelleher might have killed the critical link in his chain of command. Those zombies may not know who to shoot and who to protect."

"When in doubt, shoot. That's how we train," said Ashmore.

"Lemme see if I got this right," I said. "Our goal is to get to

Hendrian without losing anybody. We think Hendrian's interested only in the basic formula, so he doesn't need Pink. All he needs is Gladys, unless he thinks Gladys is dead. Gladys, did the head zombie ever see you?"

"Not that I know of, Al. I got here before the zombies arrived. Came back dressed as a courier. Said I was from Wilde's main office. Nobody recognized me and I pretty much stayed in the lab until Elliot got here."

"Hard to imagine anyone who knew you not recognizing you, Gladys," I said.

"Well, thank you, Al, I'm sure, but I'm pretty good with disguises. I'll bet I could have fooled even Mr. Pinkerton." She shot a grin Pink's way, which he ignored.

As our resolve began wavering I expected Pink to have second thoughts about volunteering to approach a zombie unarmed and attempt to wrestle him into position for a dart shot to an armpit from Cromwell. If he was reconsidering this audacity, he gave no sign, and instead pushed us closer to accepting the plan.

"Nobody knows what the fuck's going on. That's what I think," Pink said, surprising me out of some intense wondering what alternatives we might have.

"They're just gamer punks. Maybe they've seen a photo of me and maybe of Gladys, but after what just happened all they're doing is trying to catch us and protect Hendrian. They're not gonna deliberately kill anybody, unless Hendrian tells them to. The leader killed Elliot because Elliot was acting crazy, it sounds like. The other zombie killed the other guy because the other guy shot him. The kid'd probly never been shot before. He panicked. That's what I think."

"So you're still willing to do this, Pink?" I said.

"What else can we do? We keep blasting them with guns, they're gonna boil our guts with their killer rays. They're wearing armor, but it still hurts to get shot. It'll scare the shit out of them and piss them off."

SACRIFICE

"Where do you want me in all of this?" asked Dr. Knoe.

Cromwell responded: "I'll need a little cover, because I'll be the only one with a gun. They see that and they're liable to shoot without thinking."

"I'll be your cover, Tony," said Gladys. We all turned to look at her. She was smiling. "These are teenage nerds, remember? Probly virgins." She started disrobing. "I'll be flashing those boys like crazy, and they'll be too busy watching my little show to see anything else."

"Good idea," said Dr. Knoe, who started taking her clothes off, too. "But we should wear something. Bathrobes would be good. If we're completely nude these kids might feel intimidated. We can't risk that. If we look like we're on our way to take a shower that'll interest them as well as confuse them."

"What if they're gay?" This was Gladys.

"It won't matter that much," said Dr. Knoe. "They'll still be fascinated if we show them a little skin."

"I'll show 'em some skin, too," said Pink, starting to undress.

"What about the rest of us?" I asked.

"Al, you'll be behind with me. Bring the shotgun. We'll need the rest of you in reserve," said Joan.

"You'll be naked, too?" I blurted, without thinking. She gave me a stern look.

"No, Al, they won't need that much nudity. I might as well be a shadow in these dark clothes, and I will be armed. Anthony and Ashmore will stay behind, out of sight in case any other zombies show up.

"We don't know how effectively they communicate in those suits, but we have to assume they're in touch with each other all the time. If we're right and Kelleher's guarding Hendrian with one of the zombies, and one is out back, then we can assume there are two more who could come from somewhere if things get wild. You can shoot them with the shotguns and keep them occupied until Pink and Cromwell can get to them with darts.

"This is a pretty good plan, allowing for something to go wrong, and you know something always goes wrong."

Pink spoke up, "I'll have a hypo with me so when I get to my guy I'll jab the needle into his armpit. Tony won't hafta worry about missing it or hitting me. If I get the leader, we might not hafta worry about the others at all."

"How long before the drug takes effect?" Cromwell asked.

"They get the erection almost instantly," said Pink. "That distracts them and then what seems like a heavy acid trip is upon them in a minute."

"A minute? That can be a looong time in a firefight," Cromwell cautioned.

"OK. Not that long. A few seconds, they get this major rush. Their thoughts come tumbling out. They're stoned."

"Good. Thanks, Pink."

Gladys fetched her bathrobe from the room in the back and brought a raincoat for Dr. Knoe.

"Bathrobe would be better," Dr. Knoe said. "Doesn't Pink have one?"

Pink shook his head. "Never owned one. I have a really big bath towel. That work?"

Dr. Knoe grinned. "Better than nothing."

Ready as we would ever be, then, we launched our strike creeping up the stairs into Cromwell's supply closet.

SACRIFICE

BATTLE OF CORRIDOR B

Our attack began like probably none other in the history of armed conflict. Leading the charge were Gladys and Pink in bathrobes (Pink had borrowed Cromwell's) and Dr. Knoe in a giant yellow beach towel. The three flipflopped down the dimly lit Corridor A laughing and talking animatedly to give the impression they were on their way to a shower room. We assumed any "zombies" they met on the way would be oblivious to the fact no such room existed in the house. Joan and I followed at a discreet distance. She carried a small stack of file folders and I had a cardboard box that might have held anything but in fact concealed the sawed-off double-barrel shotgun I'd chosen because it was shorter than the pump. Cromwell, carrying the air rifle, stayed in our shadows.

As the three "shower-bound" point walkers rounded the corner to Wing B toward Hendrian's office, Pink, who was slightly behind the women, trailed a hand with two extended fingers telling us there were, as we expected, two "zombies" stationed outside the office. I turned to signal Cromwell and saw that Joan had beaten me to it and was already in a crouch with her pistol drawn and held at her side. I tilted the box I was carrying on its side and gripped the shotgun as we moved to the corner around which lay the next corridor. The only sounds I heard as we approached the corner were female voices – a startled squeal and then laughing. There was nothing to indicate alarm or fright. Then came a series of of metallic clunks and even louder female laughter.

Joan and I stepped around the corner simultaneously, guns in hand but held low and out of sight. Cromwell moved further out so Joan and I were next to one wall and he was directly opposite. I saw a commotion ahead about twenty steps down the corridor, a mix of blue and white bathrobes rippling as if from a clothesline in a wind. I glanced quickly at Cromwell, who was braced against the wall with the butt of his air rifle against his shoulder. He was sighting along the barrel down the corridor. I turned back to the commotion and for the first time saw the black shapes of two "zombies." Both were lying on the floor with bathrobed figures bent over them. I saw a crouching nude female scuttle away from one of the black heaps and grab something yellow from the floor nearby. That was Dr. Knoe retrieving her towel.

As we advanced quickly toward them Gladys made a sudden violent movement and wrenched what resembled a Darth Vader helmet from one of the fallen "zombies," hurling it clattering down the corridor. She jumped to the next "zombie" and did the same with him. Almost immediately two male voices began groaning loudly. One of them shouted "Oh! Oh! Help me!" over and over as Gladys and Pink struggled with the rest of the armored suits, trying to open them.

"They have erections. The suits are two tight," Pink explained as we drew near.

Our spearhead troops later explained excitedly how easily they'd been able to incapacitate the "zombies." Dr. Knoe had decided to carry a syringe, too, and both she and Pink had no trouble finding the armpit chink in the armor and plunging the needles in. The two suits' occupants had fallen completely for the act, both ogling the women as Gladys, using her martial arts training, executed a dazzling high kick maneuver that revealed all of her extraordinarily impressive charms as she pretended to slip and fall backwards to the floor, managing to hook her foot behind the knee of one of the "zombies" and bringing him crashing down with her. Dr. Knoe immediately jumped on the fallen enemy, losing her towel in the process, and jabbed her needle home.

Meanwhile, the other "zombie," evidently transfixed by the impromptu ballet before him, forgot about Pink until he felt his arm being raised above his head and the sharp sting in his armpit.

Now, as Gladys, Pink and Dr. Knoe tried to figure out the intricacies of the armored suits so as to relieve the excruciating penile pressures within, Cromwell, Joan and I moved into a defensive formation in the event enemy reinforcements arrived. This frenzy of activity and anticipation nearly distracted us from

SACRIFICE

noticing the door to Hendrian's office ease open to reveal Warren Hendrian looking out with his face and body language expressing perplexed wonderment. I think I was the first to see him standing there, and I am certain that if he saw me at that moment he would have noticed a look of perplexed wonderment on my face responding to the sight of the small black pistol he was holding.

I suspect my expression resolved itself into something more decisive sooner than his, as I raised my shotgun and pointed its twin barrels directly at his midsection.

"Warren, goddammit, what the fuck are you doing with that little peashooter?" I shouted. He looked up, as if seeing me for the first time, and his expression morphed into one of a young dog that's just been scolded for peeing on the rug. He stared at me, evidently forgetting the pistol, which hung useless from his dangling arm. His mouth opened as if he were trying to speak, and maybe he did mutter something, but the cacophony of voices between us would have prevented me from hearing anything softer than the shout I'd aimed at him.

"Drop the goddam gun, Warren, or this shotgun will blow you back to Yale!" He lowered his gaze to his hand, moving his lips as if decoding the predicament he was in. His fingers opened and the gun fell to the floor at his feet. He continued standing in the doorway as if in a deep shock. It occurs to me now I might well have been in shock , too, as I recall feeling surprised to recognize that the view I had of Warren was at the base of a curve-winged V formed by the side-by-side barrels of the shotgun we'd borrowed from Merle's Marina. I remembered having pulled both hammers back when we started down the corridor and I recognized with a start that my trigger finger was now pressed lightly against one of the two triggers. This realization frightened me more than seeing the gun in Warren's hand. Our standoff was over. We needed Warren now to call off the other "zombies."

I eased my finger off the trigger but kept the gun pointed at the doorway, thinking, I suppose, that possibly another "zombie" was stationed in the office. Cromwell apparently had been watching us and now moved past me toward Hendrian. I could see the barrel of his air rifle pointed ahead, so I lowered my gun and let out a sigh I hadn't realized I'd been holding in. I moved forward, too, and heard Cromwell instructing Warren to order the other Chesapeake Security personnel to stand down.

At about the same time the cries of pain from the two on the floor stopped. I could see that the armor covering their groin areas had been removed. Both "zombies" were now instructing Gladys and Pink how to remove the rest of the suits. I saw that one of them clearly was a youngster while the other appeared to be considerably older, perhaps in his thirties. I thought to ask the older one to bring an end to the hostilities but they began their hallucinogenic babbling before I could say anything. The youngster sobbed while the older one was jabbering incoherently.

An argument erupted in the doorway.

"I can't!" It was Hendrian. It came out as a scream. He was looking at Cromwell and seemed about to cry.

"You have to call them off, Mr. Hendrian," said Cromwell, his voice louder and sterner than I remembered ever hearing. "They're carrying lethal weapons, which they've already used. You must order them to stand down!"

"I said I can't! I don't know how and I don't have the authority!" Everyone turned to look at him, except the two babbling "zombies."

"Who does have the authority, Warren?" I shouted.

"I do," came a familiar voice from within the office.

SACRIFICE

THE END

I'm still pondering my lack of surprise at watching the former president appear in the doorway of Hendrian's office holding a small pistol that looked identical to the one Hendrian had dropped on the floor. Maybe it was a result of the familiarity prevailing over all else. In the years I had worked for her, campaigning and serving as her chief of staff in the White House, I'd become accustomed to seeing her take charge when all around her seemed devolving into chaos. She had a knack for calmly asserting a sense of natural, reasonable authority. Despite the pistol, the circumstances and the implications of her being the one standing there with the pistol, my chief concern was for her safety.

"Don't shoot, anybody! It's the president!" I shouted as I stooped and placed my shotgun on the floor. Joan, reacting simultaneously, was already in motion, rushing forward to place herself in front of the woman she was assigned by the Secret Service to protect.

"Ruth, give me the gun," Joan said in a voice calm but insistent. Ruth glanced around at the small crowd gathered in front of the door, then looked down at the gun she held beside her jeans-clad leg. She stared at the gun as if in wonder as to how she came to be holding it. Joan put her hand on Ruth's wrist, holstered her own pistol and with her freed gun hand took Ruth's weapon and stuck it under her belt. She leaned toward the former president and put her mouth up to Ruth's ear. Ruth backed into the office and Joan followed. As she started to close the door she looked back and met my eyes. "Al?" she said and nodded her head for me to join them.

Soon as the door was closed, Joan reminded Ruth to order the remaining "zombies" to stand down, which Ruth accomplished with a tiny transmitter she'd been holding in the hand that hadn't been holding the gun. She ordered the three Chesapeake mercenaries to remove their armored suits and remain outside the house on the rear deck.

"What's going on, Ruth?" I said. Somebody had to say it. When she turned to me with nothing but a blank expression I added, "What's with the gun?" She looked at her hand again, which apparently snapped her out of her trance. "Her," she said, swinging her head to the larger of two desks in the office. Surprised that I hadn't noticed her when I entered, I now beheld a small, trim woman with short, stylishly cut white hair seated behind the desk peering at me with angry eyes. I'd met her once before, at a White House function years prior. She hadn't seemed to age since that night.

"Ms. Usher," I said, bowing slightly. Edna Usher, CEO of American Enterprises, parent company of Wilde Laboratories Unlimited, the developer of cutting edge "therapeutic chemistries" including the wildly popular female aphrodisiac Primrose Lane and the as-yet unveiled penile and character enhancement formula known as Vulcana. Problem was, Edna, as I was about to learn, wanted nothing to do with the "character enhancement" part.

"Who wants a goddam world full of simpering touchy feelies, anyway?" she snarled, as we moved from why she'd had Hendrian hire the "zombies" under the pretext a foreign government wanted the formula (without, evidently, ever suspecting Gladys was in fact working for Nigerian Intelligence for that very reason) to the real reason she wanted Pink "out of the picture," which we both knew without saying meant dead.

"Better a world full of simpering touchy feelies than what we have now. We're destroying the planet," I said.

"Oh, that's all liberal bullshit, Geddes. The planet's doing just fine. It's overpopulated, of course, but nature has ways of dealing with that."

At this, Ruth wheeled, face red with rage and stalked across the office to the woman whose wealth and friendship had been instrumental in launching her career in politics and her elevation

SACRIFICE

to the presidency.

"I'd ask you to repeat that, Ed, but I know damned well what you just said. I am having trouble accepting it. I thought I knew you." Ruth kept her voice almost conversational, but a fierce tension hummed beneath the casual tone.

"What, little miss fancypants cheerleader's suddenly one of the hoi polloi? What do you care what happens to the stupid sheeple who let TV tell them what to think and what to buy and when to laugh and when to cry...hahahaha I'm a fucking poet whattaya know."

Ruth's voice came out cold as a winter tundra. "You've never forgiven me for beating you out for the squad, have you. All your dad's money couldn't buy you that little striped skirt you wanted so badly to impress...whom? You never had a date the whole time we were roommates. Have you ever had a date, Ed?"

"God damn you, you fucking little whore! I read Geddes's fucking book. I was so embarrassed it made me sick! Humiliating. You fucking goddam socialist whore!" Edna stood up, her face now as red as Ruth's. She shoved her chair back so violently it crashed against the wall. She started around the desk, tiny hands balled into fists.

I stepped between them and held them apart until the emotional crisis peaked and both women, still glaring murderously at each other, moved a step backward. I nodded at Joan and whispered, "Pink," motioning with my thumb and first two fingers in a manner she indicated she understood. She nodded and smiled grimly. She opened the door, stuck her head into the corridor, exchanged some words with someone and backed away from the door. Instead of Pink, Anthony Cromwell stepped into the office and closed the door behind him. Joan spoke quickly, quietly to him, causing his face to distort with obvious discomfort. I caught his eye and nodded, as did Ruth, who evidently knew intuitively what was happening.

Cromwell shrugged, shook his head and raised the air rifle he'd been holding at his side. Edna finally caught on. She shouted,

"NO! PUT THAT GODDAM FUCKING GUN DOWN RIGHT NOW, YOU FUCKING CLOWN! The rifle spat its dart into her neck with a pneumatic pop. Edna grabbed at her neck, found the dart and yanked it out, screaming in pain and rage, and hurled it across the office.

"I'll have you all killed," she said, but her tone was more puzzled than threatening. She held her hand up to her face and peered at the blood on her palm from the dart wound. She took a couple of steps backward, sat down in the chair and leaned her head against the wall. That's when the moaning started.

SACRIFICE

EPILOGUE

Happy ending? Well, a guarded yes, for the time being, let us say. We are not at the moment in immediate danger, although we're soon heading into a shit storm of trouble. Those who would have us dead, who would see Vulcana undone, see it become the forgotten nemesis of our me-first, consumption-obsessed culture, have unimaginable resources.

But don't count us out as mere prey destined to run and hide forevermore. If we were, publishing this account of our struggle would be astoundingly stupid. It's one of our weapons, this account. This might be the first revolution in history conducted solely by "psy-ops," which is military jargon for psychological operations. In this revolution what the enemy worries about not only can but will defeat him (we're thinking upbeat here, as all warriors should do).

Anybody who might be considering making odds on our chances might wish to keep several things in mind:

• Technology can amplify our potency. Social media via variable satellite dispersion gives us ubiquity with little danger of revealing our location.

• We are few and we are many. Some of us are known, which gives our movement a personality, a focal center. This helps with morale and recruitment by protecting our soldiers and allies with relative anonymity. The Chill® man filling the soda machines wears the company shirt, but each drink just might contain a dose of Vulcana.

• Vulcana is colorless, tasteless and odorless, impossible to detect without sophisticated equipment. A small amount goes a long way. It could show up in coffee urns at corporate meetings everywhere. No one would be the wiser until CEOs began sprouting erections and rolling on the floor babbling childhood memories.

- Eventually our movement will prove Bunyan's Law of Burgeoning Returns, as everyone who ingests Vulcana will soon become our ally. Meanwhile, the danger posed by WACKO (Worldwide Action Coalition Klux of Oligarchists) to stymy our attempt to save the species is real and we have information the group is allocating more cash every day toward our intended demise.

We've discussed a concern over the possible negative effect the drug might have on people suffering from psychoses. It's a valid concern. We haven't seen evidence of it yet, although Edna Usher did give us considerable pause for the first week after Anthony Cromwell injected her with a dose by firing the dart into her neck. After alternating between rage and near catatonia, however, she leveled off, smiled like a school girl on prom night and eagerly agreed to turn over the reins of American Enterprises to Warren Hendrian, whom, I should note, voluntarily submitted to an injection and has become one of the more pleasant and reasonable people I have ever known.

During her conversion, Edna revealed that Am-Ent, as stock traders refer enviously to her privately held company, owns Chesapeake Security, which has been assigned to protect The Cottage as well as Wilde Labs' executives and its employees. Secure as this arrangement might well be, Hendrian agreed with my suggestion to set up a second campus at an even more secure location. He has appointed me director of this facility, the name of which bears no resemblance to its assigned task, which simply is to crank out Vulcana in various forms, primarily liquid and ingestible tablets.

Pink's lab at The Cottage has been converted for manufacturing, as well. It can easily be adapted for further research should something unexpected occur with the existing formula. Gladys Alabi was granted political asylum and full citizenship, expedited by Ruth's friend House Speaker Edith Glick, and is now directing production at the auxiliary plant. No, she and Pink have not kissed

SACRIFICE

and made up and, no, Gladys and I have not even toyed with the idea of getting to know each other on a personal basis – at least I don't think so.

Anthony Cromwell is now CEO of Chesapeake Security and has moved his headquarters to what I shall call, for now, "my campus." Cromwell has retired the "zombie" suits and the videogame nerds who wore them. He has started a training camp for any former "zombies" who wish to develop martial skills. So far as I know, all of those we confronted at The Cottage have signed up. Sean Seawell, former Chesapeake CEO is now chief operations officer. After undergoing a Vulcana conversion he replaced Bryan Kelleher, who, after his Vulcana conversion at the hands of a nude Dr. Knoe in the Battle of Corridor B, is running the nerd training camp.

This will be my final transmission to the blogosphere, at least for the time being. I expect to be rather busy as we ramp up our production of Vulcana and launch our revolution, which we are calling Save Our Species! You can do the acronym.

This is the end. ;-)

ABOUT THE AUTHOR

Mathew Paust is a retired award-winning newspaper reporter who lives in Hampton Roads, Virginia within reasonable earshot of the booms of cannon and the clangs of their lead balls bouncing off the Monitor and the Merrimac during the tragic War Between the States. He is the author of *Executive Pink*, a satire of presidential politics, and *If the Woodsman is Late*, a collection of stories both fiction and nonfiction. Visit his website at **www.mattpaust.com**

Made in the USA
Charleston, SC
24 January 2013